Grave Concerns

# GRAVE ROBBING AND OTHER HOBBIES

JAYCE CARTER

Grave Robbing and Other Hobbies
ISBN # 978-1-83943-973-5
©Copyright Jayce Carter 2021
Cover Art by Louisa Maggio ©Copyright April 2021
Interior text design by Claire Siemaszkiewicz
Totally Bound Publishing

# GRAVE ROBBING AND OTHER HOBBIES

# Dedication

To my amazing editor, Rebecca, who tirelessly fixes
my shit and lets me know that using cock 123 times in
a story is too many.
You keep me from looking like an idiot and you never
tell people I don't know how to place commas.
Thank you.

# Chapter One

I wished a floating, nearly headless body at three in the morning were an unusual thing for me, but this was the fourth time this one had visited me in as many weeks.

A squinty gaze at my watch made me groan. *At least she's punctual.*

"Avenge me!" the apparition demanded in an over-the-top ghostly voice.

I pushed myself upright to offer an annoyed look. "Don't pull that scary crap with me, Melinda. I'm not some kid trying to contact spirits at a sleepover."

The spirit shimmered then crossed her arms and gave me the same dirty look back. *Ghosts have the worst attitude.* "Well, if you did what I wanted the first time I asked, I wouldn't have to keep bothering you."

"You want me to kill a teenager."

"He killed me. How is that not a fair reaction?"

"You ran a red light because you were trying to get your caramel macchiato to mix while complaining the barista didn't make it right. Can't really blame him for that."

She pursed her lips as though she'd blown out a huge sigh, but with her being incorporeal, no actual air escaped. "If he hadn't been driving, it would have been fine. Isn't this your job? To make things right? You were given this gift for a reason."

"I don't know why I was given this *gift*, but I know I won't be using it to murder innocent teenagers."

"Can I talk to someone above you? Like your boss?"

I groaned and rubbed my eyes as it became clear I wasn't going to be getting back to sleep any time soon. "Did you really just ask to speak to my manager? Look, if you can find whoever is responsible for me, please, be my guest and speak to them. While you're at it, tell them I'd like to quit."

Melinda jammed a bony finger at me. "Do you know who I am?"

"Someone who has ruined my sleep for four weeks."

"And I'll keep doing it until you agree to help."

The threat was good, as far as threats went. Most ghosts tried to scare me into doing what they wanted, but after a person had seen as much as I had, those tactics fell flat. The worst an apparition could do was annoy me until they lost their hold on this world and went to the afterlife. A poltergeist could do some damage, but they were few and far between, luckily.

Melinda's outline had already lost its sharpness. She'd dimmed until she was more of a shimmer than a clear picture. Another week—maybe two—and she'd drift to a whisper, then to nothing.

"And I'll keep ignoring you until you're no longer in this realm."

An entitled huff came from her. "Look at me! I can't believe I'm sitting here being ignored by some short, frumpy girl with bad hair."

I considered pointing out that my hair didn't normally look quite so wild, but she *had* woken me up in the middle of the night.

"Make peace with what happened," I told her as I rolled over, my back to her. "Because I'm not going to help you."

The bed didn't sink, but an electric feeling that said she'd neared ran along my back. "It wasn't supposed to happen like this," she whispered, some of that sureness missing. "I wasn't supposed to die like this."

"Well, that's how it always goes. Everyone thinks *their* death will be some great sacrifice, some noble leap, but that isn't what it is."

"Harrison already moved his mistress into our home."

Okay, so I wasn't entirely jaded, because an ache ran through my chest at that. Being dead sucked, I was sure, but being forgotten so quickly? Replaced? *Far worse.*

"The world keeps moving. If there's one thing I've learned, it's that no matter what, no matter who dies or how, the world doesn't stop for any of us."

"Then what's the point? Why does any of it matter if as soon as we're gone, it all goes away?"

I cuddled into the warmth of my bed, unsure what to tell her. She wanted to be reassured. She wanted me to tell her there was some great plan, that at the end of the day everything, made sense. I would have loved to tell her that because I'd love to hear it—to believe it.

The reality was that despite having spent my life surrounded by death, I had no stunning pieces of wisdom about it. I didn't know why we were all here, or what the great purpose was, or why any of it meant a damn thing.

Instead, I told her the only thing I could. "Make your peace, Melinda, because you don't want to end up where you'll go if you don't."

She wailed, the screeching of a soul that few could hear and even fewer could survive. It made my ears want to bleed, so I grabbed my headphones and cranked up the music to cover it.

She'd be gone soon, since she only ever stayed for twenty minutes or so. I'd done this long enough to know which ones would cross over and which ones who would get stuck. Melinda?

She'd get stuck. She'd cling and try to bargain until the last moment, when she faded to nothing and ended up in purgatory. Even I didn't like to think about that, about the place I'd glimpsed a handful of times that sent a creeping, gnawing terror through me.

The deep bass and rhythmic drumming drowned out her wailing, and I fell back to sleep. Eventually.

* * * *

A banging on my door at ten at night made me grit my teeth.

*Really? Last night Melinda kept me up and now this?*

Did the universe have a personal vendetta against my sleep? It didn't matter who was there, I couldn't be blamed for whatever I did. Even if it was the hottest stripper-gram I'd ever seen, I'd tell him to take his G-string on home and let me rest.

Dicks were nice and all, but at thirty-five, I'd realized sleep mattered more. Finding a willing cock was far easier than managing a full eight hours.

When I pulled open the front door, a dark-haired man stood there, his suit impeccable and his hands folded behind him like some regal prince.

It took a moment for me to realize I'd seen him before. We hadn't ever spoken, but he'd been into the small occult store I spent time at. I doubted he'd noticed me—I didn't tend to be the sort of person others spent a lot of time caring about. The sharp points of his fangs also told me exactly *what* he was.

"Ava Harlin?" he said, voice smooth and careful, my name a question. Maybe he didn't remember he'd seen me before? "My name is Kase, and I am here at the behest of Lord Raymond Colter."

And that was about the time I realized my night was going to get much, much worse, because Raymond Colter led the local vampire coven.

I'd avoided most of the supernatural world by treading along the outskirts like a mouse avoiding the trap. Others like myself—those who walked the line between human and supernatural—tended to leap right into a world they weren't equipped for. Humans playing the games of immortals never went well for the human.

They ended up dead, which was a fate I'd rather avoid for as long as possible.

"What exactly does he want?"

Kase lifted one of his perfectly manicured eyebrows. "That isn't for me to ask, and I'd suggest you not ask, either. All I know is that he sent me to collect you."

I groaned, wishing Melinda would come back. She wasn't great company, but it had to be better than vampires. The few I'd run into were always insufferable bores who thought far too much of themselves.

"Let me get dressed," I muttered. Arguing with vampires was, in general, a bad idea.

"There isn't time."

I waved down at myself—my pink fluffy bath robe with cartoon penises on it over a pair of boy shorts and a tank top—both with a quip about books being better than boys. "I'm not well versed with vampire etiquette, but I'm thinking this might not be the best outfit to go meeting royalty, huh?"

Kase traced his gaze down my body impassively, a look so uninterested it offended. Sure, fucking a dead guy wasn't my idea of a good time, but he could at least look as though I were slightly more appetizing than spoiled meat.

Though, at the same time...using 'appetizing' when talking about a vampire was probably a poor choice of terms.

"He won't care. He made it clear time is of the essence, so this way." Kase held his hand out toward a dark car parked in front of my house, someone else in the driver's seat.

There wasn't really a way to refuse that was there? I was pretty sure if I pushed any further, I'd end up gagged and tied, and while that might be wonderfully fun on my days off, I just didn't think this vampire was a fan of safewords.

So instead, I followed his lead.

He sat up front with the driver, leaving me in the back alone.

Faint whispers rattled through the cab, and I did my best to ignore them. They were the echoes of ghosts who followed vampires around. When I'd still been young and full of optimism, I'd thought they were the whispers of the souls from the vampires themselves. Eventually I'd realized the truth—they were the whispers of their *victims*. Why those whispers never went away, I didn't understand. They just kept growing into a chorus that followed the vampire everywhere, even though only I heard it.

The presence of so many whispers in the car said the two up front were not vampires I should trust. *Like anything that eats people should be trusted.* I'd sooner turn my back on a man-eating tiger than a vampire.

The ride didn't take long, and the stretches of empty road in the barren night reminded me of how isolated the desert was. Why so many vampires would choose to settle in a place with so much sun and heat never made much sense to me, but then again, no one asked for my opinion.

The car pulled past large iron gates, and the house before us didn't fit the area at all. Instead of a Spanish style—all flat stucco walls and clay roofs—this house was an old Victorian mansion with peaked roofs and oval windows near the top. A large porch sat at the front, the wood aged as though the place had been there for centuries.

Maybe it had. Who knew the truth when it came to immortals?

Kase opened my door, and I ignored the way the pebbles of the driveway dug into the bottom of my fuzzy slippers. My absurd outfit might have bothered me, but there was a benefit to looking weak and ridiculous.

It was easy to play the part of a medium when I had to, to pretend my abilities were on par with fortune tellers at fairs and the stay-at-home-moms who sold love potions along with MLM leggings. Safer, too, since *those* people were never seen as a threat. What I was, I didn't know, but I didn't need anyone else taking an interest in it—or me.

Inside the house, a young man offered to take my robe as though it were a jacket.

Keeping covered seemed a good idea, so I waved him off. No reason to walk into a room full of blood drinkers looking like a buffet.

I followed Kase not up the staircase but down. Beneath the first level, the already impressive mansion spread out into more rooms and areas than I could count.

It made sense, though. Being underground helped them conduct business even when the sun was up and reduced the chance of attack or danger. It had to suck to know only a curtain stood between someone and a fiery end.

Inside the final set of doors—two large ones that reached from floor to ceiling and were adorned with gold and jewels —was a place that made me rethink the entire thing.

Vampires stood on either side of a center aisle, the floor shiny black stone except for a middle strip of red tile. At the end of the walkway were several seats on two different levels of stage, most on the lower level, and on the upper level, just one.

Dense shadows twisted around the throne, as though a layer of living darkness surrounded the chair. I sensed *something* from those shadows, but I couldn't tell what they were. If they had ever been spirits, it had been so long ago that they were nothing but glimmers of what they had been.

And on the throne? A vampire who made my skin crawl and all my warnings go off like an old car the owner hoped would keep limping forward. He had long, straight black hair and dark skin. Flat and empty red-rimmed eyes met mine.

The older a vampire got, the less human they appeared and acted. It was as though they stopped remembering how to be human. All that showed in the absolute stillness of the one in the throne, the way he didn't even blink.

"Ms. Harlin?"

I gulped and nodded. The whole idea of not showing fear before predators sounded like great advice until facing off against one.

"Thank you for coming. I wish to hire you."

*Well…that wasn't what I expected…*

I tried to play dumb, to pretend we were talking about my boring day job selling life insurance. "I'm afraid I don't do policies for the undead since you don't really…die."

Colter tilted his head, as though unused to having to tell anyone something twice. Then again, as ruler of a coven, he probably never did. "I require your *other* set of skills."

*Well fuck.* I supposed that answered if they knew about me, didn't it? I'd thought I'd kept that side of me under wraps, but clearly, I hadn't done a good enough job.

"What did you need?"

"I need you to speak to the spirit of someone recently deceased."

Not a difficult task, nor an unusual one for those who knew my powers. Though… "I can't talk to vampires who have died." I frowned. "I mean, dead-dead. Like, deader than you are."

And that was not the best example of self-preservation I'd ever heard.

Still, if Colter was offended, he didn't show it. "No. Not a vampire." *Good.* The last thing I needed was to explain how vampires didn't have souls anymore, thus couldn't be summoned. That was the sort of thing they might take offense to, and offending things that could kill me was dumb. For beings with such hard skin, I'd found vampires to be exceptionally sensitive. "I need you to speak with the most recent person a vampire killed."

*Less good.*

I shuffled my fluffy slippers along the tile to buy time. Turning down the leader of a vampire coven was a good way to waste all that staying alive I'd done, but getting involved with the mess of a vampire who had been killing people — and the whole 'most recent person he killed' was a very bad way to put it — wasn't a great idea either.

"Murder victims are notoriously difficult to summon —" I started, trying for my best 'oh, I wish I could, really' tone.

Colter's eyes flashed red, the rim expanding until the entire iris turned ruby and bright. "You will do as I ask, and I will pay you well for your time. If you refuse, you will be lucky if a medium can find what is left of *your* soul when we finish with you. Now, let us try this again. I have a job for you."

My gulp was harsh against my bone-dry throat, but really, there was only one answer.

I plastered on a smile I didn't feel and stuck my hands into the pockets of my penis robe. "Sounds great. Just give me a shovel and point me in the direction of the corpse."

*I wish fewer of my nights led to graverobbing.*

# Chapter Two

Damp, cold mud soaked through my fuzzy slippers.

"I didn't think mediums needed access to a body to work." Kase leaned against the side of the car as we watched a few of his associates digging up a hastily dug grave. We weren't at a cemetery. No one had officially put the body to rest.

"Well, most of them are hit and miss. They take something the person was bound to and hope an echo of the person shows up. Colter doesn't seem the type to accept 'he didn't show up' as a good explanation."

"True enough. He doesn't take failure lightly." Kase turned a side-eye on me. "Of course, that was a very clever way of skipping over why you do things differently."

The bastard knew how to ask something without directly asking. Good thing I was excellent at answering without giving information.

In the darkness lit only by the headlights of the car, Kase appeared even darker than usual. His hair was pushed back and slicked with something that made it glossy. His suit fit to him perfectly, giving him the look of someone polished and powerful.

"Everyone is different," I answered.

Even if I wanted to explain to him everything—which would be a lethal mistake—I had no idea what *was* different about me. Why didn't I do things as other mediums did? What made me different?

An entire life of those questions, and I had no more answers now than I had the first time I'd seen a ghost, when I had been young enough to not remember, when the behavior had gotten me thrown into the system because my mother didn't want a freak for a child.

Kase gave up on the side-eye, choosing instead to stare directly at me. His eyes were a deep, dark brown with the thinnest red line on the outside the iris—like all vampires had. It was such a subtle detail that people usually missed it.

"So what's the woman's name?" I didn't ask because I cared, but because I wanted something to take his focus down a few notches.

He answered, yet amazingly didn't seem to lessen that intense look at all. "Her name was Rachel Deglo."

"And the vampire?" At his harsh look, I added, "What if I see a bunch of vampires in her memories? I need to know who I'm looking for."

The pause before he answered was long and full of annoyance. "Olin."

That sharp response should have told me to shut up, but I'd never been good at that. "Why'd he kill her?"

"Because she asked too many questions?"

*Well, I guess that ends the conversation...*

"Done," came a voice from one of the lackies. He had dirt on his pants and shoes, and the hunger in his gaze made me want to inch slightly closer to Kase.

Not that I trusted *any* of them, but Kase at least didn't seem hungry.

"It seems you're up." Kase motioned toward the open grave that sat beneath the large overpass.

"Right. Climbing into graves. What else is there to do in the middle of the night?" I continued to mutter as I slid down into the pit they'd dug. More wetness soaked into my shorts and I groaned at the knowledge of what I had caked to my legs.

Grave mud was the worst. It stuck and stained in way normal mud didn't…or maybe that was just my brain refusing to let go of how it had been touching a dead body.

At the bottom of the pit, Rachel's mangled corpse rested in a twisted pile. I was grateful for the darkness, because it meant I couldn't see the details. Some things even I had trouble scrubbing from my brain, and I didn't want to know what the body looked like, what had been done to it.

Vampires tended to *enjoy* their meals, and it often showed in what was left over. That was one reason they took such care to hide their kills, because they could be quickly painted as a serial killer.

Which wasn't so far off.

"How long do you expect this to take?" Kase crouched at the top of the pit.

"Why? Important date?"

"Yes. It's called the sunrise, and sadly it isn't the sort of thing I can reschedule."

I leaned down, the scent of rot having taken hold already. Seeing spirits was one thing. I couldn't avoid that, no matter how hard I tried. They found me, as if drawn to me, knowing I could see them when no one else could.

That wasn't nearly as bad as *this* though. Calling forth a spirit required focus. It was becoming a conduit for the spirit, a way for them to interact with the world. It felt as though something had slipped inside me and left behind a sticky residue once gone.

However, since Colter wouldn't let me off the hook, I didn't have other options. One quick chat with the spirit and I could take myself home to wash up.

Kase staring at me made me uneasy, but I pushed that from my mind. Instead, I closed my eyes. My stomach rolled at the way flesh gave beneath my fingertips, at the clammy chill of it. *Don't think about it.*

I breathed through my mouth to avoid the scent, nice and slow, and tried to focus as I reached through whatever it was that connected me to the afterworld. When I did, it rushed over me, through me, and even breathing became challenging. It felt like sucking whipped cream into my lungs, made me want to cough it up.

Instead, I sank into it, accepted it, reached further into that abyss that always welcomed me, always felt as though it pulled me in.

The body created an anchor in those weeks until a spirit left this realm entirely. By connecting to that other realm, that power, along with the body, I could drag the spirit back, no matter where it had ventured.

It wasn't something I did often — grave digging never led anywhere good — but I'd done it before in rare cases.

I grasped in that abyss, calling forth the spirit. The prickling sensation I was used to didn't come. That filling as the spirit took up space inside me, as it spoke through me, none of that happened.

The trail the spirit had left was long and narrow, but at the end? When I expected to find the spirit…

Blackness. Emptiness. A void that made me open my mouth and let out a bottomless scream that tore at my throat. My chest wouldn't rise, frozen as if that mist had turned to ice around me.

The burning, choking sensation swamped over me just before I passed out.

\* \* \* \*

Coughing woke me, the sort that made me worry I'd throw up. It felt like the time I'd overestimated my swimming ability at the beach and inhaled a few mouthfuls of sea water.

Even with the frantic hacking, nothing came up. Worse, a chill inside me remained, something dark and ugly and void, as if it had hollowed out a spot inside me that would forever be empty.

"Breathe slowly." Kase's voice brought me back to the present, to the realization I'd been passed out with a vampire around.

My hand flew to my neck to check for wounds.

A dark sigh. "I didn't bite you."

"Can never be too careful. You might have gotten peckish." My words came out rough, as though covered in gravel and shoved through a too-tight throat. Still, I pushed myself up to sitting, finding myself back in my own home. The curtains were drawn, the room dim, but it was my bed.

The comforter of which was now covered in the same mud I'd had on me. *Just wonderful.*

Being back didn't reassure me nearly as much as it should have. Somehow having Kase in my room was far too personal. He didn't sit on my bed — thankfully — but watched from the foot. The still way he stood unnerved me, the way all old vampires did.

And there was no mistaking him for being anything other than exceedingly old.

"What happened?" I croaked out the question, a pounding in my head as I tried to recall past that horrible sinking feeling I'd encountered.

"I was hoping you would be able to tell me. You touched the corpse, then your mouth opened and a sound came out."

"It's called screaming. With how many humans you've killed, I'd think you'd recognize it."

He lifted his dark eyebrow, as though not surprised I'd think that, but rather that I'd say it out loud.

*So maybe insulting him isn't smart.*

He shook his head. "You didn't scream, Ava. The sound that came out was nothing I've ever heard. It was like the wind over the ocean. Your eyes turned white, as well."

The memory of the darkness pulling me in swamped me again, a sinking void that wanted to devour me. I leaned forward, trying to slow my breath. "How did it stop?"

"I ripped you away from the corpse. When the connection was broken, you fell unconscious."

"Wonderful. Thanks for that."

He didn't speak, didn't smile, just stared as if he wasn't sure what to think of me.

*Welcome to the club.*

Something about living my life with a constant awareness of death had made the idea of dying less scary. Sure, I didn't *want* to die. Who did, really? Even if the afterlife didn't frighten me the way it did people with less information, I also wasn't looking to make the leap any time soon. I doubted they had coffee worth a damn, there. However, demystifying it had also loosened my tongue through the years, and that loose tongue was probably what would send me to the afterlife.

When I did go, I planned to find a medium and bug the shit out of *her*. Maybe it was petty, but I figured I'd earned it. It was like hazing. I might hate it when I had to experience it, but I was sure as hell going to pass that trauma onto the next person.

"What does this mean?" Kase folded his hands behind his back again, a stance that seemed pompous.

Then again, he *was* pompous. It showed in the way he walked, the way he spoke. I'd thought at first that he was a glorified errand boy for Colter, but now that I could really look at him, I realized it wasn't the case. He was far too old and powerful for anything so simple.

It took a moment to recall his question. My brain wasn't ready to return to real life. "I have no idea," I admitted.

"Not the best answer."

"Probably smarter for me to lie and tell you what you want to hear, but honestly? I've got no clue. *That* has never happened before."

"Explain what you do know."

I took a deep breath and turned so my feet could rest on the floor. It made me feel slightly more in control. "I follow the trail the spirit leaves, the one that tethers it to the body. It thins the longer a soul is still here, but if they haven't left this realm, it's there. If they have, I don't have a trail at all. There *was* a trail." I spoke those words carefully, as if to really drive that point home.

There *had* been a trail. I'd grasped it, been able to follow it. The time I had tried such a trick with a soul that had already moved on was like touching sand, with nothing to hold onto.

Kase didn't interrupt me, only stared as I continued to try to explain.

"At the end, where the spirit should have been, there was nothing. Just a huge empty void."

"Could the soul have moved on right at that moment?"

I considered it, the god-awful timing it would take for such a thing to happen. Still, I shook my head. "I don't think so. The tether would have disappeared. It was there. It was just broken, like something had snatched the soul away." I risked staring directly at Kase. "What the hell was Olin? What aren't you telling me?"

Despite it not showing on his face, I could *feel* his surprise at the question. So, he wasn't used to people asking him things? People probably took one look at him — once they knew what he was — and did whatever he said. Vampires tended to have that sort of influence on people. It wasn't magical — it was fear.

Anyone who didn't fear vampires was an idiot. There were so many things that prowled this world, but I doubted any had a worse reputation for being cruel and dangerous.

I knew better, though. Kase was scary, sure, but he made sense. I understood him.

There were things I glimpsed in the afterlife from time to time, the parts of it that were normally safely sealed away, the twisting shadows and flame-covered monsters, and I knew Kase wasn't so bad.

"I told you once before, but I will offer the same advice again, since you seem to not learn quickly. Stop asking questions. They will be the end of you."

"They haven't been yet."

"You haven't dealt with me before, either."

And that made me realize Kase might just be worse than that void…

# Chapter Three

Having Kase out of my house was the best feeling in the world. Funny that a looming, dangerous vampire would bring down the vibes of a place, but he did.

He'd needed to report to the coven, so after a day full of little conversation and one awkward attempt at playing board games, I'd been only too happy to see his ass leaving the moment the sun dipped behind the mountains.

He'd given me a check for the job—a more-than-generous one—and warned me against speaking of the events to anyone.

It was almost enough for me to consider working for them again.

At least, until I recalled that sinking void and that I was trying to talk to someone *they* had killed.

It was probably best to not entangle myself any further with murderers.

Still, no matter how I tried to shake off the feelings, I couldn't. It was in the memory of that pit, the darkness. What *was* that?

In all my years of dealing with spirits, I'd never encountered anything similar. What did it mean?

Ignoring a lot of the supernatural world was easy because it didn't affect me. Who cared about vampires or werewolves or their nonsense? However, this was *my* area of expertise. I understood the dead, how spirits worked, and this wasn't following the rules I'd spent my life mapping out.

A knock on my door drew me short. People visiting me wasn't ever a good thing. It wasn't like I had girls' night friends who might show up out of the blue with wine and rom-com movies. A second, louder knock made me groan.

Not answering wasn't a choice, and ignoring it wouldn't solve a thing. The big bad monsters in the world didn't let flimsy wooden doors stop them.

I pulled it open, prepared to find god only knew what.

Thankfully, it wasn't all that bad.

"It's a bit late, Troy. Isn't it?"

Troy, my neighbor, offered me his bright smile that never failed to melt me. He had that silver-fox thing down, with his neatly cut, graying hair but extraordinarily fit body. His eyes were a blue so pale they looked silver. The man had to be in his late forties or early fifties, but with him being over six feet tall and having the frame of a fridge, I was never too disappointed to find him on my porch. How one man could be every hero in every small-country-town romance at once, I didn't know.

"I just got home and saw your lights on. I thought I'd stop over." His voice held an odd wariness and a tightness to his cheeks that sharpened the edges of his smile.

*Maybe he's having a bad day.*

He worked as a detective for the local police station. No doubt he had some days where he saw things he'd rather not, and those days brought him to my porch. Then again, I understood how an empty house could weigh on a person, especially on those bad days.

Even with my own shitty day, I couldn't turn him away. Troy was too nice a person for that. I moved backward and nodded toward the kitchen table.

Troy always made my place feel small, but when I hit the button on my kettle and turned around, my home grew even tinier. His gaze moved around the room, his motions slow and almost predatory.

Despite his unfairly deep voice and his size, Troy had *never* unnerved me like this. Maybe it was his *I'm a good guy* persona that made that all seem less threatening.

His gaze darted to mine as if he'd noted my discomfort. He gave me another smile, though it still held the sharp edges. "No caffeine," he said. "I think my heart rate is fast enough."

I nodded and pulled down two cups along with herbal tea.

*Don't be stupid—you know Troy. You're just paranoid after dealing with the vampires.*

"Did you have a visitor earlier?"

The question made me frown. "I thought you just got home?"

"I did." My kitchen chair complained as it always did when Troy sat. My cute little finds from a thrift store hadn't been made for a man his size. "My front camera picks up your driveway, too, and I saw a big black town car here all day.

*At least he didn't see me being carried in.*

"I also went back and saw you were carried in early this morning."

*Well fuck.* "And you didn't check on me? I'm insulted."

He shrugged. "You went outside later, when I was reviewing the video, so I knew you were okay. It just seemed a good time to come check on you in person."

When the kettle beeped, I poured hot water into over the tea bags in the mugs. "Everything's fine."

"I've lived next door to you for six years, Ava. You've never been carried home before. Is everything okay?"

*No, not really.* Somehow, I didn't think my sweet neighbor — no matter how good-looking — was going to be much help when dealing with a coven of vampires, a missing soul and whatever else was looking to screw me over.

Still, even the offer helped the loneliness.

"Yeah. You know how it is. I had a little too much fun. It happens."

He took the cup of tea when I handed it over, his smile not returning. Instead, his expression screamed disapproval. The graying hair helped. "And the person who brought you home?" There wasn't any mistaking his tone about Kase.

*Jealousy?* Doubtful. Troy hadn't shown any interest in me in all the years he'd lived next door. I figured he saw me as an annoying little sister at best. He probably visited me because he felt responsible, since I had no family of my own, and that made him the one to lecture me about proper courting practices. He was for sure the type to take in neighborhood strays.

I shrugged as I took a seat across from him. "A friend."

He snorted softly then took a drink. After a long moment, he set his cup on the table. "Be careful, Ava.

Sometimes friends aren't as…friendly as you might hope."

The words felt ominous, especially when he darted his gaze to my throat.

Except, that was insane. I scolded myself for being so damned paranoid. It had to have been my night. Digging up corpses and getting sucked into mysterious voids were the sorts of things that would put anyone on edge.

Troy was perfectly nice, had always been a wonderful neighbor, and he was most likely looking for a hickey so he could lecture me about drinking too much and going home with men I didn't know.

He opened his mouth, and before he could start the lecture—I'd never been a fan of them—I interrupted him. "I need you to look into a missing person."

*That* got his attention. "What for?" Some of the time he seemed like such a sweet, fun neighbor, but every once in a while, he gave me a look that reminded me of how he must look to criminals. I suddenly understood why he was a detective and almost felt the hot light of an interrogation room.

"A friend of a friend kind of thing. I just need you to see what you can find on her, see if there's anything that stands out."

His eyes narrowed, and somehow, they looked even brighter. That blue-silver seemed to shine as he studied me. "I'm serious, Ava. If you're in trouble, I can help. Whatever it is, I can help you."

Damn, that was tempting. Having someone else on my side, someone I could run these things by. Except, I immediately thought about Kase, about Colter, about Olin, about all the other horrible things that were in a part of the world Troy needed to be nowhere around, and that made the decision easy.

I couldn't let him get any more involved than I had to.

"No, I'm not in any trouble. I just need whatever information you can find on her."

He nodded, though the sharpness in his silver eyes said he didn't fully believe me.

Even so, he took the piece of paper I wrote down everything I knew about Rachel on and tucked it into his pocket.

Getting more involved was the last thing I should be doing, but something about the void, about the way some small part of me *still* felt frozen meant I couldn't just walk away.

\* \* \* \*

The night wore on after Troy had left, and sleep didn't come easily. It never had.

When it finally happened, when I finally relaxed enough to close my eyes, the same dream as always hit me. The mist came, surrounding me, swallowing me. It was thick, dragging me under it, filling my lungs until I clawed at my throat. It choked me, made me wake exhausted and gasping.

That inability to sleep left me sitting outside my favorite occult shop, waiting for it to open.

Gran never opened early, but I'd planted my ass on the bench outside at five. It let me bask in the silence and watch the sun creep up above the mountain line.

When she did show—at eight sharp—I didn't fight the smile I had.

She was odd in all the best ways. The woman was in her sixties and didn't like anyone. She was prickly, hard-headed, and yet few crossed her.

What she was, I had no idea. I'd asked once, and she'd laughed, saying that if I had to ask, I wasn't ready to know. It wasn't the most helpful of answers, but I'd also gotten used to that from her. She made cryptic puzzles seem straightforward.

"Morning." She unlocked the front door, then let me in behind her.

The shop smelled of sage and incense and blood. I always ignored that last one, too unsettled by it to consider the why.

Some questions were better left unasked, let alone unanswered.

"You're up and about early. Tea?"

"Sure." I slid onto the stool at the far end of the sales counter as she went about turning on an electric kettle—the same type as the one she'd bought me for my housewarming present. Really, it was a nice present, considering she could have gotten me something far scarier from her store.

"Are there any other ways spirits leave this realm? They go to the afterlife, to purgatory or become a poltergeist, right? There are only the three options?"

She poured something into the tea, but I'd long ago stopped asking what anything was. She hadn't poisoned me yet, and I didn't see that changing. "Yes. Spirits do not belong to this world but are anchored here by the physical body. A reaper cuts the bond at the moment of death, and when their tether fades, the spirit moves on."

Just the mention of reapers made my skin crawl. Of all the things that were out of my weight class, reapers had to be the meanest. They weren't living or dead…but were more powerful than either.

Thankfully, I'd never had to deal with one. Would I even see them if one appeared? I could see spirits and the things in the afterlife I'd glimpsed, the horrors that glimmered through our realm, but perhaps reapers would have been too different.

Which served me fine. If I never had to see such a thing, I'd chalk it up to a win.

"Why are you asking? In all our years together, I've never known you to be an overly curious girl."

That felt like an understatement. "Curiosity is a dangerous thing in my position."

"Ignorance is *always* more dangerous, dear."

I sighed at the lesson she'd tried to teach me before. It was easy for her to say — she was part of that world. I'd seen it in the way others dealt with her, when old vampires would walk in and treat her with a reverence that reeked of fear. It was so easy to want to know about things that could keep me safe.

What would knowing do for me? Only drag me farther down a path that would get me killed. "Humans don't last long in that world. We aren't built for it."

"And yet every time you try to avoid it, every time you try to pretend like you're no part of it, you end up in worse trouble."

"That isn't a lesson. That's bad luck."

"Luck is often the best teacher of all. The others you talk about — the mediums, the two-bit witches, the telepaths — those humans have to work extremely hard to become part of this world. They have to chase it. You? It won't leave you be."

"Your world is a fucking stalker, then."

She smiled, the winkles in her face deepening with the action. "Fate gets what it wants, Ava, no matter what we think about it. Now, explain to me what happened. No more being coy."

The story came slowly, as if by telling it I could figure something out I'd missed before. Not that it helped—I ended up as confused as I'd been before.

"Close your eyes," Gran said.

When I did, her fingers brushed my wrist, warmer than I'd have expected, and far stronger.

She touched me, and some of that coldness, the place inside me that had seemed frozen from the void, thawed.

No, not thawed, but retreated as though the heat inside her forced it to flee.

Shivers took hold, making me tremble as that coldness thinned but spread and seemed to try to escape her.

I *felt* her hand wrap around it, as though she'd reached inside me and taken hold of that freezing darkness.

I opened my eyes to find her hand, fist closed, in front of me. She opened her palm and mist drifted out, as though she had a piece of dry ice hidden there.

It had me leaping backward, off the stool, but she didn't react.

Instead, she lifted her tea and took another sip.

"What the hell was that?"

"I know I've mentioned before that all connections are two ways, have I not? When you tried to call that spirit, you reached for it and found what?"

"Darkness."

She tapped her finger against the cup. "You only saw darkness. It was like the spirit was in the deepest part of the ocean. You couldn't see it, but it *was* there, and you swallowed water as you looked."

"That's what you pulled out of me? That's what I could feel?"

She nodded. "You could have expelled it yourself if you knew it was there, but you don't like to know such things. That was growing inside you, filling you, taking over."

"It looks like what's in my dreams…"

"Does it?"

Even as I felt myself again, as that place inside me that had been frozen now warmed, I couldn't rid myself of the thought that something had been there.

"I don't understand."

"Unfortunately for you, you will soon enough." Her eyes went white, the creepy way they turned when she wasn't there anymore. I never quite got used to it. "There are things in the darkness, Ava, things you've only glimpsed before."

Memories of those things, of the monsters I'd seen only through the corner of my eye, the ones I'd looked away from as though if I never really saw them, they couldn't hurt me. "I don't know what you're talking about."

"You do. They can't see you, but they will. You've looked into the shadows too long. It's looking back, and it will see you."

Which was not the most reassuring statement I'd ever heard.

# Chapter Four

I welcomed the dull monotony of my job when compared to the craziness I'd gone through the last few days. I sat in the office, making phone calls, tracking leads. Life insurance might have been the most boring occupation in the world, but that was exactly what had drawn me to it.

No one who sold insurance did anything important. They lived long, uneventful lives and died safely in their beds at an old age and with lots of money going to their beneficiaries.

That sounded like a good plan to me.

Life was far too eventful without tempting fate by having a job that welcomed trouble, too.

Despite my best attempts to keep my attention on the task, I couldn't help but venture off. I recalled that void I'd found at the end of the tether, the mist Gran had pulled from me and her haunting final words before I'd decided the entire day was too strange and I needed to get back to the boring normality of work.

"You have a new client to see you," my receptionist said, peeking into my office.

"I don't have anything on my schedule."

"He just came in." She leaned in farther and dropped her voice. "Trust me. You *want* to take this one."

Her conspiratorial tone told me everything I needed to know. He was good-looking, and she was forever hoping to get me laid. Good help was hard to find, and help that kept an eye out for my love life was even harder.

Still, being set up right now was *so* not the time. I had vampires watching over me, a missing spirit and something from the void staring back at me. I didn't see how dating could fit into that equation anywhere.

Still, a client was a client, and I could always use more of those. "Okay," I said before running my hands over my dark hair to straighten it. It was doing what it did — which was being wavier than I'd like it to but not wavy enough to look purposeful.

When the door opened again and the client walked in, I tried not to stare — I really did. Who could blame me, though?

This man had grunge-hot down to a science. He had long hair that went past his shoulders — medium brown with red undertones. Scruffy, *haven't shaved today and might not tomorrow* stubble rested over his chin and cheeks, and he had a T-shirt just tight enough to show off his muscular arms. He also had tattoos that wound up his bare arms, over his throat, as if they'd grown there naturally. How much of him was covered in the black flames?

I was all for discovering it, for tracing each mark. *For science, of course.*

His clearing throat made me realize I'd been gawking. Not just slyly looking but mouth-hanging-open ogling.

*So much for being professional.*

He stuck his hand out over the desk and offered a devastating smile. "I'm Hunter."

*Of course his name is Hunter.* Somehow it fit, as if it were as unique and dangerous as the man before me. I clasped his hand, but instead of shaking it like I expected, he tugged me in and pressed a kiss to my knuckles.

His lips were hot, and his breath seared me as he kept his eyes locked on mine. It was only his lips to my knuckles, yet I could almost picture that same smirk, those same whiskey-colored eyes staring up at me from between my legs.

*Down, girl.* As soon as the thought came, my cheeks heated, and I yanked my hand away.

Hunter only smiled wider, as though he'd caught the stray idea and didn't mind it a bit.

Which was probably just him amused by the fact that he turned on every woman in a nine-mile-radius. Who could blame me, really? It had been far too long since I'd had sex, and he was essentially walking sex.

"Please, sit," I said as if that could wipe away the entire interaction thus far and paint me as a professional.

Thankfully, he did. It meant I had to look at less of him.

"So, you're here for life insurance?"

He nodded, tossing his arm across the back of the chair. It was an awkward angle, and yet it only made him look more like some fantasy rebel. "Sure. I'm curious, though. You don't really seem like the insurance type."

"What does an 'insurance type' look like?"

"Frumpy. Boring. A balding man in his sixties sleeping with his secretary because his wife won't talk to him anymore. That type."

I pressed my lips together. What was there to say back to that? As insulted as I wanted to feel, that was exactly why I'd gotten into the business, wasn't it? Well, I mean, minus the balding and wife part—I didn't much want either of those. The rest of it, though?

"I'm not going to discuss that," I snapped. "If you're here out of some joke, just leave. I have work to do."

He lifted an eyebrow, an act that made the light hit his eyes and turned them almost red. "Feisty, aren't you? And here I thought this entire trip might be boring. I hate being bored, you know? At my age, there isn't anything worse."

"And I hate having my time wasted. You might make for nice scenery, but I'm busy. Thank you for stopping by." I made sure my 'thank you' sounded as much like *fuck you* as possible. Sure, he *was* nice to look at, but I had so many other things to deal with. Pretty boys who wasted my time couldn't make it on the list.

He laughed and pushed himself out of the seat. I didn't stand, trying my best to ignore him entirely. Better that then risk staring again.

"This isn't over."

"Yes, it is."

He set his hands on the desk and leaned in close enough to force my gaze up and to his amber eyes. He was only a breath away. "No, it isn't. If you thought no one would sense what you did, that sort of power, then you're even more foolish than you look."

*Power.* His words chilled me. He couldn't mean what had happened with the spirit, could he?

*Exactly who — and what — is he?*

I opened my mouth to ask, but he took the opportunity to run his thumb across my bottom lip, silencing me. "I'll see you around, shadow-girl. Count on that."

With that, he left. The heat of his thumb remained on my lip, as if I could still feel it there, teasing me.

*What the hell just happened?*

\* \* \* \*

"I thought you weren't allowed to come in without an invitation." I carried my to-go container of food past Kase, who sat in the recliner of my living room as though he were entirely welcome there and hadn't broken in while I had been gone.

"Superstition. We've encouraged quite a few of those over the years to throw people off our trail."

"It's also called manners."

He waved that off but didn't rise from the seat. "Manners are for humans."

"You sure like reminding me you aren't one."

"Why hide it? You already know the truth, so why pretend? Besides, who would *want* to be human? You all scuttle about your short, little lives, oblivious to the world around you."

"Do you even remember being human?"

He pursed his lips as though thinking. "A little. I remember it smelled horrible. Filth everywhere, everything wanting to kill or eat me. Not much miss."

I went into the kitchen, leaving him behind in the living room. If he wanted to talk — and I'd guess he did since he'd shown up at my house — he could follow me. I took a seat at the kitchen counter and flipped open the top on my food.

*Carne asada fries.* The best food for hangovers or life crisis. Which I was having, I wasn't sure. Maybe both?

He lifted his lip as though the food disgusted him.

In turn, I took one slow, noisy bite, making sure to smack my lips, just to annoy him.

Sure, annoying him was stupid, but it seemed they wanted me alive. If they hadn't, I wouldn't have been able to say a word before he ended me.

"So what misfortune brings you here? Last I checked, I did the job you forced me to, and I was paid for it. That ends our little transaction."

"Why are you still looking into Rachel's death?"

I paused, then narrowed my eyes. "How would you know that?"

"You drove by her grave again."

Okay, sure, I *had* done that, but I hadn't gotten out. Some strange pull had taken me there, as if by parking for an hour and staring at the spot I could understand what had happened, as though I could make sense of it all. As much as I didn't want to get involved with the vampires, I still had this drive to understand Rachel, to understand that void. Nothing had come to me, though, and by the third time a very shady-looking car had driven by mine, I'd taken off.

How had he known, though…?

"You were stalking me?"

"Not me, no. I have underlings to do such menial tasks."

*Harsh.* Still, I refused to be annoyed by not being seen as important enough to warrant his personal attention. "So why did you have someone following me? I can't believe one little human is worth that?"

"It is common procedure when outsiders work with the coven, to ensure they aren't spreading information they shouldn't. It is a security measure."

"It's rude."

"Haven't we already discussed that?"

I opened my mouth but snapped it shut before speaking. He was right, and seeing as he didn't appear to care about rudeness, scolding him for it was pointless and I didn't care for wasting my breath.

Thankfully, he spoke next. "You need to let this go, Ava. You have no reason to be involved in this case any longer."

"You can't ask me to stick my nose into it then get mad when I don't let it go."

"I am fairly certain I can get mad about that, and you would not care for that happening."

"But I don't understand what happened."

He didn't seem moved at all by that. "You are a human, Ava. You are exceedingly fragile. Are answers worth your life?"

"You were the one to call on me first. How can you act like you've got any high ground on this? You weren't too worried about my safety when you wanted me to grope a corpse."

"That is not true. I personally accompanied you and did not leave until you were well and safe. However, you continuing this line of investigation will put you into danger when I am not there to help."

"Well, Kase, I never *asked* you to help."

Kase didn't respond, and I went to pick up a piece of my food as a signal to him that we were done with the conversation.

A knock on the door had me ready to toss my fries across the room. What did a woman need to do to get a little solitude? All I wanted was to eat my greasy, fattening fast food in peace. The rest of the world — especially the supernatural one I wasn't even a part of — could go to hell.

When I didn't answer, the door opened. I thought I'd locked it.

"Ava?"

I straightened at Troy's voice. Getting him involved with Kase was a very bad idea. Troy was overly protective, and I doubted Kase wanted a police officer anywhere near coven business. What if Kase decided that as a detective, Troy had become a threat?

I rushed off the seat, wanting to get rid of Troy before the two could see each other.

In the living room, I stopped in front of Troy, trying to block his path, despite him being far larger than I was. "Hey, what's up?"

He looked past me as if he *knew* someone as in my kitchen. "I have those files for you."

"Wonderful. I'll just take them then —"

"Who's here?"

"No one."

He huffed and shifted to the left as though to walk past me. I went that way with him, like two people in an aisle both trying to get out of the other's way.

"It's the same car from before."

"Black town cars a dime a dozen. Look, maybe tomorrow we'll get together and —"

"I didn't know you had a pet." Kase's voice had me glancing over my shoulder and groaning.

Why couldn't anyone listen? Troy ignored me, Kase ignored me.

*A pet?* The odd statement drew a frown.

"What are *you* doing here?" Troy's voice—always deep—had dropped another few octave until it rumbled more like a growl more than actual words. It sent a shiver up my spine and made me want to take a step backward.

"I have business with her," Kase said.

"No, you really don't. This isn't a safe place for your kind."

*Your kind?* The statement made me realize something I'd never considered before.

Troy knew about vampires. He had to. There was no other explanation for what he'd said to Kase.

"You know what he is?" Even as I turned toward Troy again, he didn't look my way.

Instead, his eyes flashed impossibly bright and locked on Kase with an intensity that made me glad they weren't on me. He might know what Kase was, but he likely had no idea how old or dangerous he was...

"You have no claim," Kase said as though the threats from Troy were no concern of his. "She bears no marks, and her home has no wards. You have nothing here to protect, dog."

"Neither do you."

Suddenly I was less concerned about keeping either of them alive and more bothered by them talking about me as though I were a local fire hydrant they both liked to piss on from time to time. "No one has *any* claim here." I waved around at the room. "This is *my* house, which, by the way, you *both* broke into."

Troy did give me a look that seemed more than a little indulgent, as though it was adorable that I thought that. "I didn't break in. I wanted to make sure *that* hadn't hurt you."

"I broke in," Kase said without a shred of regret. "We have business to attend to, business that isn't any of that thing's concern. Why don't you put him in the yard while we finish our talk?"

A growl echoed through the room, dark and dangerous and loud enough that I had a moment of glancing around as though a bear had somehow made its way inside.

Instead of that, however, what I found was Troy, eyes like flashlights, throwing their own light out. That lovely silver-blue now glowered like twin full moons. He bared his teeth and instead of the flat, white teeth I was used to, long, sharp canines flashed.

Everything became clear then.

Troy was a werewolf. The nice neighbor who I'd let in so many times wasn't at all what I'd thought.

"Both of you, out!" I pointed at the door.

The men stopped and turned toward me, giving *me* a look as though I were acting crazy.

I was over it, though. I was tired of them screwing up my life and my sleep. "Out, *now*."

Kase moved backward as if my look were as frightening as I wished it were. "We are not finished talking."

"Oh, I am. I have a job I was at all day. I have been up at night dealing with your nonsense. I'm human, as you love to point out, and humans require carne asada fries and sleep."

Kase lifted his dark eyebrow as he stared at me, but I didn't budge.

I deserved a night, damn it.

He nodded. "Stay out of our business, Ava, or you'll find it just might kill you."

"Would you miss me?" I asked the question with as much snark as I could shove into the words.

"No, but I'd have to find a another human to help if we needed another spirit contacted, and I'd prefer not to have to learn any new names." He nodded, an oddly old-world gesture, before casting a look of pure hostility at Troy. Still, he said nothing else before walking out.

Troy's gaze remained locked on Kase until the black car pulled away, and right then he looked every bit the dog Kase had called him, as though he were watching a mailman drive away.

When he had left, however, Troy's shoulders lifted once then lowered, as though he took one deep breath and let it go, before he turned toward me.

"Out."

He frowned. "Ava—"

"I am not doing this with you tonight."

"We need to talk about this."

"No, we really don't." I gestured toward the door, and when I walked closer to him, he backed off.

Did he not want to get close to me, or did he think I wouldn't want to get close to him after realizing what he was?

It didn't really matter, as long as he was leaving.

"What about what I found out about your missing person?"

"Tomorrow. For tonight, take your werewolf ass home because I am marinating myself in hot water until nothing can bother me."

I advanced on him as he backed up until he ended up on my front porch. He set his hand out on the door to keep me from slamming it, then leaned down until he was far closer than he'd ever been before. "You will come over tomorrow morning, Ava, and we *will* talk."

My breath caught at the way he spoke, at that intensity in his gaze I'd never seen before, the way that his overbearing attitude had grown a new, dangerous edge. I leaned in, drawn by the heat of him, but as soon as I did, I wondered what the fuck I was thinking.

I stepped back and closed the door in his face.

I was old enough to know that a hot bath was *always* better than whatever he was offering.

# Chapter Five

The steaming water was heavenly. It soaked into my body, into the soreness and exhaustion of my muscles. I'd added a fizzy bath bomb, so the water had turned a light blue and had tiny, dried flowers through it.

I wasn't a girly girl, but I loved my hot baths. I'd lie there until the water turned cold, until my fingers and toes turned pruney and the scents and bubbles made me feel like a delicate fucking flower myself.

I'd draped my arms over the sides of the tub, and for one moment, my gaze settled on the white scars that covered both my forearms in swirls and almost-beautiful designs. My stomach dropped as it always did when I spotted them, when I had to remember they were there.

It was funny that I could go so long without noticing them. I chalked that up to a mixture of long sleeves and a wonderfully stubborn mind.

The creaking of a door drew my attention away and made me groan at yet another potential interruption.

"Whoever it is, I suggest you go away. I'm armed."

I wasn't armed, of course, and even if I were, I wouldn't have a clue what to do with an actual weapon. It was just the sort of thing people said bravely into the darkness when they had nothing else going for them.

Which was about where I was.

Not that I really thought anyone was there. Sure, I'd ended up on the radar for a couple vampires and a werewolf neighbor, but that didn't mean anyone else was looking for me.

Another sound brought my attention back to the moment. I sat up as I scolded myself for freaking out when it was the house settling—nothing more. Old houses creaked like old men.

It certainly was *not* a killer vampire.

I got out of the bath slowly then pulled my robe around me—my good old penis robe, freshly washed after the whole corpse-mud ordeal. The tile chilled my bare feet, and I stepped slowly so I didn't slip.

I'd never forgotten the spirit from a few years back who had died after a nasty shower fall. Spirits wore whatever they had on when they died, and it had been an awkward couple of weeks as he'd visited me every day in all his naked glory.

I refused to go out the same way.

A strange sensation came over me, something I couldn't place. It was cold, like that void that had been inside me, like the mist I traveled through to try and find the woman's spirit, like my dreams. Except, this didn't frighten me.

It was deep, and cold, but somehow familiar.

I took the stairs carefully, gripping the railing as I went, trying to peer into the darkness of my living room.

Was it Kase? Had he decided he didn't care for a human telling him what to do or where to go? Or perhaps Troy figured waiting until morning for something between an apology and a lecture was just too far.

Except, I *knew* it wasn't them. I could feel it deep in my bones, the way I knew when the sun rose without looking outside, the way I knew when a predator was staring at me.

Whatever was here wasn't anything as trivial as a vampire or werewolf.

And what sort of fucked up world did I live in where vampires and werewolves were *trivial*?

When I reached the ground floor, that chill worsened. I struggled to breathe, and the darkness wasn't run-of-the-mill, as if someone forgot to turn on a light. It was deeper, as though light wasn't just absent but devoured. Something was there inside it, shifting, *staring* back at me.

My wrists burned, as if fire licked along the edges of the scars there. It crept up my arms, searing me, and when I would have screamed, something closed over my mouth.

It muffled the sound, kept it from escaping.

"Trust me. You don't want it to hear you." The voice took a moment for me to recognize.

*Hunter?*

Still, the shadows in the mist swirled as if agitated, shifting enough that a breeze blew through my hair. It moved in a circle, like a small tornado, before leaving.

It didn't go through a door, didn't dissipate. It just disappeared, leaving a vacuum in its wake.

Still, Hunter didn't remove his hand from my mouth. It made me realize he was also entirely pressed against me, and despite it not being possible, he felt better than he'd looked. His skin was warm, even through my robe.

He took his hand off my mouth but didn't move away. "Stay still," he whispered against my ear.

"Why? Is it coming back?"

"No. I just really like looking down your robe."

As soon as his words sank in, when I moved past the adrenaline and the purr of his voice, I realized that yes, my robe had bagged open and he had a perfect view down the front.

I elbowed him, but he didn't seem to even feel it. He released me, though the way he did it implied my little move hadn't meant a thing.

"I am so tired of people breaking into my house," I said.

"You aren't human, and you don't have any wards. That's the same as a 'come on in' sign in our world."

"I *am* human."

"Sure, shadow-girl." He sent me a conspiratorial wink, as if we were on the joke together.

"No, I actually am. No funky teeth, no freaky eyes. Human." I pointed at my face as though that drove the point home.

He waved at himself. "No funky teeth, no freaky eyes. Very much *not* human. Sure, though, if you want to pretend, I'm not one to turn down a bit of good roleplay. You want to be innocent Little Red Riding Hood? I'll play the wolf."

His suggestion derailed me. How could it not? Any girl who claimed she hadn't had entirely inappropriate dreams about the wolf in that story was a damned liar. Once I'd reached a certain age, 'all the better to eat you with' had taken on a very different meaning.

I pictured a dark, heavily wooded forest as I ran, something on my heels, gaining ground. His warm breath on my neck when he caught me…

Suddenly I didn't care what he'd said, why he was there or what exactly he meant by him *'not being human'*.

Until I recalled he'd broken in, and clearly him showing up at my office wasn't a coincidence.

He snorted. "I liked where your mind was going before."

"What are you doing here? And what was that thing?"

"Don't we have better things to discuss? Or we can do away with talking all together."

"I don't sleep with people who might kill me, but thanks."

"If someone might not kill you, are they even worth sleeping with in the first place?" He walked over to the couch and sat with such an exaggerated motion that it was as if he fell. "As for what *that* was? Well, that's more difficult to explain."

"Try."

He let out a long, slow sigh. "Whatever you did the other night sent a hell of a shockwave through the underworld. Did you really think things wouldn't follow it back to you?"

"I didn't do anything."

"Just like you're human? Right."

"What was that thing?"

"A bottomless pit of hunger, mostly. It was a remnant—a creature from hell that feasts off souls. Usually they stick to hell."

"And it was in my living room why?"

"My answer to that won't change, no matter how many times you ask. It came looking for food after the other night." He kicked off his shoes then put his feet up as he stretched out on the couch, as though planning to stay.

"What are you doing?"

"It's late. Unless you're offering a spot in your bed..."

"I don't think so."

He chuckled as though he expected nothing else. "Then it looks like I'm sleeping here."

"You can't just invite yourself to stay at my place."

"Of course I can. I mean, I'm pretty sure I just did."

"I don't even know you."

"I'm Hunter. I don't plan on killing you tonight, and when I fuck you, you'll be begging for it. So unless you want to start begging now, run along and we'll talk more tomorrow."

I stood there, mouth hanging open, with absolutely nothing to say back to it. What did a normal person say back to something like that? It wasn't really like I could throw him out physically or call the cops, given all that had happened, and he *had* saved my life.

Worse?

I was pretty sure if I dealt with him much longer, I might just do as he claimed, so I hurried up the stairs.

So much for a bath to relax me—an even worse tension ran through me, and it would take a lot more than hot water to resolve it...

* * * *

Hunter was gone when I woke, and I had no idea what that meant. He didn't strike me as a vampire, given his normal teeth, yet he certainly wasn't human. The fact that he'd left before the sun came up made me hesitate, but he'd come into my office during the daylight hours, so again, probably not a vampire.

Troy had left a note on my door reminding me to come over when I was up and about, and by ten in the morning, I didn't think I could avoid it anymore.

He always kept his house perfectly. He was the sort of down-home guy who spent every Saturday morning working in his yard. There had been more than a few times I'd drunk coffee on my balcony during those Saturday mornings and watched the show.

Not that I ever was *too* obvious. I would hold a book as though I was totally not watching my extremely hot neighbor mow his lawn.

When I knocked, it took a long moment for him to answer. He was too on the ball for him to have not been near the door, waiting, and yet the pause made me suspect he'd done it for me.

Did he not want to make me feel crowded? *Maybe.*

He nodded and moved away.

*So, we're pretending everything is normal?*

It was my first time inside his house, but it lived up to all my expectations. Everything was worn-in and cozy, as if he'd bought it years before and loved each piece.

Then again, he *was* a werewolf, which meant his age was a far trickier thing to work out.

Supernaturals didn't age. *None* of them. Werewolves and vampires stopped aging when they turned, and mages stopped aging when they gained control of their full powers after some weird ritual. It meant he could be in his early fifties or he could have been three thousand years old, and I'd have had no idea.

"You look like you're thinking," he said as he spooned food from a pan to a plate when we reached the kitchen.

"I'm wondering how old you are," I admitted when he set the plate in front of me.

It was piled high with eggs, bacon, grilled veggies. Then again, werewolves had to eat an extraordinary amount to keep up with their metabolism.

Troy chuckled as he sat across from me with his own plate which had, amazingly, even more food. "Worried I'm three hundred?"

"Add a zero and you have what I was thinking. I don't mind the whole silver-fox thing, but I might draw the line at grandpa wolf."

He choked, hitting his hand against his chest to dislodge the food he'd inhaled due to my little comment. After catching his breath, he gave me a chiding look. "I was made into a werewolf when I was forty, about thirty years ago."

"You were only forty?"

"Last I checked, telling someone they look older than their age is considered rude."

"Not my fault you look like a hard forty."

He huffed, the sound of a man amused when he didn't want to be. "I'm just one of those people who went gray by thirty."

"Look, I'm not complaining."

"No?" The lift of his eyebrow was all too tempting, as if I'd shown my hand.

Instead of answering — I didn't need the complication of letting the werewolf next door know how incredibly handsome I found him — I changed the topic. "So, you said you had information?"

He leaned back and pulled a file from the kitchen counter, then tossed it onto the table next to me. I opened it and flipped through the two scant pages. "This is it?"

"I don't know why people expect the police will have huge files on everyone. I hate to burst your bubble, but most people are exceptionally boring, and the police take little notice of them. Rachel Deglo was thirty-two, sold makeup for a living and had two cats. That's everything there is to know about her."

"How would she end up on the radar of a vampire?"

"People don't need to do much to end up a victim, Ava. Just being in the vicinity of a vampire is enough." He dropped his voice, as if making a point.

I closed the file and met his gaze. "Go on, lecture me. I know you've been dying to do it."

"Kase is *not* someone you should trust."

"You know him? And here I thought it was rude to assume all you supernaturals knew each other."

Troy's expression didn't soften. If anything, he seemed more frustrated by my not taking him seriously. "Kase is second in line in the local coven. Everyone knows him. Many say he actually runs it more than the leader does."

"Colter looked pretty in charge when I met him."

Troy's stillness came back, that edge that said he was trying not to look as bothered as he was. "You met Colter?"

"He's the one who called me in to work the case."

"No one sees Colter, Ava, especially not on some low-level job. Even the consultants who work for the coven never actually meet him."

So why had I? Why would I meet both Colter and Kase? And could Kase actually be as powerful as Troy seemed to think? I pressed my lips together as I considered it. It was hard to imagine Kase as being like Colter. Colter had been terrifying—he'd reached that point in being a vampire where he barely seemed like a person anymore. Kase, however, despite a few times when he would go still in that terrifying way, wasn't the same.

"You still haven't explained what they want with you or why you know what I am or why the idea of vampires and werewolves doesn't bother you at all."

"Don't talk to me like that." I pointed my fork at him. "Last I checked, you never told me you get all furry every full moon, so maybe you don't pretend to be innocent here?"

He leaned back in his chair. "Fair enough. I told you I was turned about thirty years ago. That's where my story pretty much starts and ends. Your turn."

I opened my mouth then snapped it shut. When was the last time I'd told anyone anything?

I didn't talk about myself, ever. I tried very hard not to think about whatever I was, to pretend it didn't exist, that I was just like everyone else.

Yet, Troy stared at me in that way that said he wasn't going to give in. The last time I'd seen that look was when I'd run over his hedges on accident, and he'd waited until I'd admitted it.

The bastard could outlast me for sure.

Better to get it over with and just rip the Band-Aid off. "If I said I could see dead people, would it sound too cliche?"

"A medium?"

I *hated* that question. Not because I had a problem with mediums, but rather because I wished I had something so easily definable. It would make my life much simpler to be able to say exactly what I was, for better or worse. Instead, I always had to follow up every clarification with *well, sort of.*

"Not exactly. Mediums use basic magic to draw in a spirit, and even then, it's only the echo of one. Some are more attuned to that sort of magic, or drawn to it, but they're just doing a spell that's already been created. That's why mediums are next to useless, why they can't give any real information. They can only call up a reflection of who the person was before they went to the afterlife, like an imprint left here."

He didn't talk over me, didn't seem to doubt me. Instead, he nodded for me to continue.

"I can talk to the real spirit. I see them all over, but I can also call them if I have access to their body before they move on."

"And the vampires needed you to talk to Rachel why?"

"Because the vampire who killed her went missing, and they wanted to figure out why."

He pressed his lips together for a moment then shook his head. "Ava, you don't want to get involved with this. If you already know the vampire killed at least one person, why help look for him?"

I set my fork down a little harder than needed, and it clattered against the plate. "I didn't *volunteer*. It's not like I put out a paper ad for the job. Kase showed up at my house in the middle of the night and there wasn't any saying no. When I tried to get out of it, Colter made it clear it wasn't a request I could turn down."

A flash in his eyes, the way they brightened, reminded me he wasn't anywhere close to human. Still, he reeled the reaction in quickly. "That explains why you started helping them. You came to me for information after you'd already found her body, though. Don't look at me like that—corpse smell doesn't wash off well, even after a shower. If you did what they wanted, why are you still looking into this?"

"Because when I tried to call forth her spirit, there was nothing there. It was like she was gone."

The memory of how that dark void had sucked me into the blackness made me shudder and close my eyes. I'd never felt so lost before.

I *knew* what happened after death, so fear hadn't meant much to me. Even if something got me, I had no question about where I was going. That made it easier to accept death. It wasn't an end, only a change of address.

Death had always been safe but life? That was the scary thing.

However, when I had stared into that void, I'd realized there were parts deeper and darker than I'd ever known.

And *that* terrified me.

A warmth on my arm made me open my eyes to find Troy's hand on me. The touch was sweet, and far too personal.

I extracted my arm from his grasp, unsure how to respond or deal with his sympathy.

Thankfully, he didn't call me on it. He picked up his fork and took another bite, chewing slowly, gaze down.

I could almost hear his brain working, moving back through all our interactions, seeing them through a new lens.

Hell, I'd done the same since I'd found out about him. Suddenly, the time he'd laid bricks for a retaining wall in his front yard held new meaning. He'd done it with no shirt, and it made sense now how he'd managed to lift them all. Hell, with werewolf strength, he probably could have moved the pallet all on his own if he'd wanted.

*And wouldn't that be a sight to behold?*

The fact he turned into some sort of dog-creature occasionally was something I chose not to think about. I'd never actually seen a werewolf change, because that required getting far closer to them than I'd ever wanted to. I preferred the very hypothetical knowledge I got from Gran rather than anything more hands-on.

*Of course, hands-on with Troy would be…*

A growl from him had my back straightening. How the hell did a sound like *that* come from a human body?

He stared at me with such intensity that I took my lip between my teeth. How did I become so easy with just one little growl?

As quickly as he started it, however, he silenced it. His slow inhalation made me wonder… *Can he smell me?*

My cheeks heated at the idea that he knew exactly what I'd been thinking.

"So you won't let this go?"

It took a moment to recall what we had been talking about. "No, I can't. I don't understand what happened, but I need to figure it out."

"Why?"

"Because this is all I have. I've always understood *this*, if nothing else. It's like you finding out you couldn't shift for some reason. Would you turn around and go 'oh, well, guess that doesn't matter?' No. You'd do anything you had to to figure out why it happened, to make sure it didn't happen again, wouldn't you?"

He chuffed, the sound reminding me of a dog. "Be very careful, Ava. No matter what skills you have, you're still human, and humans tend to get trampled in our world. Call me before you dig any deeper."

I pushed my plate forward and rose, nodding. "Sure. I'll call."

*Like hell.*

I went to leave but Troy grasped my arm, halting me. He didn't look up and into my eyes at first, as though he had to calm himself. After a moment, he lifted his gaze to mine, and again, that brightness startled me. I would have pulled backward if his grip weren't so solid.

"Call me, Ava. I don't want to find your body because you were being stubborn."

I gulped at the seriousness of his tone, at the crushing weight of his gaze.

All I could do was nod before he let me go and I could get out of the house.

*That* was my neighbor? The sweet but strait-laced silver fox next door had just all but eye-fucked me while giving me that 'do as I say' voice that made my knees weak.

If I'd realized that was what was inside that man, I'd have taken up nude sunbathing years ago.

# Chapter Six

*Another* knock on my door had me ready to move somewhere tropical, with no forwarding address, so people couldn't find me. Years I'd lived here, and unless they were delivering food, I'd had all of two people over — Troy and the religious woman who I only invited in because she tended to clean my kitchen while telling me about her cult.

The thought of leaving town had merit, but when another knock happened, I had to accept that for today my house would be a destination stop.

Of course, the man on my front porch wasn't one I recognized.

And I would have remembered him...

He seemed young, early twenties as best, with hair shaved at the sides and pushed up and back on the top. His eyes were a bright green that caught the sunlight. He wore a jean jacket over a white T-shirt, and tattoos showed at the cuffs. Did he have sleeves? They weren't the same kind as Hunter's, who had an almost ethereal flow to the marks, as though they'd been grown rather than tattooed. This man had clear images in it—koi, skulls, flowers. He had every type imaginable, like he'd gone into a tattoo shop and treated it like an all-you-can-eat buffet. Across his chest sat the strap to a messenger-style bag that was slung across him.

I held right to the door, and as much as I hated it, the thought of calling out to Troy did occur to me. Strange people showing up hadn't been a good thing so far, and I did have a man who turned into a wolf just next door. That was the sort of advantage that was best to use.

"Just what have you been letting into this house?"

The words caught me off guard, and it took a moment to catch up. "What?"

"It smells like a swamp."

"Well, that's incredibly rude. I'll have you know I am an excellent housekeeper."

The man chuckled and crossed his arms. "It's adorable you pretend to be human and misunderstand." He went to move past me and walk into the house.

I put my arm out, across the door frame, to bar his way. "I don't let strange men into my house."

"Well, that sounds boring." He twisted his lips into a grin that was downright breath taking. I was tempted to let him in just because of that smile. It was hard to say no to a man who could smirk like *that.*

A moment before I gave in, I remembered I wasn't a cat in heat, nor was I crazy enough to invite random men into my house for sex romps. I wasn't twenty anymore.

He must have read my moment of stupid sanity for what it was and saw it was over, because his smile widened. "Kase called me."

Talk about a dose of cold water. It seemed Kase's name worked better than a bucket of ice for my libido. "Why would he do that?"

"He wanted to make sure nothing got you during the day."

"Yeah, well, thanks, but I don't need some kid to protect me. You look like a hard stare could knock you over."

His chuckle said I hadn't offended him. "Having no wards on your home is a very stupid choice. It's a miracle you haven't been offed already."

I considered saying no. I could walk back into the house, make myself another cup of coffee and pretend none of this was real.

However, that wasn't realistic. The man didn't seem the type to give up, and if Kase had sent him, well, Kase didn't take 'no' well either.

I pressed my lips together and offered an unhappy snort before stepping backward. "Come on in, I guess."

He followed me into the kitchen, which seemed like the perfect place for entertaining—close proximity to both food and knives.

*Yep. Invite men whose name you don't even know into your house. Brilliant.*

"Grant."

I turned to find him across the kitchen island from me.

"My name's Grant. See? We aren't strangers anymore."

I narrowed my eyes. "Stay out of my head."

Just the idea that he'd crawled around in there, that he'd picked up my thoughts made my skin crawl. It was yet another reason I didn't care for getting near the supernatural world.

In the regular world, I didn't have to worry about someone reading my mind. It just wasn't a consideration. However, in *this* world, mages could manage it.

Which told me exactly what Grant was.

Mages were almost worse than other supernaturals. Vampires were clearly not human. Werewolves might pass for a while, but at least their *other* side looked like the monster it was.

Mages could pass easily for human and were, in many ways, the most closely related to humans. It meant a person had no idea what they were dealing with until they saw exactly what mages were capable of. Reading minds was just the tip of that very dangerous iceberg, of course.

He smiled as if my scolding didn't matter. "Sure. It'd do you more good to learn how to block people, though. Not everyone is as upstanding as I am, willing to do as you asked just because you asked so nicely." He tilted his head, his green eyes studying me. "Which makes me wonder why you've left so much to chance. No wards? Not even a charm to help keep you safe? Never learned to even feel when someone was reading your mind seems awfully stupid."

"It isn't stupid," I snapped.

"No? So explain it to me."

"If you walked past this house and it was warded to the teeth, what would you think?"

"That someone who lived here valued their life."

I shook my head. "You'd know that whoever lived here knew about your world. You'd take notice. If you walked past it and felt nothing, though, you'd keep on walking. Trying to protect myself from your world only lets people know I'm aware of it. For a human, *that* is far more dangerous. Sometimes a locked door only tells people there's something worth breaking in for."

He lifted his dark eyebrow then let his gaze drift over her from head to toe, as if forced to reevaluate me. "That might just be smarter than I'd given you credit for."

The praise was unexpected and entirely unwelcome. I didn't need him to tell me it was smart. I'd lived to thirty-five because I knew how to survive on the outskirts of their world. "So, as you can see, I don't *need* any wards on my house."

He huffed before walking to my fridge and opening it as though he lived there, the arrogant bastard. "Sorry, but Kase paid me well to make sure you were protected. Flying under the radar is great and all, but that ship has sailed. Our world has taken an interest in you, and that means your whole unlocked-door theory is over with."

I blew out a slow breath, grappling with my temper. "Well he clearly doesn't understand boundaries, does he?"

"Vampires rarely do. They're territorial and possessive and, for whatever reason, Kase seems to want you to stay alive. I'm here to ensure that. Once I have the wards up, almost nothing will be able to enter."

"Almost?" The qualifier caught my attention.

He let out a dramatic sigh. "Right. Let's run down the fine print. Upon setting up the ward, you will need to invite in any being of this realm. Once invited in, they will be able to enter again any time they want until that welcome is revoked."

"Will I need some special spell to make it work?"

"What is this, amateur hour? No. Just a 'come on in,' works fine. If you want to revoke an invitation, in my experience 'get the fuck out' is quite effective. The ward works less well against humans, but any supernatural being will be unable to pass without an invitation. Expectations are anything noncorporeal, such as spirits, poltergeists, or any god or demi-god creature. Additionally, anything not of this realm, even if bound temporarily by a corporeal form from this realm, may be able to break the boundaries of the ward. You're looking there at certain demons—again, usually smoke or mist-based—reapers, hellhounds, wardens—"

"You know, listing things that I have no idea about doesn't really help."

Grant pulled a water bottle from my fridge and twisted the cap off. "It comes down to this—it will keep out almost everything dangerous you'd have to worry about. You'll be bound to the ward, so if someone tries to break it—and it is possible to break with enough time—you'll know about it first."

I thought about how Hunter had snuck into my house the night before, how Kase had broken in, how Troy had just walked in, not to mention *whatever* that thing in my living room had been. Clearly my attempt to avoid the supernatural world wasn't working, since they seemed apt at breaking in anytime they wanted, like my house was a train station.

"Okay," I said with a nod. "Let's ward this bitch."

* * * *

Two hours later and I knew for sure I never wanted to be a mage. I'd expected lightning and fire and other amazing things like some light show.

Instead, it was a lot of quiet muttering and wandering through my house. I'd put my foot down when he'd opened my underwear drawer, though. The pervert hadn't even bothered to pretend to be sorry. He'd only laughed and made a joke about warding panties.

"This is taking forever," I complained from the couch as he stood at the front door, his back to me, his hands moving in strange ways that seemed purposeful and almost beautiful — at least if I hadn't stopped caring so long before.

Grant didn't answer right away, a delay that implied his task took all his attention.

Finally, he turned. "One more thing. I need your blood."

"Whoa now." I rose and took a step backward. "I thought I had to worry about that with Kase — not with you."

Grant reached into the bag slung across his body to pull out an ornately decorated knife, one with a far larger blade than I was comfortable with. "I need to bind the ward to you. Blood speaks to blood the best."

I held my hand against my side. If he seriously thought I was going to let him *cut* me, he was bat-shit-crazy. "The whole point of this was to keep me safe. I'll probably get tetanus from that thing."

Grant waved me over, as if that motion alone would convince me to stop arguing and do as he requested. "I don't need much. Don't be a baby."

"I don't think not wanting some weirdo to slice me open is being a baby."

"I'm not trying to slice you open. I just need a couple of drops. You won't even need a Band-Aid when I'm done."

I gritted my teeth, but that seemed reasonable. Gran had told me blood was a common element to magic, but I hadn't planned on it ever being *my* blood being used.

After tapping my foot on the ground, I came over. He held his hand out, and I placed mine in his.

Grant's hand was warm and surprisingly strong. Mages were physically as frail as humans, using their magic as their main offense and defense. It meant they weren't incredibly fast, strong or tough like the other beings in their world. Perhaps that was why it surprised me to find his grasp so solid.

It distracted me well enough that I missed when he brought the knife closer, and when he sliced it along my palm, it took a moment for the pain to catch up.

And when it did? I tried to yank away but again — that grip. Grant slipped the blade into his bag in a practiced move then held my hand — palm down — over the threshold. He spoke in a language I didn't recognize, the words as smooth as if he had said them a hundred times. Blood dripped from my palm and spilled on the concrete of the small porch.

I yanked away, cradling my bloodied hand to my stomach. "What the fuck?"

Grant lifted his hands, though the one he'd used to restrain me was covered in my blood, which was *not* as reassuring as he probably meant the action to be. "Sorry, but that's how it had to be."

"You know cutting someone's palm is incredibly stupid! It makes using your hand harder and there are far more nerve endings there, so it hurts more than if you did the forearm. You are the worst mage *ever*."

He chuckled. "That's why we do it there. Everything requires a sacrifice, a give and take. You were getting protection, so you needed to give blood and pain. You can feel it, though, can't you? How the spell connects to you through the blood?"

I frowned, stretching my hand and closing it into a fist, ignoring the wetness of the blood. "No. I didn't feel anything other than you cutting me. You clearly screwed it up."

He paused, closed his eyes, then shook his head. "No, it's working. You really can't sense it? It should have hurt when it formed."

"Well, it didn't."

He pressed his lips together. "Strange. Well, it still worked, so you don't have any reason to be annoyed."

"That isn't the point. You can't go slicing people open without even asking them."

"If I'd told you I needed to cut open your palm, you'd have complained. I've found that when something needs to be done, it's better to just do it rather than waste time arguing." He shrugged as if it didn't matter at all to him.

"I revoke your invitation," I snapped.

He cracked a wide smile as though I'd just charmed him. "Sorry, but it doesn't work with me. I set the ward, so it automatically allows me through."

"And you just failed to mention that either."

"I prefer not talking about things that might get me into trouble. If you didn't like it, you'd complain, and didn't we just have a talk about how I feel about complaining?"

I curled my hands into fists. He was a mage, which meant if I punched him, he'd at least feel it.

Self-preservation kept me from doing it. Even though Grant didn't seem the kind to turn me into a smoking pile of ash for one little punch, he certainly *could* do it if he wanted.

Instead of risking that, I opened the front door and pointed.

"What?" Grant shifted his gaze from the door to me and back again, as if he couldn't work out the meaning.

"Leave."

"You can't be serious. One little cut and you throw me out?"

"It's not a little cut. Besides, you did your job, so you can leave now."

He crossed his arms. "How long are you going to be mad about that?"

"How about until it heals?"

He huffed, then walked out. "Fine, I'll go. I left my card with my number on your counter. If you have problems with the wards, call me."

*Like hell.*

I shut the door behind him—well, slammed it really—and stared at the key hook. I could so easily grab those, pack a bag and leave all this behind. Kase. Troy. Hunter. Grant and his stupid knife. Olin, Rachel, Gran, ghosts—everything that made my life so damned complicated. They could all be just figments in my rearview mirror.

Driving until my credit cards gave out sounded amazing.

Except...

That void haunted me. It wouldn't go away, wouldn't let me close my eyes without remembering it.

Boys didn't matter.

Big scary voids mattered, and I was going to find out what it all meant.

# Chapter Seven

Troy looked as though he could strangle me when I walked up to the apartment I'd found online—the one listed for Rachel.

I hadn't called him, of course. I'd figured I could slide through a window and no one would be the wiser for it.

The glare he offered me said I'd been wrong.

"I thought I told you to call me when you needed something."

"I didn't need anything."

"You were planning to break into her apartment."

I crossed my arms and tried to meet his glare head on. I'd done that enough times before, willingly annoyed him and enjoyed the frustration in his expression. However, those times I'd been human and so had he—as far as I'd known—which meant that edge to his face held a lot more danger than it had before.

Not that I thought he'd ever really hurt me. Troy, even as a werewolf, struck me as the most level-headed and dull supernatural I'd ever met.

Honestly, Kase could learn a thing or two from him.

"What are you doing here?" I asked instead of answering his pointed question.

"You've walked by this place three times. I had a unit surveilling it, and they called in a suspicious brunette with blue eyes. I figured it was you."

"So am I getting arrested?"

"Not today."

I offered him a playful smile, as if it would make him more inclined to help. "And here I thought I might get to see your handcuffs."

He did that surprised snort again, one that sounded like he'd choked on his own spit at my joke. After swallowing and trying to play it off as if it hadn't happened, he leaned in close. "You shouldn't play games like that, Ava. Supernaturals aren't something to toy with."

His expression made me want to see how far I could push him. Could I make him lose that amazing control of his? Did I even want that? Sure, I had no problem looking when it came to Troy—who wouldn't want to look at that?—but touching was a whole different matter.

So I nodded, and he took a step backward as though we both needed that space.

"Are you going to let me in?" I asked.

"I shouldn't. I feel like the more access I give you, the worse you'll behave. I've already told you to leave this alone."

"And we both know I'm not going to do that."

He let out a soft sigh. "Which is exactly why I'm going to let you in, when I'm here, so I can assure you don't touch anything you shouldn't and also that you stay alive."

"I don't think some girl's apartment is all that dangerous."

"Tell that to the dead woman."

Troy had a point, and while him lumbering behind me wasn't my idea of a great, relaxing time, at least I didn't have to keep looking over my shoulder.

And no one would arrest me.

*Win-win.*

Inside the apartment was like most of the ones I saw for thirty-somethings who lived alone. In fact, it reminded me a lot of my own place, other than it being a bit smaller.

Though, judging from Rachel's picture collection, she had more friends and went out much more than I did. She didn't need so much space at home.

The décor was all faded, almost gray wood with pops of green and orange. On the walls were sayings like, *Smile, because it helps*, and *Friends make life worth living*.

The pseudo-intellectual feel-good sayings made me instantly dislike her. Sure, we might pick the same color schemes, but if I ever decided to go the whole decal sayings route, I'd go with *It takes forty-two muscles to frown, twenty-eight muscles to smile, but only four muscles to reach out and slap something* and *It probably could get worse*.

Troy stood back and silent as I went around Rachel's living room, finding nothing useful. She seemed to be a reader. That always felt a bit like a self-important thing, like people who said they meditated.

I, on the other hand, had a bookshelf full of books I never read. The cracked spines on Rachel's collection said she either bought used or read often.

Her house pointed at a good life. "So if she had friends, family, a great job, what was she doing around Olin?"

Troy let out a long sigh, as though we'd had this conversation many times. "She didn't need to be doing anything for Olin to target her. You're looking for a connection that probably isn't there."

"There has to be something."

"Why?"

I turned toward him, frustration bubbling over. "Because I need to understand what happened! I can't close my eyes and not feel that void, pulling me in and drowning me. I already have nightmares every goddamned night of my life—I can't have that thing living in my head, too. I've got a limit of shit I can deal with and this crosses the threshold." I hadn't even realized I'd started to shake, that my breaths had turned rough and ragged, until Troy grabbed me and tugged me against his chest.

Which was crossing all sorts of lines for us, and yet I couldn't push him away. It was a sweet gesture and far too welcome. His heart pounded, strong and steady, and I closed my eyes to listen.

He ran his hand up and down my back, and I breathed in his wild scent. Where Hunter smelled of fire, Troy was like rain, like deep forests in the darkness.

*And maybe a bit like wet dog.*

I shuddered to let the excess energy slide from me. When I did, he released me, and I very pointedly did *not* look right back at him. Instead, I glanced around the room. *Let's pretend that moment didn't happen.*

"Maybe she was just at the wrong place at the wrong time…"

"I know that isn't a comforting answer, Ava, but I've dealt with a lot of vampire kills over my life. I've rarely found a good reason they died. No matter how much I looked into it, no matter if the guilty party was brought to justice or not, I never found anything that made me feel like there was a reason behind it. It was just bad luck."

I nodded and looked at a picture of her on the wall, at how she looked so full of life, so different from the corpse in that pit. "Does her family know she's gone?"

"No. Even if you told us what shallow grave the coven put her in, I wouldn't go find it. The remains vampires leave create questions that there are no good answers to. I wish her family could have closure, but discovering her mangled corpse won't give that. It'll stay a missing persons case."

"Do you know where she was killed, at least?"

"Here. Magic has a scent to it, and it's all over her bedroom. I'd guess the coven had a mage clean it up."

Suddenly the apartment, which had seemed quaint, held a darker edge to it. I could almost *feel* the blood, as though it hadn't been cleaned but rather hidden. It made my stomach roll, and I pressed a hand there.

Troy didn't try to reassure me again, instead using a finger against the bottom of my chin to lift my face and meet my gaze. "*This* is what they are, Ava. I know vampires can seem alluring, that Kase can come across as charming and civilized, but they are killers through and through."

"And you aren't?"

His lips thinned. "No, Ava, I'm one, too. Why do you think I keep trying to get you to keep your distance from us all?"

*Well, at least he's honest...*

* * * *

I sighed as I put my feet up on the ottoman in front of my couch. As annoyed as I might have been about Kase demanding the wards, I had to admit, they *did* help me to relax.

Nothing weird had happened since the sun had gone down, since arriving home from Rachel's apartment. That felt like some sort of record for recently. No huge swirling darkness, no people breaking in, no being kidnapped in the middle of the night.

It was downright boring, which I planned to enjoy the hell out of.

I had a cup of tea held between my palms, the sort with chamomile and lavender, meant to relax a person before bed.

Not that I ever drank it. Honestly, I hated tea. Still, Gran always told me I needed to drink it, and every health article said a person should have some to relax.

So I liked to make tea and pretend I was the sort of girl who actually would drink it, who did yoga regularly and had a great skin-care regime. Then the tea would get cold and I'd pour it out, blaming my lack of drinking any on it being tepid rather than my absolute hatred of the gross leaf juice.

My plan was to pretend with my tea until the heat went away, then take myself to bed with my favorite vibrator and remind myself that I did not need any of the men who seemed to be orbiting me.

*None* of them vibrated, which made them a distant second in the race for my heart—or more honestly, my vagina.

A knock at the door made me drop my head back.

*Again?*

When I got there, I found Hunter standing on my porch, his eyebrow lifted. "Decided to put up wards, huh? And you sure were not fucking around about them, either."

I leaned against the doorframe, annoyed to find he looked even more handsome than he had the last time. How it was possible, I wasn't sure. That long hair of his was down and messy and it made him look like some rebel bad boy who I shouldn't let in but who I really, really wanted to. "Well, it kept you out, so it seems like it was worth it."

He snorted and mirrored my stand, leaning against the open screen door. "If I wanted past them that badly, I could. Sure, this is the Fort Knox of wards—kudos to the mage who set it up—but I've got my ways."

"So why haven't you?"

"I figured I'd ask real nicely, and you'd let me in."

The worst part of his words was how sure he was about them. The arrogance in them, the way he looked at me as if he knew I wanted him, that it was only a matter of time, all made me again wonder just what he was.

"Well, I'm sorry to disappoint you, but *that* won't be happening."

"Sure. Whatever you say." The asshole *winked* at me, as if it were all some funny joke between us. "Any sight of what came looking for you the other night?"

"What was it?"

He shrugged.

"You don't know?"

"Not exactly. Believe it or not, I'm not an expert on every bad thing that crawls around in the shadows. I know it was looking for you and that if it had found you, it probably didn't want to just sell you some cookies."

"How did you know about it at all? *What* are you?"

"It's considered rude to ask that."

I leaned closer to him but kept the ward threshold between us. "I am so tired of people keeping what they are from me."

"Does it really matter? I mean, in the scheme of things, knowing what someone is doesn't tell you anything. Humans can be just as treacherous as anything else, so what's the point with the question?"

His eyes danced with a certain amusement, but deeper than that?

*Flames.*

They reminded me of the tattoos that swirled over his arms and throat. How was that possible?

The more I saw him, the more I doubted those tattoos had been put there by any artist. They had an otherworldly quality that made them seem darker, impossible and almost as though they moved on his skin.

We stood so close that only the thinnest barrier remained between us — the ward. No doubt if I let him in, we'd end up in bed.

And who could blame me?

*Look at him!*

He was the poster boy for a man I wasn't supposed to want. He looked like any wet-dream-created biker, and I was suddenly very aware of my entire body.

The last quickie I'd had—because I tended to stick with no-strings sex—replayed in my mind, and I was sure that would pale compared to what he could give me.

"Let me in," he all but purred in a voice *so* seductive and tempting that I nearly did so.

"It's not a good idea."

"So? Make a bad choice with me, then. I've seen you for years, shadow-girl, years of wanting you but not knowing exactly where you were. Let me have you finally."

*Years?* The words crept past all that mindless, stupid lust.

"What do you mean you've seen me for years?" Was he some sort of weird supernatural stalker?

He inhaled slowly through his nose, then went unnaturally still. "Invite me in."

I shook my head. "Not a chance. You realize watching a girl for *years* is creepy, right?"

"Ava, you need to let me in, right now." His face had shifted, changed to an expression of absolute seriousness.

However, given he'd just admitted to watching me for years, I wasn't inclined to take his seriousness as something that mattered to me. Maybe his sudden emergency was nothing more than a pesky erection he felt needed immediate attention.

And while I would have been only too happy to attend to it prior, his own admission had dried up my lust like one of those towel infomercials.

I took a step away from the door. "You need to leave."

Those flames in his eyes consumed the entire iris, and in that there was no question—he wasn't anything close to human, and nothing I knew anything about either.

The wards gave me a comfort they hadn't before. Beyond vampires and werewolves who lacked an understanding of boundaries, I was thankful *that* had to stay outside.

"You don't understand," he pressed and seemed to try to enter. The ward functioned not like a wall but more like drying cement — too thick and heavy to pass through. He couldn't make progress, though the muscles I could see and the cords in his neck all stood out as though he gave it his best try.

*I could kiss Kase right now.*

I shuddered. Nope. That was *far* too much.

Still, I took another step away as he let out a roar I swore I'd heard in my nightmares before. It was dark and inhuman and chilled me.

I didn't notice a sound behind me at first, nor did the way the hair on my neck stood occur to me. I was too taken by the sight of Hunter trying to get through the ward.

An electric sensation ran down my spine — one I knew far too well — and I turned.

Behind me stood Melinda, but she wasn't on schedule. It was hours early for her to show, and she'd been unfailingly punctual.

"I don't have time for this," I told her.

She tilted her head as she floated forward, lowering herself until her feet touched the floor as though she were walking. It was eerie. Melinda had *never* been silent.

That was when I really saw it, though, the thing I'd missed because I'd been so focused on Hunter.

Melinda was untethered. That leash that had connected her before to her corpse, the one that had held her to this realm, was gone. Which could only mean one thing, something that terrified me far more than whatever it was trying to force his way through my wards.

Melinda was a poltergeist.

I opened my mouth to invite Hunter in, but before I could make a sound, Melinda rushed forward and wrapped a freezing, ethereal hand around my throat.

I never would have guessed it would be *Melinda* who ended up killing me.

# Chapter Eight

My vision wavered as Melinda cut off my air. It was easy to think of spirits as harmless inconveniences, and they usually were.

I could ignore a spirit. The worst they could do was freak me out, threaten me, but they had no ability to affect the physical world.

Poltergeists happened when they snapped the tether to their body and *remained* in this realm. They were rare, but because they were neither of this world or the next, they could interact with living things.

And by *interact,* I meant strangle the ever-living shit out of me.

I kicked, but my feet went through her body. She wasn't fully corporeal or fully ethereal, and I had *no* idea how to counter such a thing.

In the past, when I'd come across one, running away was my go-to option. She didn't seem inclined to let me do that, though.

"*You* should have done as I said!"

Another roar echoed in the background, and her gaze shot up. She bared her teeth toward Hunter.

Which was a very strange reaction.

Neither spirits nor poltergeists tended to take notice of humans or supernaturals—other than vampires, who they avoided. They might make fun of them, but they were never afraid.

That was *fear* on Melinda's face.

I should have let Hunter in, risk to my virtue be damned.

I hit the ground hard, and it took a moment for me to realize what had happened. I'd slipped through her hand. It seemed she was still learning to control her powers, to remain corporeal.

I opened my mouth to invite Hunter in but only a painful croak escaped. My throat burned, and I knew without a doubt I'd sport some nasty bruises.

They'd be hard to explain to people without them thinking I was into some sort of kink. Worse, given my constantly single status, the coroner would assume auto-erotic asphyxiation. At least my eulogy would be entertaining.

I crawled backward, scooting away from Melinda as she waved her hand, like that would make it work again.

She narrowed her gaze. "I asked you for one thing! That's it. You could have done that for me, and I wouldn't be *here*."

Typical self-entitled bitch. Her one thing had been murdering an innocent teen who already lived in guilt from the accident. Still, I had a moment of wondering what my life would have been like if I'd done what spirits wanted.

What if I started taking requests like some sort of concierge to the afterlife? Killing off people who had wronged them, setting shit right?

Would I have avoided being murdered by a rich lady who wore an ugly tracksuit while doing it?

She rushed forward, and I brought my arms up together to protect my face.

As soon as I did, a burning sensation ran through my arms, over the old tattoos, expanding and coursing over my skin until it lashed out. Melinda struck the wall—damaging the plaster there—her body fully corporeal. Her eyes widened, as if she understood what had just happened no better than I did.

Well, at least we were in the same boat together.

When she pulled herself from the plaster—bits of it raining down around her—a plume of smoke passed me.

When it was between her and I, it took form into...*Hunter?*

A butt-assed naked Hunter, who I had to admit, looked even better from behind...

He let out a growl that knocked more pieces of plaster from the wall before he lifted his hand toward Melinda.

I opened my mouth to warn him, to tell him exactly how dangerous she could be, but still nothing escaped.

It turned out I didn't need to worry. More of that smoke drifted from him and surrounded Melinda.

An unholy scream left her, something made of pure agony, just before she dissipated. Not like fading out of existence, but as if whatever Hunter did had devoured her.

When she was gone, when even that electric sensation I got from her being around faded away, only then did Hunter roll his shoulders and put his hand down.

He twisted, and I jerked my gaze up. It had to say something about how unnerved I felt when I didn't feel the urge to ogle even a little.

The sound of terror Melinda had let out, the way those tattoos had moved around, as though made up by that smoke, the fact a man could look and act as casual as Hunter and do *that* made me suddenly not care what his dick looked like.

He crouched then grasped my chin and lifted my head, staring at my neck. A slight *tsk* said he didn't care for the marks. "She almost killed you. I don't think even you can outrun death."

When I tried to speak, the words came out hoarse and rough, but at least I could talk. "What *are* you?"

"The person who saved you. Isn't that a good enough answer?"

I pressed my lips together—no, it really wasn't—but he only lifted me against his chest as though it took no effort at all. All that warm skin made me realize that my whole 'not interested in his dick' stance hadn't lasted long, especially as he walked up the stairs carrying me.

What he was really didn't matter, did it?

It wasn't until I lowered myself onto the bed that I realized just how much I hurt. As it turned out, getting tossed around by a poltergeist wasn't something I could just brush off.

Really, there were far better ways to have fun if someone was going to get bruised up.

Hunter walked in, a cup in his hands, and a few of those things came to mind.

Getting thrown around by him wouldn't be so bad.

*Really? You are twisted.*

85

Somehow, even though he'd dressed again, I couldn't wipe away the memory of how he'd looked naked. It seemed entirely unfair that a man could look that good.

He wasn't a man though, was he? I suppose a supernatural metabolism could do wonders for the physique.

He sat on the bed on my side, since I was up against the headboard, and handed me the cup.

I took one glance inside and curled my lip. "I hate tea."

"Why do you have so much of it, then?"

I shrugged, not willing to explain my forever falling short attempts at healthy living.

He chuckled and nodded at the drink. "Have it anyway. It'll help you feel better."

"Did you do something weird to it?"

"Just honey. It should soothe your throat."

I sipped the tea and…amazingly it wasn't bad. Then again, the almost sickly sweetness of it said he'd put a hell of a lot of honey in it. Enough sugar in anything could make it good.

Sure enough, after I swallowed the hot liquid, the burning ache of my throat seemed to ease.

"That shouldn't have happened," I whispered.

"Poltergeists are nasty creatures. They don't follow a lot of 'shoulds'."

I shook my head. "Melinda shouldn't have turned into one. Sure, she was a raging bitch, and I had my money on her resisting until she ended up in purgatory, but a poltergeist?" I sighed and rested my cup on my folded legs. "Melinda wasn't the type. She wasn't strong enough. It doesn't make sense."

"Sometimes there isn't an explanation. I know shit seems less scary when it all makes sense, when it follows clear-cut rules, but that isn't how life—or death—works. Sometimes shit happens. Sometimes someone is born weird"—he gave me a meaningful look—"and sometimes someone who shouldn't have become a poltergeist does. Trying to make sense of it all will only drive you crazy."

I sighed when I couldn't argue. Wasn't that part of what I'd learned over my life? Shit didn't make sense. Why did I get tossed away by my family? Why was I born like I was instead of like everyone else? The truth was that clinging to what should have been never helped anyone. It had only prolonged the pain.

If someone ran over my foot with their car, I could spend weeks trying to figure out why, trying to track them down and discover the great meaning behind it, or I could suck it up and move on. Knowing why sure as hell wouldn't speed up the healing.

He tilted his head, his gaze on my forearms.

It prickled at me, that unease when people noticed what I'd tried so hard to hide.

"It's nothing," I muttered and turned my arms to hide the white scars.

Hunter grasped my wrist and tugged my arm into his lap. He traced the raised scaring. "It's something."

I refused to look at the marks. I'd spent far too long staring at them in the past. "Anyone who says tattoo removal works is a liar. It might pull out the color, but it sure as hell leaves scars."

"And who put them on you?"

"How do you know it wasn't a stupid, drunken teenage mistake?"

Hunter lifted an eyebrow as he peered at me. "Because these aren't just random designs. This symbol is an enchantment." The stroke of his finger across the scarred skin left the sensation of burning behind it, but it wasn't a bad feeling. Hell, it made me want him to keep doing it. "It's a symbol to hide you from the dead, Ava, to keep them from seeing you. I suppose that makes sense why the thing in your living room that first night couldn't find you."

"No. They're tattoos someone put on me when I was three because my parents were drug addicts."

"You were that young when you got them? Do you remember it?"

I shook my head. "I just have the records. I was found outside a fire station, with the fresh tattoos on my arms. I figured they had to be on drugs. What other explanation would there be for doing this to a kid?"

Hunter eased my other arm out after setting my tea on the nightstand. He again traced the scarred design left behind from a lot of expensive and painful procedures. "This one keeps you hidden from the living world."

I huffed. "Trust me. The living world can see me."

"It doesn't work by making you invisible but just…less noticed. Have you ever felt like you walk into a room and people just don't seem to see you? They pass you over?"

As soon as he said it, that familiar pain lanced through me. How long had I felt unseen? Sure, if I spoke directly to someone, if I was in their way, if they were looking for me specifically, they'd notice me, but otherwise?

I was the one no one seemed to notice. They'd walk past me without a word. They'd pick others instead of me. In a room full of people, I'd be the one by myself.

I'd chalked it up to being exceptionally awkward, as though they knew just by looking at me not to expect any great conversations, which led them to choosing better people to speak to.

"Why would someone curse a child?" My parents had screwed me up plenty. Them abandoning me had left its fair share of scars. The idea that they'd somehow had managed to actually put a spell on me that further ruined my life seemed unbelievable. Hadn't they done *enough?*

"These aren't curses, Ava, they're marks of protection. Whoever put them on you figured you needed safety from not only the living, but the dead, too." He continued to trace over the marks as if consumed by them. "And they weren't put there on a whim. This takes serious power to perform, and nothing that takes power comes cheap."

I couldn't believe that. I'd spent years furious, saving for so long to remove the black marks that had marred my forearms, shamed by them. So many people had looked at them, tried to pretend as if they hadn't seen them like some unsightly spinach in my teeth. I'd accepted that my parents were twisted assholes who had permanently marked me then thrown me away.

The idea that I'd gotten it all wrong was too much for me to accept right then.

"You're wrong," I said.

"I'm not. Trust me, Ava, I can feel the power off this thing. There isn't a lot that can throw a poltergeist into a wall like that."

I shook my head. "My parents were freaks and these are the proof of it." I pulled from his grip and angled my arms toward him.

When I brought my forearms together, an odd burning started, something that reminded me of when I'd tossed Melinda into the wall. How had I never done that before? How had I never realized they had power? Doing in that moment had been instinct, as if I'd somehow known what would happen if I did... Maybe that same deep-buried instinct had prevented me from doing it before?

Before it expanded, before whatever happened before happened again, I found myself flat on my back.

Hunter had pinned my hands to the bed beside my head, trapping me beneath his large, strong form.

I'd known he was big—it wasn't easy to ignore that—but having all of that against me was a far different matter than knowing something logically.

"I don't mind rough sex, but I'd prefer not to get thrown across the room before we even get started. How about you not point that mark at me?"

"It's never done anything to anyone before."

"Well, I saw what it did to that poltergeist, and I don't want the same treatment."

"Are you telling me you're a poltergeist?"

He chuckled as he shifted his hand so he could stroke the inside of my wrist. The touch was innocent—he wasn't rubbing anything intimate—and yet I could feel it rush through me as if his fingers were between my thighs. "What do you think?"

"I've never seen a poltergeist act like you." I frowned as I tried to make my brain work despite how he touched my wrist, despite how he crowded me and made me want to arch against him. "And you weren't able to enter my house without my invitation, at least not easily. Plus my secretary could see you."

He traced my bottom lip with the edge of his warm tongue, and I *tasted* flames. "You don't invite poltergeists into your bed?"

"I didn't invite you."

"You did, just not with words."

"That's what people with boundary issues say."

He curled his lips into a grin before he bit down softly on my bottom lip, a sting of pain that made me arch up, that made me press my pelvis to him in a blatant and desperate offer. So, he wasn't wrong.

I did want him, more than I might have ever wanted anything else.

And it stilled me for one moment. "Are you an incubus?" The thought he might be causing this reaction in me, that I might be being played by him, managed to snuff out the desire for a moment.

"No, I'm not an incubus, and I haven't forced you to feel anything."

"So what *are* you doing here?"

He pushed up enough to trace his gaze down my body, and despite me wearing pajamas—these ones with cartoon coffee mugs—he stared as if I were clad in expensive lace lingerie. "I'm sure you can figure that out. Are there many reasons a man would be on top of you in your bed?"

I narrowed my eyes. "You aren't a man."

"Maybe not." He rocked his hips forward, and I shivered at how his hard cock rubbed against me. "Though I think I'm man enough for you."

I set my hands on his chest and pushed, surprised to find again just how solid he was. He didn't have any fat on his body, as if every single inch were firm muscle. That sort of body was inhumanly strong.

*Damn it.* I had stopped pushing and instead curled my fingers in as though to grip his pecs.

The warmth of his tattoos drew me, as well. The skin was raised over them, and I swore the black marks were a good ten degrees warmer than the rest of his already-heated body. They pulsed beneath my palms as if currents moved through them.

It made me recall the smoke that had poured from his fingertips, how the marks had moved on his body as if alive.

"Stop thinking," he whispered before leaning closer and brushing his lips to mine. More of that wonderful taste filled my senses. It was heat and danger and darkness.

Whatever he was stopped mattering. I saw spirits. A werewolf lived next door. A vampire kept screwing with my life. Who the hell *cared* what Hunter was? If he wanted to kill me, well, he'd had plenty of opportunities for that well before my pants ever came off, so worrying about it didn't matter.

I slid my hands around his impressive chest, over his sides, then dug my fingers into his back as I returned the kiss.

Hell, forget *returned.* I deepened it, wanted more, *demanded* more. I wasn't a passive woman, hadn't ever been someone willing to accept whatever I was given. When I teased my tongue across his full bottom lip, he parted for me, and it was like tasting brimstone itself. Heat, smoke, fire — it all felt as though it could consume me, and I'd happily accept it.

He groaned and dragged his hand down my throat and over my collarbone. He slipped the thin strap down to bare my breast, and his rough palm scraped against my nipple.

Something about seeing ghosts, about knowing there was more to a person than their body, had always made me worry less about how mine looked.

It was a detriment at times when I didn't care about dressing up, but it helped in sex. I didn't give a fuck if my hips were perfect or my breasts perky or my waist small enough. My thighs spread out when I sat because they were thighs, and anyone who didn't like it could fuck off.

It meant when Hunter scooted down to drag his tongue over my nipple, when he bit softly at the curve of my breast, that I could allow the delicious sensation to wash over me without the slightest concern about how I *looked*. Judging by the cock he ground against me, he liked what he saw well enough. No reason for me to be worried if his dick thought I was fine.

My flesh stung where he'd nipped me, a lingering sensation that said I'd bear a mark. If the mark had been on my throat, or my shoulder, I might have felt differently. I didn't care for something that others would see, but this felt so much more intimate. I imagined my bra rubbing against the mark tomorrow, how it would remind me of this moment—of hopefully others to come—and it would take me back to here as surely as if he were whispering in my ear about it.

Hunter grasped my sides, spanning his hands over my ribs, reminding me of just how large they were. He dragged them down until he reached the waist of my sleep shorts. He curled his fingers into the band, then met my gaze, a question in his eyes.

A question like that had only one realistic answer. When a man as good looking as Hunter was there, offering, the answer was always *fuck yes.*

A nod from me had him shifting his lips into a smile. He pulled the shorts from me, tossing them aside. A deep sound that sounded much like the one he'd made at the door—a growl but far too low for any animal I'd ever heard before—came from him. His gaze was locked on mine, so intense that I struggled to look anywhere else. The light brown looked darker in the dim room, but I had no doubt he could see every last detail.

He spread my legs around him and dragged his palms up, stroking the sensitive expanse of skin.

Hunter leaned forward, his large body bowing and crowding as he moved to lie flat between my thighs. It forced my legs to spread more, to accommodate his ridiculously wide shoulders, but that was a hardship I didn't mind suffering.

Especially when he swiped his tongue up my slit. The sensation was overwhelming, and his tongue was *so* incredibly hot. He seared me as he dove in, as he placed his large, strong hands on the insides of my thighs to pin me open and still for him.

Damn, Hunter knew what he was doing.

Or maybe it was just a matter of enthusiasm going a long damn way. He wasn't acting as if he were just putting on a show, as though he were only interested for as long as it took for him to get credit for having done it.

Boy, I had dealt with enough of *those* sorts of men, the ones who took one quick lick and wanted a medal for best lover.

Instead, Hunter moved like a man for whom this *was* the main event. He slid his tongue through my folds, teasing me, shifting between gentle, light touches and hard, demanding ones. He used his lips, the flat of his tongue, the tip. He traced around my clit after pulling the hood out of the way.

It didn't take long before I moaned and tried to lift my hips against his solid grasp. He didn't relent, reminding me of a predator who had caught his prey and intended to play with it for a while before the kill.

A deep sound left him, dragging a shiver from me. Fire roared inside me, clouding my head, making it so all I could do was feel what he did. I cupped my own breasts, needing more — everything — chasing my own release. It was wild, an odd sense of connection to something I couldn't name, couldn't identify. Funny to feel that with someone I didn't know a damn thing about.

He nipped me, the sting leaving me gasping. Not that he let me recover. Instead, he delivered punishing licks to my clit, zeroing in there, driving me past my own ability to resist.

The orgasm that crashed over me was so powerful that my brain shorted out. The waves of pleasure rolled through me, overwhelming and shocking. A break inside me, all the things I held so tightly, the worries I refused to acknowledge, the stress of trying so hard to live a life that wouldn't accept me, my inability to find a place I fit in — they all drifted away.

Along with the orgasm, I found a moment of peace.

At least, I did until Hunter dragged his tongue over my drenched and sensitive pussy. I peered down, over my body, to find his gaze locked on me, his face framed by my thighs. He offered a slow, meaningful lick up my cunt, flames in his eyes as clear as anything. "I've been watching you for *years*, shadow-girl. If you think I'm about to stop at one measly little orgasm, you're dead wrong."

Maybe I should have been terrified by such a declaration, especially since he said it as though I had no choice in it, as if he were informing rather than asking.

Instead, something in his eyes, in the ease I felt after the first mind-blowing orgasm, they all made me think...maybe he was onto something.

When something had their teeth so close to my sensitive parts, maybe that wasn't the best time to argue, anyway.

I certainly could suffer through a few more orgasms.

If he *insisted*.

# Chapter Nine

Somehow, waiting for a vampire to answer his door felt oddly…normal. I'd always thought it strange when a vampire had a smartphone, like something didn't fit. It was as if I expected them to always live in old castles, travel by horse and wear cloaks. It felt rude for Kase not to adhere to blatant stereotypes.

His porch was covered, the door set back so he wouldn't risk becoming a crispy pile of ash if he opened it on a particularly sunny day — a necessary thing for a vampire to consider.

The door opened, and Kase lifted an eyebrow as though I were the last person he expected to find.

Which was an entirely stupid reaction since I'd called him first and he'd given me the address to his private residence.

He stepped backward and held his arm out like some grand gesture.

I nodded as I looked around his place. The townhouse was somewhat narrow and decorated in that minimalistic modern style. Black and white everywhere with a punch of red — a bit too on the nose for my taste. Still, it fit him. Rigid, everything in its place, nothing unneeded.

"This could have waited until nightfall," Kase said as he closed the front door, locking it behind me.

A moment of fear made my heart stutter.

He stilled, remaining beside the door, coming no closer. "Are you afraid now?"

"Maybe being alone and locked in a house with a vampire was a bad idea." I swallowed hard.

"If I wanted to kill you, Ava, I could have done so at any time."

"Yeah, but I could have made you work for it at least. I might get killed, but I plan on making it as annoying for my killer as possible."

That crease appeared in his cheek, the one that said he was amused even if he didn't show it. "I assure you, you are perfectly safe here."

"Not feeling hungry?"

"Not particularly. I fed last night, and even if I hadn't, I have far more control than that."

I had a flash of him sinking his fangs into a woman, of how her eyes would glaze over in pleasure. It didn't *seem* pleasurable to me, but I damn well knew vampires had a way to make victims think it was. I chalked that up to the same idiocy that made women want bikers, fixer uppers and stiletto heels.

Him talking about his control made me wonder about his age. Asking vampires how old they were was considered rude, yet the question perched on my lips. Kase didn't strike me as all that young — especially with what I'd heard about him being the true power behind the coven. As vampires aged, they tended to gain better control and needed to feed less often.

They also tended to be far less human…

It was a toss-up on what was worse.

His gaze landed on my throat, on the bruises from Melinda, and that unnatural stillness took over again. After a long moment, he asked, "What happened?"

"Poltergeist." The response came out softly, uneasy. I did *not* like being the focus of all that intensity.

He either noticed my discomfort or simply had moved on, because he nodded and walked past me. "I trust that was handled since you're still breathing and here?" He gestured toward the couch before going to the freezer.

"Yep. Poltergeist is gone." I took a seat where he'd indicated.

"How did that happen? As I recall, they aren't all that easy to get rid of."

"A friend was there." I paused. Kase knew more about supernatural things than I did, right? "Do you know what can just disintegrate a poltergeist?"

Kase sat beside me, his movements unnervingly smooth, and pressed something to my throat. A moment of shock struck me as coldness soaked into my neck.

*An ice pack?*

Again, it surprised me how human he could seem.

"There are a few different ways poltergeists can be cast out. Holy men—"

"I highly doubt he was a holy man." The memory of how Hunter had licked me had my cheeks warming.

Kase didn't acknowledge my statement, simply kept listing options. "Necromancers, some demons, some mages."

I took the ice pack from him so I could hold it against my neck myself. I didn't care for him being so close to my pulse... "There was smoke that surrounded the poltergeist. In fact, the man turned into smoke before he looked like a human again."

Kase lifted his lip, showing off his impressive fangs. I would never understand how people couldn't know about vampires, not when their teeth looked like *that* all that time. All the stories of their fangs retracting or only sharpening when they were about to feed were bullshit. They *always* looked like rottweilers. I think people just tended to only see what they expected to see, and we humans were great at explaining away anything we didn't want to believe.

"Hellhound."

"What's a hellhound?"

Kase set his arm over the back of the couch and crossed one ankle over his other knee. How he could look regal even when *relaxing,* I didn't understand. "They're demons who reside in the underworld."

"So like...demon werewolves?"

"No. They're not called 'hounds' because they resemble dogs, but rather because they patrol the underworld to ensure nothing gets out that shouldn't. They also track down such things in our world when they do escape. It is rare for them to venture into our world unless on a hunt." The way he spoke made me take notice. His words were careful, as always, but clipped slightly. Was that concern?

"Are they dangerous?"

"*Everything* is dangerous. I explain this to new vampires who believe themselves invincible. I once knew a vampire, one of the strongest I've ever known. He thought himself beyond the point of needing to worry about humans — or anything else. Then, one day, he crossed the wrong person. A human walked into his home and set it aflame. He burned inside along with the human, and that has always driven home the point No matter how weak something seems, no matter how strong something else seems, *everything* is capable of being dangerous."

I swallowed at the weight of his gaze. "And hellhounds?"

"Even the coven gives hellhounds a wide berth when we discover them in our territory. While they rarely care about anything in the mortal realm beyond their hunt, they also care little about getting rid of anything in their way. You should be very cautious, Ava."

I nodded, then handed the ice pack back to him. When he took it, he frowned at a red mark that remained on the white pack.

"Sorry." I turned my hand over, the one Grant had cut, to find that sure enough, I'd managed to tear open the scab.

"What happened?"

"Grant needed my blood for the wards."

He frowned, as though he disliked the idea. "He could have done less damage."

"That's what I said, but he said it was about the *sacrifice* of the action."

Kase lifted his thumb to his mouth and pressed it against the tip of his fang. He didn't grimace, didn't show any reaction to the wound.

Blood welled at the top, a red so dark it was almost purple.

Which sent me bolting. I jumped to my feet, wanting that blood nowhere near me.

Kase didn't grab me—and I knew damn well he could have, because vampires were terrifyingly fast—but he stared. "Really?"

"I may not always love my life, but I do love being alive. No thanks to *that*." I waved at his thumb.

"How can you be so ignorant of our world? You can't be turned into a vampire from a little blood."

"That sounds like men who say a girl can't get knocked up because it's just the tip."

"I am sterile, so that isn't an issue I deal with." Kase spoke with such flatness of his voice, I almost missed that he'd made a joke, even more so because he so quickly moved on from it. "To be changed from mortal, a person has to die. My blood will help to heal you, but it won't change you since I, again, don't plan on killing you."

I pressed my lips together, then responded slowly. "You know, I normally don't spend so much time around people who have to keep telling me they don't plan on killing me."

"Would you rather I not tell you that?"

"I'd rather you not *need* to tell me that."

He made a soft sound that didn't acknowledge what I'd said as he held out his hand.

I took one deep breath, reminding myself that as unnerving as it was, he *could* have killed me whenever he'd wanted to.

*And he still can.*

*Fair point.*

I set my hand in his palm, and he held his other finger above. Fat droplets of blood fell from the mark on his thumb and onto my wound. It was cold, which was an incredibly odd sensation. I had always pictured blood as warm, and the thought of cold blood made me want to gag. I could only imagine it coagulating and clotting.

Even so, before my eyes, the cut in my hand knitted back together. It narrowed, the skin repairing itself, until only a faint white scar remained. It ached, but rather than the sharp pain that had been there before, one that would make me wince when I moved that hand, it reminded me of the day after a little-too-strenuous a workout.

The deep red remained there, like a stain, even after the wound had closed.

"What did you want, Ava? You didn't come over just so I could heal your hand."

*Right.* I'd asked to come over for a reason, hadn't I? Funny how quickly Kase could drive us off topic.

I extracted my hand from his grip. "I want access to Olin's place."

Kase blinked slowly, spaced out as though he had them timed. I got the sense it was about hiding his annoyance with a topic he'd already discussed with me and felt over. "Getting involved in vampire affairs is unwise. You did as you were hired to do, Ava, and you were well paid for it. Now is the time to take a step backward and accept this is no longer your problem."

I shook my head, wanting him to understand. "This isn't a vampire affair. I'm not getting involved in vampire politics. I don't care about your secrets or your plans or anything like that."

"So why? You've stayed out of such things for as long as I've known you. Why are you suddenly interested in involving yourself the games of supernaturals?"

"Because this is *my* world. I said I don't care about the vampires and I don't, but something that is happening is affecting *me*. Something appeared in my living room — this dark, shadow — and when I looked for Rachel? This shadow was inside me, had to be pulled out. Whatever happened to Rachel isn't over — everything inside me says it isn't — and the vampire is my only lead."

Kase didn't move, only stared at me as though trying to work through what I had said.

He finally nodded and rose, reminding me that he was quite a bit taller than I was. He gestured for me to follow as he went down his hallway and into an office. From the desk he pulled a set of keys, then jotted down an address on a scrap of paper. "This isn't official, of course. The coven would not care for a human to go traipsing through a vampire's liar."

"So why are you helping me?"

"Because you would do it no matter what, and I'd prefer this need for answers you suddenly have to not kill you."

"I didn't think you much cared if I kept breathing."

He caught my hand, the movement quick enough to make me jerk back. Still, with his grip, I couldn't go far. He dragged his fingers along the bruising at my throat, the chill from his touch almost as nice as the ice pack he'd given me. "I believe I do care, so go only during the daylight hours and be very cautious. Other vampires are not as trustworthy as I am." His gaze skirted down my body, and for once, something about him didn't seem so cold. "You have proven yourself detrimental to even my self-control."

The moment he released me, I all but leapt two feet back. *That* was the last thing I'd expected.

What the hell was wrong with men in my life suddenly? They, as a group, had ignored me most of my life and in the past week deemed me irresistible?

I swallowed hard at the heat in Kase's eyes, though he remained back, as if proving he wouldn't give chase.

Fuck that, though. I still ran.

I had answers to find, and I sure was hell wasn't going to find them if I got tangled up with a vampire like Kase.

\* \* \* \*

Olin's lair reminded me that vampires were as different as anything else. Whereas Kase's had been modern, understated and entirely human-appearing, Olin's was anything but.

I'd entered with the keys Kase had given me to find it dusty and full of mold. Light streamed in through boarded-up windows, highlighting the dust that hung in the air.

He couldn't have been there any time in the last few weeks.

There was furniture, but it was all old. Not well-loved or cared for, either. A few pieces reminded me of things one might find in the older areas of the south, where grandmothers kept rocking chairs that had belonged to *their* grandmothers.

Had Olin kept these pieces from his human life? Dragged them from lair to lair like some tether to his long-lost humanity?

Why didn't Kase, then? Why was he exempt from that sort of sentimentality or did he just hate his human past so much?

I pushed away the thought. It didn't matter, really. The cobwebs over the door told me Olin wasn't there, and I had bigger mysteries to handle than the vampire who I had no business thinking about.

There were no pictures on the walls, nothing modern, as though Olin had stopped adjusting long ago. The house sat in a small suburb a few miles outside the main city, an old area that had a mixture of homes that had been in the family for generations and windows covered in foil.

It was the sort of place where neighbors didn't bother one another and kept to themselves. Perfect for a vampire who didn't want to be disturbed.

I explored the main floor but found nothing of interest. In fact, I'd almost believe he didn't stay there at all, given how few personal items there were. The rooms were decorated only so far as pieces of old, broken furniture were placed in their respective spots, but there was no real decor, no dishes in the kitchen, no fridge.

A door sat off the kitchen, ajar, and when I pushed it open, stairs descended into the darkness of the basement.

*Right. Go down into the creepy murder basement.*

A moment of realization hit me about just how stupid this idea was. Sure, I had no reason the believe Olin was here, which meant mold spores and the occasional spider were the worst dangers I faced. That other part of me thought...*what if?*

What if I were wrong? What if Kase was? What if an angry, vicious vampire waited at the base of the steps?

What the hell was I thinking? I had a vampire, a werewolf, a mage and a hellhound – apparently – who all had offered to help. Going into dark basements felt like it counted as part of that offered help, and was definitely something one of the non-mortal beings should be shouldering.

Then the void came back to me. Rachel's face, the sensation of Melinda's hands around my throat—they all hit me.

Whether I wanted it to be my problem or not, it *was*.

I reached into my bag and wrapped my fingers around the thin piece of metal Gran had given me years before. It was made of something amazingly strong and sharp enough to easily pierce anything. I'd discovered that the first time I'd kept it in my purse and reached in without thinking. It had taken six stiches to close the wound. Since then, I'd been more careful.

Still, it was useful enough to keep.

Piercing a vampire's heart was enough to kill them, and the best part was that it didn't require a wooden stake or silver. Anything that could make it through their exceedingly hard skin would work.

I'd asked Gran about that, back when she'd given me the weapon. The idea of a sharp stick taking down a vampire seemed insane.

*'So you poke them with a stick and what? The magic falls out?'*

She'd looked at me as if I were an idiot—it was a look she had down pat—and snorted. *'What do you think will happen if I pierce your heart?'*

I'd frowned. *'Well, I'd die, but there are a lot of things that could kill me that a vampire would shake off.'*

She'd grinned, then leaned closer. *'They heal fast, but piercing their heart isn't the sort of thing one can heal from quick enough. One good, well-placed jab, and if it doesn't kill them, it will weaken them enough to give you a chance to run.'*

*'That's all I get? A chance?'*

*'Would you rather not have a chance?'*

That had always stuck with me. It was the most I could hope for, just a *chance* to run.

The steps creaked beneath my feet, and I grasped the railing with my free hand. The darkness made it impossible to take in any details, especially since my eyes hadn't adjusted yet. Whereas Kase had his house properly sun-proofed so he could be in the main living areas, it seemed Olin went with the dark and dank basement idea.

As I moved through the space, down the steps, I tried to breathe softly, as if that would help hide my presence.

At the bottom of the stairs, I squinted to try to pick up the details. No light streamed in at all, telling me he'd at least properly light-proofed the basement. Slowly, the specifics of the room came into focus.

A couch, a desk, a computer that looked as if it had never been touched. No doubt the place he actually slept might have been even better hidden. The whole 'coffin' idea had come from vampires trying to reduce the risk of getting caught in the sun. A well-made coffin could survive most things.

I searched slowly, listening for any sign of movement. The last thing I needed was to end up surprised by...

Well, anything.

I pulled open the drawers of the desk, sorting through the items there. Bills, paperwork, things that were oddly normal. It was weird to think of Olin sitting down at the desk, a credit card in his hand as he called in to pay his car loan. If the learning curve for new technology was so high for old people, imagine how it was for vampires pushing five-hundred years.

As I went through the items, I caught a few details about Olin.

He drove sports cars—there were loans for at least three different ones—and the payments were as much as my rent. He never used his computer, which I could tell by it having a mouse with a ball and the monitor taking up half the desk.

All in all, I found nothing about Rachel, nothing that gave me any insight into where he might have gone or what he might be into.

What was I hoping for? Maybe a large pentagram drawn in blood on the floor that let me go, 'oh, look, he's into some weird demonic shit.'

Instead, I got glimpses of his life, and it wasn't all that different from mine.

Well, less trash reality TV and more murdering, but otherwise?

*The same.*

I dropped into the chair in the corner of the room, less dust flying up than I'd expected. He must have sat in that place most of the time. A table to the left had books piled up on it, and as I examined them, I knew Olin and I could never be friends.

I loved to watch the show about college-aged kids who drank to excess and slept around and cried about it the next day while Olin read classic literature bound in leather.

I picked up a book that reminded me of the ones at Rachel's and flipped open the pages. A paper slid from the pages of the book and fell to the floor.

I leaned over to grab it, then lifted it close enough to make out the image in the darkness.

*Rachel and...Olin?*

The two looked happy. Olin's arm was wrapped around her waist, pulling her against his side as he leaned in to make up for the height difference. They both grinned, their gazes skirting toward one another as though even that small amount of time to snap a picture was too long to *not* gaze lovingly at one another.

Had they been together?

The thought was strange. Sure, I knew logically that some women liked vampires. It wasn't something I understood, but people had weirder kinks. The idea of curling up with something that wanted to kill me seemed like a horribly bad idea. Sleeping with a vampire was like sleeping with a man-eating tiger.

I mean, sure, Kase was good-looking. Even with that slightly unnatural look to his skin, the ever-so-translucent tint older vampires got when they kept the shade of their skin but lost the glow from the sun.

And, okay, so he was built rather well, at least from what his tailored suits showed, but even then...

A hot killer was still a killer.

I tucked the picture into my jean jacket because it haunted me. I recalled Rachel's twisted body in that pit, imagined the way she'd died. For a moment I was thankful that I hadn't found her spirit. Those killed horrifically could be a challenge to talk to. They'd suffered a trauma, and death didn't wipe that away. She'd not only been murdered — which let's be honest was a pretty terrible thing to happen — but it was by someone she *had known*. The way she was pressed against his side showed trust.

I turned the corner to take the stairs and something caught me. I didn't even have time to evaluate what it might be. All I saw in my head was the lifeless form Olin had left Rachel as.

And he'd even *liked* her.

I doubted he felt so positively toward me.

I swung the thin spike at the person who had grabbed me, ready to end them. 'Live and let live' also meant the opposite.

*Fuck with me and I'm going to give killing you a good try.*

The spike found nothing but air, and my hand was knocked aside. Something solid but without temperature caught my wrist and threw me backward. I hit the wall hard enough to drive the breath from my lungs and remind myself that being tossed around was not my idea of a good time.

Instead of the snarling Olin I expected, however, Grant stood in the dimly lit room, his hand lifted toward me.

I couldn't move. My wrists were pinned to the wall, my body just as stuck. Even when I jerked, nothing budged.

"Would you let me go?"

He smiled and closed the distance between us. "You still look rather feral. Maybe it's best to keep you exactly like this." He took the hand not lifted—no doubt that one was busy keeping me stuck there—and traced his fingers over my jawline. "Plus, you're far easier to follow if you can't move."

I narrowed my eyes, so he let out a soft laugh and released me.

The sudden change made me lose my balance, and I fell forward—against him. The bastard had probably planned that, because he caught me with ease.

It made me look up into his face and realize how young he seemed. Where Kase looked like something ancient, Grant seemed like a kid barely out of high school. He *wasn't* of course. In fact, given that mages, once they came into their full power, stopped aging like every other type of supernatural being, he could have been far older than Kase.

I hated not being able to tell.

It took *far* too long for me to realize I was staring, that I was studying his face with an embarrassingly thorough level of attention.

When I pulled back, he let me. "What are you doing here?"

"Kase seemed to think you sneaking into a vampire's lair alone wasn't such a good idea. Do you have any idea how you unsettle him? It's a bit pathetic, though fun to watch."

"So you're going to just keep following me?"

"Are you going to keep doing stupid things that make me *need* to follow you?"

"We both know the answer to that is yes."

"Then you have yourself a very handsome, hilarious shadow."

*Just what I needed.*

Grant put his hand out, then gestured. It took me a moment to realize he wanted the stake.

I set it in his palm, and he lifted it to study the strange piece. "Impressive. Where did you get it?"

"A friend."

"Some friend." He twisted his wrist to examine it from every angle. "I haven't seen one of these in a very long time."

"It's a piece of metal."

"No. Well, I mean, sure, in the same way a car or a computer is. It might be made of metal, but it's more than that. It's enchanted. These marks?" Grant turned to stand just beside me, his arm brushing mine, as he pointed at the scribbled marks on the side that I had assumed were either decoration or from me shoving it into my purse for years. "It's pulsing with magic. You really can't feel that?"

"I'm not all that magically sensitive," I admitted. "I can walk through most wards without noticing them."

He lifted his dark eyebrow but didn't address the statement with more than a soft hum before returning to the topic at hand. "Well, there are protection runes here and here that help to keep the bearer safe. In addition, the tip is reinforced for strength. A normal stick wouldn't pierce a vampire's heart, but this? It wouldn't take much force to work its way in. Who gave you this? No normal witch or mage could have made this." Even as he spoke, he handed it back to me.

I tucked the weapon into my purse, more careful with it than I had been. Suddenly I felt bad about having tossed it in the junk drawer for so long. "Just a friend who runs an occult shop. Actually, I was headed there next, if you wanted to come with me."

"I figured you'd complain about having a shadow like you did yesterday."

"Yesterday I hadn't broken into a vampire's lair. Besides, I have a feeling you'll follow me anyways."

His smile was devastating, and for what was not close to the first time, I worried.

Sure, him coming along, especially after I'd seen how well he managed to pin me, was a smart move. After the poltergeist, after stalking a killer vampire, after a missing spirit, a little muscle couldn't be a bad thing.

But when he smiled like *that*, I thought back to Hunter, back to what an easy hussy I apparently was, and I was only thankful where we were going.

I doubt Gran would let me fuck him in her store, so my virtue was safe.

Or at least as safe as it had ever been.

# Chapter Ten

"Oh, fuck this."

I turned to find Grant with his gaze pinned on Gran, his color paler than it had been before we'd walked in, his green eyes wide.

He hadn't seemed to recognize the store, but the moment he'd seen Gran, he'd uttered the curse.

Gran only smiled. "Hello, Grant."

"Nope." He shook his head and took a step backward. "You know *her*?"

I turned my gaze between the two like some tennis match, unsure where to look. "What's the problem?" I'd seen people give Gran a lot of respect, but I'd always chalked that up to her age more than anything. Maybe an odd amount of professional courtesy?

That wasn't what was on Grant's face. He was *terrified*.

And for a man who had just flung me against a wall, a man who Kase trusted to take on Olin should he need to, that was an unnerving thing.

"She turned me into a goat!"

I fully about-faced at that, staring at Grant as if he'd lost his mind completely. "A goat?"

Grant shook his head. "Nope. No fucking way. Kase can take his money and shove it, because I will *not* do this. Nothing is going to screw with you while you're around her, so I will be outside, you know, the place where normal people don't turn other people into fucking goats."

The door slammed behind him like some final punctuation to his hissy fit.

Gran's laugh meant I didn't need ask if she'd done it. People didn't giggle like *that* unless they were guilty as shit.

"Really? A goat?"

Gran lost whatever composure she had then, her laughter deepening until she had to lean forward to catch her breath. "A girl goat."

"Why would you turn him into a goat?"

"It was a long time ago, but rest assured he deserved it." She straightened, then smoothed her hands down the loose gown she wore. Her silvered hair was pulled back into a messy bun and her withered skin held years of lines. "He walked into one of my old shops with all the confidence, as if he were the biggest thing around. I rather like explaining to men who think that that they are not, in fact, the most dangerous thing there is. I've discovered a few days as a goat tends to teach them some humility, and I rarely need to give the lesson more than once."

"But if *you* can deal with him that easily, why on earth would Kase hire him to protect me? What? Was he some sort of bargain, coupon bodyguard deal?" I slid onto the stool beside Gran.

"No, Ava, he's rather talented. He can handle your protection. He might have been overly full of himself but if he weren't powerful, I wouldn't have bothered with the lesson. Plus, he was kicked out of the guild, which makes me likes him more."

"Oh, so not only is he a goat-man, but he also got kicked out of the *one* group he's supposed to be in as a mage? This is getting better and better."

Gran sat on the stool across from me, the same slow way she always did, one that said she was in no hurry and would do things at the exact moment she intended to—and not a second earlier. "The guild is like a boy's club. Him not being in it doesn't change his abilities."

"So he's not that bad?"

"I never said *that*. I said he's capable of protecting you, if you're into a man doing that." She scoffed at that, as if the entire idea was one of the dumbest she'd ever heard.

"Well, mostly I'm into not dying, and since vampires, werewolves and hellhounds are out of my range when it comes to protecting myself, I think I'll sit this one back and rely on goat-man."

She snorted. "I've always said you were capable of more than you realize."

"Yeah, but that's just what everyone says now. It's the new age, participation-trophy thought process. We're all special and capable of more. I may not have had parents to tell me that, but you've done it."

Gran caught my hand, her grip solid for a woman who had to be in her eighties. "You don't get it, Ava." Her eyes went white, the freaky thing I'd seen from time to time that always forced me to remember she was very much not normal. "There's more inside you, and so much less. If you ever stopped hiding, if you ever stopped being afraid..." She shivered and shook her head, releasing me. "You might terrify us all."

I stared down at my hand, at where she'd clutched, tiny red half circles in the skin from where she'd dug her nails into me.

An unease crept through me, one I had every time I stopped to think about exactly what I was.

And, like always, I shook away the thought. I *was* human. Maybe I had skills most didn't, but like so many other humans, the unique ones, the ones who were cursed with something different, I was still human.

Instead of arguing with her—what was the point when Gran never listened?—I switched subjects. "What I really need is a spell."

She took a deep breath, her eyes returning to normal, her regaining the look of an old woman. "Well, then you came to the right place. What sort of spell?"

"I need to hold a seance."

\* \* \* \*

Grant looked far less tough leaning against the wall across the street from Gran's shop, pouting. He had his arms crossed and his green eyes locked on the door, so the weight of his gaze struck me the moment I exited the building.

He was something between pissed and properly put in his place, like a dog who had been thrown out of the house when guests came over.

I crossed the small street since Grant didn't seem willing to come any closer to the shop than that. "Okay, so tell me, what did you do?"

He huffed and shook his head. "Does it really matter?"

"Well, I mean, it was goat worthy, so I feel like it's a good story."

He let out a long sigh. "It was just after I gained my immortality. I'll admit, I was a bit of a dick. It's a weird moment, to realize you're not aging anymore. It's like the entire world opens up, like you have something you never thought you would before. When we grow up, we're held to certain beliefs, to certain rules, and with one swoop, it all changes."

That youngness he'd had didn't seem so obvious anymore, as he spoke about how it used to be, about how people changed and grew.

He uncrossed his arms and tucked his thumbs into his pockets. "So I went into her shop—it was somewhere else at the time—and I was acting like some big-shot mage in some little human's occult store. I deserved to be taken down a few pegs, but her—" He pointed at the store. "She's dangerous."

"She hasn't turned me into a goat, yet."

He shook his head. "You know how things like to announce they're dangerous? You have the red hourglass on black widows, the stripes on a tiger, the brighter colors that say 'stay the fuck back,' right? Dangerous things like others to *know* they're dangerous because it means fewer fights. Some things, though, the really lethal things, they don't give a fuck what anyone thinks. Gran has looked like *that* for years. I talked to someone who knew her two hundred years ago, and she looked exactly the same. Whatever she is, with the power she has, she could look like anything, but she chooses to look like some harmless old woman." He whistled low. "Let's just say that isn't the sort of being

I want to mess with any more than absolutely necessary."

I turned to gaze at the shop, trying to connect the woman I'd come to know with the person he was talking about. It seemed impossible for them to be the same, for her to be whatever he seemed to think.

She was odd, sure, but she'd looked after me, helped me understand when no one else would.

Could she be as dangerous as he'd said?

Then her words to me turned sinister, threatening. If she was what Grant thought, what exactly did she think *I* was?

* * * *

I rubbed my eyes as I looked around the large, open room Kase had rented for me. It was in an office building, and I didn't bother to ask how he'd managed to secure it so quickly. In fact, the entire floor seemed empty.

It was better not to ask such questions.

I could have done this in my own living room, but death magic *always* had a scent of brimstone that was impossible to get out of carpets.

I didn't want *my* house to be the one stinking after all was said and done.

Kase held up the item I'd asked him for, then set it in my open palm. Rachel's heavy necklace—the one she'd worn both when she'd died and in the picture— was cool against my skin. "Are you sure about this?"

I shook my head. "Not really. Magic like this, it's not much fun."

"Why didn't you just call a medium? They'll do this sort of thing for a good cost."

I curled my fingers around the necklace. "Because if someone else did it, they might have lied, or didn't find the echo, or who knows what." I shook my head. "I need to do it to be sure. I mean, letting the echo of a murdered woman speak through me? That's not my idea of a good time, but it's the only way to know exactly what happened."

"We know what happened. He killed her in her apartment. I saw the room. There wasn't much ambiguity."

"But *why*?" I pulled the picture from my pocket and held it out to him. "They were happy, Kase. You failed to mention that to me, that he *knew* her, that they weren't just strangers. How did he go from *that* to brutally killing her?"

Kase peered down at the picture, his lips pressed together in a tight line before he handed it back. "I wasn't aware he'd started seeing a human." His tone was low, careful. "He was always impulsive, but I hadn't expected *that* from him."

"*That*? Like humans are beneath you?"

He tilted his head, as if I'd missed the point entirely. "Humans are different from us. They pose dangers to vampires, and it rarely ends well."

"*We're* the dangerous ones?" I didn't bother to stifle the laughter.

"We are dangerous to one another. Vampires are able to kill humans without meaning to, but we are also weaker during daylight hours. Incorporating humans into our lives, into the times when we are vulnerable, also gives them an ability to do us harm. Such relationships are frowned upon."

His words confused me. I was sure that last time, in his place, he'd looked at me like something more than just friends.

*Maybe it was just lunch time...*

I shook away the thought. Why did it matter, since I wasn't planning on anything with Kase? He was what a gambler would call a losing hand. Other than the way he filled out his suits, he had zero positives. Judging from the whispers around him, he'd killed more than his fair share of people, he drank blood to live, he couldn't go hiking on a nice sunny day and... what was that last one?

Right, he was *dead.*

So getting offended that he thought it was as bad an idea as I did was altogether stupid.

I tucked the picture back into my pocket.

"Have you ever done this before?" He nodded toward where I'd drawn a circle in salt.

"No. It should be easy enough, though. Gran gave me everything I needed, went over the basic spell. I'm not a medium, so it isn't quite as easy as it would be for one, but with the right tools, anyone can manage it."

"I will stay," he said as if we had already discussed and come to a conclusion about it.

"No, you actually have to go. Spirits, even echoes, don't care for vampires."

He lifted an eyebrow as though that were the worst excuse he'd ever heard. "I doubt spirits care much."

"Oh, they do." I fought the shudder at those whispers. I had to think that it was *those* that warned off spirits, that they could hear them as I could. To be fair, it was a warning I should probably heed as well.

Spirits had a better sense of self-preservation than I did.

"Perhaps you are the one who is actually afraid," he pointed out.

"Shouldn't I be? I am chasing down some crazed vampire who killed at least one woman I know of. Seems worthwhile to be wary of vampires."

Kase folded his hands together behind his back. "Not of me, no. And seeing as you are chasing a killer, despite what I've said, I don't feel you have enough good sense to be afraid."

I licked my bottom lip, not even bothering with trying to sort out my feelings. Since when did fear and arousal become so fucking similar that I couldn't tell them apart?

I dropped my gaze. "I'm not kidding, Kase. Something about vampires scare spirits off, and it might make it harder to catch an echo."

He took a step backward, as though he realized I needed the space. "Okay. I'll go. Let me know what you find out."

I nodded, relieved when he did as he'd said and left. Why was it that it was so much harder when he was there to think?

It left me alone in the room with just the salt and the candles. I could have called someone to come over. Not a regular friend—I didn't have many of them—but one of the many new friends I'd accumulated.

Hunter might have come, if I'd had any idea how to actually contact him. Instead, he seemed to show up whenever the fuck he wanted. That didn't make him overly useful.

Plus, after Melinda's reaction to him, maybe he wasn't a great companion when dealing with spirits.

Besides, I didn't *need* anyone else.

I was tough. I'd been knee-deep in death all my life. A little seance was the least of what I'd dealt with before.

The candles crackled when I lit them. I turned off the light, then sat in the center of the circle, my eyes closed.

I tried to relax—I really did. This needed my complete attention, for me to center myself and reach for an echo of who Rachel had been, for what was left, imprinted on the world.

And yet, each time I started, each time I tried, I remembered her body.

I really *didn't* want feel that, to experience those last minutes of her life.

The scent of the candles, the burning wick, they filled the room as I rolled my shoulders and tried to focus. The necklace pressed into my palm, the slightest of currents there I could feel, a connection to her.

A creak made me jump, my heart speeding.

Instead of some huge danger—maybe another poltergeist or Olin himself—I was alone other than the snap of the flames.

A deep breath helped my heart to slow, but what was the point? When had I become a fucking chicken?

It didn't matter, because the choices were clear. I either had to give up or do the one thing I'd never live down.

So I pulled my phone out and dialed.

# Chapter Eleven

Troy held up two containers of food like some conquering hero returning from battle. Thank fuck I'd called him.

Anyone else would have mocked me, but not Troy. After shutting the door to the office, he peered around the salt and candles. "So, serious work going on?"

The fact he'd come over without question, without making me explain what I was doing or why, made me smile. It was an odd feeling, and one I wasn't sure how to deal with.

I took a seat in the circle, and Troy stepped over the line of salt and candles. He sat cross-legged beside me, then set the food containers down in front of us. He paused as he looked at them. "The food won't mess up the whole flow of this, right?"

I gave him my best 'you really are an idiot' look and opened the container of food closest to me. "You think a few nachos are going to throw off the cosmic flow of a spell?"

He huffed as he opened his own container — tacos. "I don't understand how this all works. In case you've missed it, we werewolves like to avoid magic."

"Says the man who turns into a wolf." I lifted my eyebrow.

"Point taken." He popped a piece of the shredded beef into his mouth, chewed it slowly, then swallowed again before speaking. "So how does this all work?"

I thought about it, trying to figure out how to explain it. Troy being a wolf was the only reason he could be there at all. Spirits didn't care much about werewolves. I had to figure it was because they were, in many ways, far more 'natural' than the other types, which was probably why I could do a seance and not worry about him being there.

It was also why spirits had no problem bothering me, despite a werewolf living next door.

That was the first time living close to a vampire sounded like a benefit. If Kase shacked up nearby, maybe I could manage full nights of sleep without anything weird showing up.

"A seance can be done by anyone, and it is really just catching the echo of a person, the imprint they left behind. It doesn't take a medium because it uses basic energy. It's like the different between a mechanic and someone who can change the oil of a car."

"That doesn't sound so bad."

I shifted, then sighed softly. "It means I'll have to relive her death. That's what I need, to know what happened to her, what Olin did to her, so the echo will be the last hours of her life." I shivered as I thought back to the body. "I really *don't* want to relive that, though. Dying is the sort of thing you're only supposed to experience the one time."

Troy stared at me for a long moment, his silver eyes so familiar. "Don't forget that all of us immortals die. Trust me. I know what you mean about it being something that should only happen once."

"I've never thought much about how werewolves are made," I admitted.

His words were slow, measured, as if recalling something he tried not to think about often. "To become immortal, a human's life has to end. It's true of any type of supernatural. For werewolves it requires a massive infection. A tiny cut won't do it. Every werewolf was mauled by one that came before, and we all died in agony." His voice didn't tremble, but the shadows in his eyes told the story.

I'd known a werewolf needed to be bitten to turn, but had no idea the extent. Troy seemed bigger than life now—werewolves had an amazing amount of strength that helped them seem that way—but to think he'd been stalked and attacked by a wolf seemed impossible.

Werewolves didn't look after changing quite like they had before. They tended to become larger and more muscular—talk about a good workout plan—which made me wonder what Troy had looked like back when he was human.

"I'm sorry," I said softly, unsure what else to say.

Troy shuddered, as if that would dislodge the memories of whenever it had happened, then offered a tired smile. "I wouldn't be who I am without it, right? But, yeah, I get it. I wouldn't want to sign up for experiencing that again. There's no other option?"

I shook my head. "I've run into walls over and over again. Trust me. I've been looking for another option, but this is it. It's all I've got, but it isn't exactly coming easily."

He nodded, then rubbed his fingers along his chin. He looked good pensive like that. It was hard to ignore or forget.

Honestly, he looked even better when not at least slightly annoyed with me.

Troy closed the food and pushed it toward the side of the circle to give us room. Afterward, he shifted his position and crooked his finger at me.

I must have sat there too long, wondering just what the fuck he was talking about, because he caught my arm and tugged me toward him. He settled me in front of him, his large, warm body behind me. His breath was slow and deep and even if I hated to admit it, it was calming.

Something about him eased me. Whereas Kase put me on edge, Hunter amused me and Grant annoyed me, Troy felt like a solid wall behind me, something unmovable.

Which was hilarious, given he changed into a wolf…

"If you just wanted to get handsy, you could have asked," I said.

He shushed me, then set my hands on my knees. "Relax."

I huffed softly. Relaxing wasn't something I was good at, and honestly, doing it when he was *this* close was impossible.

I opened my mouth to argue, but he pulled me against him.

"Follow my breath, Ava. Nice and slow." His breathing warmed me, and I did as he said, following the inhalations and exhalations.

Slowly, the tension drained from me. I leaned more against him, his steady heartbeat thumping evenly.

*In. Out.* Amazingly, it all worked. My heart slowed, my muscles unknotted. It felt nice, the ability to close my eyes and relax into the snap of the candles and Troy's scent.

He smelled wild, like a forest at midnight or the flicker of stars.

"I'm sorry I never said anything," he whispered.

I didn't pretend to misunderstand. "Why didn't you?"

He slid his thumbs against my hands, the touch gentle and calming. "Because I assumed you were human. Humans and werewolves don't mix well."

"So I keep hearing. And again, I'm *still* human."

"So you say." He moved his fingers to drag them over the tops of my thighs. "I didn't want to endanger you, but since you seem to put yourself in danger all the time, maybe it's safer if I'm not so far away."

"Why are you so worried about my safety?"

"Because I've seen what happens, Ava, when people try to live in a world they aren't equipped for." He spoke like someone who truly had seen. It wasn't something hypothetical, or something that had happened to someone else. It was personal.

But he hadn't always been this person, had he?

Still, I didn't ask more. We weren't that close, for me to poke at his wounds, for me to expect him to tell me whatever had taught him that. Or, maybe the more honest answer was that *I* wasn't ready to know…

Thankfully, he didn't force me to respond and kept talking. "I still wouldn't think twice about you if I thought you'd live a safe little life next door. I'd already decided to back off, to keep my distance. You were something I looked forward to catching glimpses of but knew I could never have. Then I saw Kase, and I realized you had already ventured into a world you had no idea the dangers of, and I thought…maybe I'm not the worst thing out there for you."

His touch teased me, even through my clothing, and I didn't look at him like a stranger. He wasn't the hot guy next door, the one who was nice to look at but always out of reach. Instead, he was right against me, offering—well, I wasn't sure what he was offering but it was more than nothing.

I drew a deep breath and stopped fighting.

I stopped fighting him, the fear, the unknowns. What I was, what any of this meant, I let it all go. His presence behind me let me do it.

And the second I did, a shock ran through me that made my back straighten and my mouth open in a silent scream.

*This* was why I hated seances.

Spirits always showed at the worst times.

\* \* \* \*

Seeing the world through someone else's eyes was always disconcerting. I was me but I was *her* too. I felt what she did but still knew what I did.

So while I wanted to shudder and scream at the sight of Olin, Rachel was there too, and she smiled.

Olin was even larger, even more intimidating than he'd been in the picture. He smiled, the tips of his fangs showing as if Rachel—I—were the best thing he'd ever seen. We stood on her front porch.

Words between us escaped my lips, but I didn't say them. I was nothing but a passenger, someone to feel and witness Rachel's echo but unable to do a thing about it.

*"I didn't think you were coming over today."*

He smiled wider and pulled me into his arms. His kiss was deep and familiar, the sort that happened after years together.

This *wasn't* just some fling. These were two people who loved one another, and it started an ache inside me, a desire for that, a reminder I'd never experienced it.

He broke the kiss but not before running his fang along my lip. A drop of blood welled and he licked it clean, a heat in his eyes as though that were the best foreplay.

And Rachel? She moaned.

To be wanted like that…

*"I missed you too much,"* he said, his voice deep and accented. He hadn't tried to lose the accent as most vampires did, hadn't seemed to want to acclimate to the world around him.

They laughed and went inside. He never strayed more than a foot or two away, as if he couldn't stand to be any farther from me. Rachel, for her part, never took her gaze from him.

What would it feel like to really have that?

And how could it have gone the way it had? Suddenly I doubted Olin could have done this, that he'd been part of it at all. It didn't seem possible.

She made food, and he helped to plate it, to grab items from upper shelves. It was a dance that showed they often made meals together. She ate hers, and he waited, speaking with her, insisting she finish it, as though he'd forgotten humans weren't cars that needed a specific amount of fuel to function. Still, the care was obvious.

After the meal, he pulled her, me, us? — I couldn't keep it straight — to the bedroom.

Okay, so experiencing sex through someone else was weird. I felt like some perverted voyeur intruding, but it wasn't as if I could do anything about it. I felt everything, the way Olin's lips pressed against my throat, the way his cock stretched me when he slid in deep, the bite of his fangs against my pulse and the draws as he drank deep. Every last touch was mind-blowing and personal in a way that made me as lightheaded as the orgasms he drew from me.

At the end, when he used drops of his blood to seal the fang marks, when I was breathless from the sex, the missing blood and the entire event, we stretched out in her bed in silence.

*This* was what being with a vampire could be? The ease? The simplicity of it all? It seemed impossible.

The quiet of the moment drifted away, however. I *felt* something different, something dark. Not Rachel but *me*.

Across the room stood a shadow, something so dark it drew in all the light around it. I couldn't make out what it was, especially because Rachel didn't *see* it.

Olin shifted, an unnatural movement, jerky and harsh and lacking any sense of fluidity. He turned and instead of the eyes he'd had — that softness, that affection — they were entirely black. He had no expression over his features, as though he were empty inside, as though he'd been wiped clean by something else.

Rachel realized at the same moment I did, and that understanding? The ability to look death in the face, to *know* she was doing to die? It shook me to the core, reminded me that no matter how *nice* some of these supernaturals could seem, they were only a hair away from being able to be this.

The ripping of his fangs into my throat kept a scream from escaping. Olin's body was heavy and strong and Rachel had no chance. She couldn't even budge him, no matter how hard she flailed and shoved.

I wished I could say things went dark, that they faded out like some sex scene in a movie, but instead, it was all too clear. Each time he struck again, each chunk he tore away, I felt it all. Hell, even after Rachel had lost consciousness, I *still* experienced the horror.

And in the corner through it all?

That shadow.

It hadn't been Olin at all, not really.

The enemy was whatever that shadow was.

When it finally ended, when I came back to my own body, I patted down over me, digging my fingers and nails into my throat to make sure I wasn't missing pieces.

Hands grabbed me, and it wasn't until I breathed in that unmistakably *Troy* scent that I even remembered he was there at all.

I shivered, trying to force the memories that weren't mine to carry into the tiniest area of my mind, to lock them away where they couldn't hurt me.

That shadow had killed Rachel, had forced Olin to do it, and even though I'd stayed out of such things in the past…

I couldn't anymore.

I was going to find that son of a bitch.

# Chapter Twelve

Seeing Gran somewhere other than her shop always threw me for a loop. It was like when a kid saw their teacher outside the school. I knew, logically, she went elsewhere and yet finding her not surrounded by the potions and talismans and the scent of incense felt wrong.

Not that I was about to complain when she showed up at my house out of the blue. She'd never done it — in fact, I didn't think I'd ever given her my address — but Gran was the sort of person who didn't get turned away. She could have shown up drunk and belligerent at two in the morning and the right choice would be to let her in and be nice about it.

She'd yet to say *why* she'd come, but again, one didn't rush her.

She grimaced when I offered her the tea. I'd never mastered that skill. She pushed the cup aside, making no attempt to pretend she planned to drink it, despite my making it. "I've had extra customers, Ava."

"Isn't that a good thing?"

"No. The thing you learn is that the more people who turn to religion or spirituality, the worse things are going. No one needs the gods when everything is going well."

I frowned. "Is it whatever I'm dealing with? Because this isn't about Olin, not anymore. It can't be."

She leaned forward, her forearms on my dining room table. "It's something big. I can feel it in my bones, like a storm rolling in. It aches. I'm not the only one, either. That's why people are coming—that's why they're looking for talismans and spells, because they may not know *what* is coming, but they know it isn't good."

I thought back to the chill I'd felt from that shadow, a fear that went deep, like it was primal, like I knew it on some old level, like looking at a snake. "I'm out of my depth, Gran. I don't understand what I'm even looking for."

"The funny thing is that you don't often have to look. You're a nexus in this, something all the spokes go out from. It doesn't matter what you do, where you go, you'll get drawn into it."

"Does that mean I'll win? What is this, fate? Because fate hasn't done much for me."

She laughed, an old chuckle full of years and experience. "Fate is a bitch, Ava, and it doesn't decide answers. Fate is like a sociopath with too much time. It sets up the pieces, keeps shoving people in the direction it wants, but the outcome? It has no idea. So you, Ava, you're the center cog. This is circling you. The thing in your living room, Olin, Melinda, the shadow, Fredrick…it is all moving around you."

"Fredrick? Who's that?"

Her eyes had gone white again, that freaky pale way they did when she wasn't looking at anything. She swallowed, and damn if I didn't see fear in her face...

Then she blinked slowly, and each time she closed her eyes some of the white leeched away and the color came back. When they were regular again, she looked at me. "What?"

"You said Fredrick. I don't know Fredrick."

"Did I?"

A bang on the door happened a moment before a crash. I jumped to my feet, but Gran didn't budge.

Before I could do anything else, three men strolled into the kitchen, their steps casual as if they hadn't just broken in.

The men were huge, and they walked with the sort of confidence that made me slow down and take notice.

Confidence was always bad.

The man on the left looked between Gran and I, ignoring her as soon as he saw her as if she were unimportant. "Ava Harlin?"

Saying no was probably a good idea, right? I mean, if I wasn't Ava, that meant I wasn't involved in all this bullshit. I could be Cathy, a woman who didn't have people breaking into her house.

Ah Cathy, the wonderful, normal, boring woman who never had werewolves or vampires bothering her and certainly wasn't attacked by poltergeists.

But I wasn't Cathy, so I stared at the newcomers and nodded.

They took a step forward, but Gran tapped a finger on the counter. It was a single loud click of her nail, and somehow it stilled them. "In my day, an alpha showed up himself."

*Alpha?*

136

The words were enough for the men to pause. The one in the front drew his shoulders back, puffing out his chest. "Alpha is busy. He doesn't have time to run down every little errand. What business is it of yours?"

"She's a friend."

"And you are?"

Gran's eyes flickered white, and in that moment, I saw something else. It was like a reflection, just a flash of another person. Not an old woman but someone of twenty or thirty, with white eyes and black lips and without the ravages of age she'd always worn.

Was that what Grant had been talking about? Was that what she really looked like without the glamour?

As quickly as it happened, it disappeared, and the three men backed up as if terrified.

Then again, even a glimpse of it had shaken me, and I at least knew her.

"You're not going to let us take her?"

Gran smiled. "I didn't say *that*. I just want you to make sure you and your alpha understand that I expect her back in the same condition. Your pack isn't known for its restraint. We may not be near a full moon, but I'd rather mutts not maul my friend because they have poor impulse control."

She stood, and despite her being less than five foot tall and ninety frail pounds — at least by how she looked — all three of the hulking males backed up.

"I'll tell the alpha, and I'm sure he'll guarantee her safety," the first wolf said.

"Good. Also, leave one of your boys to fix her door. It's rude to break a girl's things, you know."

He nodded, then gestured toward the front door. "We'll go take a look at it now. Please, Ms. Harlin, when you're finished here, meet me outside?"

*Oh, it's 'please' now. Guess they're more afraid of Gran than I thought.*

They seemed to retreat from the kitchen with the same speed of someone fleeing a tsunami.

Once alone, I turned a look on Gran. "If you could scare them that much, couldn't you have told them I wasn't going with them?"

"I could have, but you should go."

"Why?"

"Fate." She smiled and waved me on.

The wolf by the door was on the phone when I passed. He paused, bowing his head. "I'm shit with construction, but I'm having a buddy come over. We'll fix the mark in the drywall and the lock."

By the car stood the wolf who had spoken in the house, the other already behind the wheel. When I neared the car, he opened the door for me.

"At least tell me where we're going. Did Troy set this up?"

*If so, I'm going to kill him.*

"Troy?" The question in his voice said *no, Troy hadn't had anything to do with it.* "No. The West Coast alpha wants to speak to you."

"What for?"

"I'm afraid I don't have the details. I assure you, though, you will be safe."

I stared at the dark interior of the car, basic self-preservation screaming at me to not get into it. "At least tell me his name."

"Fredrick Graves."

*Fredrick. Well, look at that. Gran was right.*

Apparently, it was another step deeper into the mystery, whether I wanted to go or not.

* * * *

The pack house didn't look much like I expected. Maybe I was biased from the coven mansion, but this seemed more like a frat house than any place of power.

It was large, down a very long and winding driveway. Out in the desert, a person could see for miles because there weren't many trees, but the wolves had managed to buy up land that rested between two small mountains, giving them privacy.

Then again, when people wanted to turn into wolves and run around, space was probably a benefit. That tended to be the sort of thing HOAs frowned upon.

The actual house was large but not ostentatious. A smattering of smaller places sat around it, making me think that the property was more about the land than the building. The alpha might live there, in that large central house, but others in the pack had built their own abodes nearby.

It was something about werewolves that had always fascinated me, that need and draw for others. Vampires formed connections only because a lone vampire could be taken down with far more ease than a community. Werewolves, however, were driven to live near their kind, to spend time together.

I guessed that was the entire pack mentality.

"This way," the man who had sat in the back with me said, his tone far more respectful than it had been when he'd busted into my house.

Not that I planned to push that envelope too far. I had a feeling Gran's warning only worked when they were close enough to remember how scary she was. *Move too far from the threat and people got stupid.*

Inside the house, a few mulled about. They had the air of comfort I'd seen from people at their parents' houses in that it wasn't *their* place, but they'd spent enough time, made enough memories that it *felt* like their space as well. They watched me with the disconcerting look the others had had, back before Gran had stepped in.

Clearly, they weren't a fan of me being here.

We moved through the living room, down a hallway and into a brightly lit kitchen that had white cabinets. It was a country style, somewhere I could picture a woman making pies and other things I had no idea how to make. Sure enough, a woman with a streak of flour over her cheek stopped when she saw me. She smiled, her hair pulled up into a messy bun, seeming friendlier than the others. "You must be Ava, right? I'm Sarah."

When she took a step toward me, the werewolf with me stepped between us. "I don't trust her," he said, voice low. "You shouldn't get too close, not until alpha is here."

Sarah was small, her features almost pixie-like, and she planted her hands on her hips and stared at the large man as though he were some unruly child. "Are you telling me what to do?"

He shifted. "Alpha put me in charge of making sure she doesn't cause any trouble. If anything happens to you, what do you think happens to me?"

She patted the man's cheek. "Fredrick knows I do what I want. Now, run along. I believe I can handle one little human." The man huffed, the sound of an annoyed dog told to go lie down, before he left the room.

"Impressive," I told her. "In my experience, men don't listen that well."

She laughed before going back to the counter and turning a ball of dough out onto the floured surface. "I've lived here a long time. The trick is to make sure they know their place."

"Yeah, but they so rarely do."

She kneaded the dough, the rhythmic motion calming, almost mindless, as though she'd done it a million times before. "Well, werewolf packs are different. We take our position from the more dominant wolf in the pairing. In my case, that's my mate, Fredrick. Because he's alpha, I am given the same respect. Though, I've been ordering that wolf around since long before Fredrick became alpha."

I shifted my weight, uneasy in the domestic setting. I'd never grown up with a mother—or anyone—who baked, who did these things. The entire pack was like a family, and I had no idea how to interact with that. "Why am I here?"

"We need your help," Sarah told me. "I understand you helped the vampires?"

"Help isn't really the right word. They threatened me, so I did what they said."

"In our world, those are the same things. When we're dealing with such important matters, you can't let it go to chance."

"Does that mean you're not asking either?"

She smiled, though this time I saw the edge in her expression. Whether it was due to her mate—to Fredrick's alpha tendencies—or her own tenacity, I had no idea. Still, it showed that while she might bake and seem sweet, she had her sharp points. "No, dear. We're not asking."

*So much for making friends.*

Thankfully, it only took another moment for Fredrick to show, so I didn't have to stay with the scary Suzy Homemaker long. As it turned out, I much preferred people who looked as frightening as they actually were.

That was just playing fair.

Fredrick offered a kiss to his mate's cheek, then turned his attention to me. "Ms. Harlin."

*So, he must have talked to his lackey and heard about Gran's threat.*

"I hear you need my help."

He held his arm out to gesture toward the back of the house, then waited for me to move. Once I did, he spoke. "Let's go discuss it in my office."

His office was more practicality and less style. I recalled Kase's, all minimalism and everything in its place—nothing like here. Fredrick had piles of papers stacked all over, with drawers only partly closed. It didn't have that musty scent of somewhere rarely used, though, telling me he somehow worked around all that mess, that he actually used all those items.

He nodded at the chair, and instead of sitting behind the desk, he took the other chair beside me. It put us near, and I really wanted to be nowhere near any werewolf, especially one who evidently wouldn't be giving me a choice about helping.

"I understand you did a job for the coven recently."

"Like I told Sarah, I didn't have a choice. Besides, I couldn't find anything out for them."

It was best to leave off the part where I did later find things, or that I was *still* trying to discover answers. There were times to tell people all the wonderful things about me and there were times to just shut up.

This was a time to shut up. Incompetent people were left alone.

"Right." His tone said he didn't believe me. "I realize that people think the three main factions don't speak to each other, that werewolves, mages and vampires have lines we don't cross. That is true for many of the lower-downs — often by choice — but those of us in the higher rungs of society, we do talk. Not officially, but we know what's going on. There are much bigger threats out there then our petty squabbles."

"So why do you even have the squabbles?"

"Because eternity is boring and we need something to do." His light eyebrow lifted, as if to imply it was stupid that he needed to explain that at all.

Well, some of us didn't live forever, so what would I know about it?

"Could we get to the point?"

Fredrick nodded. "You helped them because a vampire killed someone they hadn't expected him to, then went off the radar. I've had similar issues. All older wolves, steady ones who I've never had a problem with before."

"You have wolves who are killing people and you want me to get involved?" I pointed at myself. "Human. Crazy werewolves aren't my area of expertise."

He didn't smile, didn't seem amused by my attitude at all. "Wolf. Just one."

"You said — "

"I do not allow unstable wolves to roam free, Ms. Harlin. They are no longer a threat. However, ending them was premature, it seems, since the problem hasn't stopped. I figured we had a few old wolves who lost control, but now? Especially with the vampires and mages reporting similar instances? It seems it might be a bigger issue."

"None of this explains what you need *me* for. My entire job was simply to figure out what had happened — to find the vampire Olin, if possible — but I couldn't do that. I'm not a detective, Fredrick, I'm not some investigator who can go figure out what happened. I can talk to the dead — that's it. I don't see how it's useful here."

Fredrick took a long moment to answer, and I shifted in the silence. It felt off to be stared at, and it reminded me he wasn't alpha because he was weak, no matter how he looked. "I have run out of options. I don't know where else to turn. You, however, are the only one who is connected to this through the vampires. Perhaps if you look, you can see connections we have missed if you speak to this wolf, to Paul."

I sighed, because it was his desperation that pulled me in, that made me pause. He might not be giving me a choice, but it was because *he* had no choice. He had werewolves killing people, and that wasn't a problem anyone in charge wanted.

Before we could continue the conversation, a crash outside the room and snarling stilled us.

Fredrick lifted his gaze, but he didn't appear surprised. Instead, his expression wavered between annoyed and mildly concerned.

I rose, but he remained sitting when the door to the office slammed open.

Troy stood there, his chest rising and falling, looking less like my charming, stable neighbor than he ever had.

In his silver eyes, the ones I'd always found so calming, I glimpsed the wolf that hid inside, the one that was at least partly in control at the moment, and I couldn't believe he'd managed to hide it so well.

Troy snarled, a low and threatening sound that vibrated through the room. He had his lips curled up to show his teeth and...*yep*, his canines had shifted to sharp points, the start of a transformation. His body seemed impossibly larger, as if he'd become taller and even wider.

"Calm yourself," Fredrick said. A strange rush of power went through the room. It didn't stick to me, sliding over me as most magic did. When it struck another man outside the door, his shoulders dropped as if he couldn't refuse the command.

Troy shuddered but showed no signs of calming down himself. "Don't try that with me," he growled out in a voice that was *nothing* like his own. "We *both* know you can't command me."

Fredrick remained sitting, though he sat rigid, as if ready for an attack. "As you can see, Ms. Harlin is unharmed. I simply require her help."

"You will not get her involved in your problems," Troy snapped.

I lifted a finger. "Right here, so you don't need to talk about me as if I'm not."

They both ignored me.

"She's unclaimed. She doesn't require anyone's permission."

And *wow* did that sound sexist. And also vaguely familiar. I thought back to Kase saying something similar about me back when he'd run into Troy that first time.

It didn't mean anything to me. Were they saying humans were claimed by werewolves the way vampires took in 'pets'? As a helper under that werewolf's protection?

Again, my lack of knowledge of their world annoyed me. Maybe I should have been paying more attention over the years, but I'd been hoping to never need such information.

"Claimed or not, you knew better. I've left you be, not interfered if your business, in pack business, and in exchange, you've left me alone. Right now, you're in my business, and I don't appreciate it."

Fredrick rose slowly, as if trying not to further agitate Troy. "This is an easy request. We have a wolf in custody who's affected by the same thing as the vampire she's investigating. We need to understand their connection, and right now, Ms. Harlin is our only lead."

"So you want her to go play nice with a wolf who is a killer? We both know I'm not allowing that."

"He is properly restrained in silver, Troy, and has three of my best wolves as guards. She will be perfectly safe."

"Not a chance."

Fredrick glanced in my direction but continued to speak as if to Troy. "The wolves we've caught and put down murdered a total of twenty-six people. Four of them were children, and eight were people the werewolves cared for deeply before the incidents."

My stomach dropped. Twenty-six people? Children? The abstract idea of some random wolf killing random people was something I could bury my head in the sand over, but when I considered the reality...

It was like the picture of Olin and Rachel. It became real. The werewolves weren't just anyone—they could have been Troy.

"No," Troy assured Fredrick, though his tone carried a hesitation.

I already knew *his* plan. Keep me out of it and safe while he did something about it himself. He wasn't uncaring—he wouldn't ignore murdered children—but he wouldn't want me anywhere near it.

*Too bad.*

"I'll do it."

Troy and Fredrick kept arguing back and forth as though neither heard me.

I repeated myself, but again, they ignored me.

Finally, I stepped between them even though they stood tall enough they could have just looked over my head. "I'll do it. This is important, Troy, and if I can keep anyone else from dying? I have to."

He met my eyes, frustration in his expression, a desire to keep me safe while he probably was figuring out I'd do what I wanted no matter what. "This is dangerous, Ava."

I offered a smile I knew didn't reach my eyes. "I get bothered daily by dead people. I know how dangerous the world is, no matter what. I still have to do something."

He pressed his lips together, then uttered a soft curse that sounded odd from him. Finally, he turned his glare on Fredrick, one so menacing I nearly took a step backward as well. "I'll go with her, and if you want to meet with her again, you *will* go through me."

"You haven't claimed her," Fredrick insisted.

"Do you recall what happened to the last person who came between me and my mate?"

Fredrick swallowed hard, the first *real* show of fear. He nodded. "Very well."

Troy caught my wrist and tugged me against his side, as though he wanted no chance of anyone else being near to me.

Fredrick reached out with a card — to Troy, not me. "This will be the meeting place. I expect another five days to finish transporting Paul, but they will contact you when it is ready."

Troy nodded before escorting me out without a goodbye to Fredrick. No one looked at us as we left, except for Sarah, who stared as if she could unman Troy with the knife she had clutched in her hand. Not that Troy took any notice of her.

Once outside, I shoved away from him. "What the hell was that about claiming?"

"Nothing." He stormed forward to his truck, then held the passenger door open for me. "Get in."

I crossed my arms and planted my feet. I'd stand there until I was old and gray if I had to. "Not until you explain what you meant. That is the second time someone talked about me being unclaimed. What does it mean?"

He released a snarl — similar to the one he had inside but one with far more frustration. It seemed dealing with me was even more annoying than dealing with the pack. "Humans can be claimed by werewolves. When they are, any other werewolf can't touch them, can't harm them. Because werewolves are possessive, it also means other supernaturals tend to give them a wide berth."

"So what? Wolves just go around collecting humans like cattle, like vampires do?"

Troy shook his head. "Werewolves only claim a single human, and only when they take that human as their mate."

*Mate.*

Even though I didn't know exactly what that meant in werewolf terms, it sure as hell wasn't hard to guess. I licked my lips as though they'd suddenly gone dry. "So I'm your…" I couldn't say it.

He looked at the ground and scuffed his shoe along the dirt. "We wolves don't get to pick this, Ava, at least not our human half. The wolf chooses our mates, and we're just along for the ride."

And…*wow*…that statement stung *far* more than I'd have ever expected it to. Not only was he admitting I was his mate—clearly he was never planning on telling me—but he also managed to make it clear he would have *never* chosen me if he'd had a say in it.

"I didn't mean it like that," he said, his voice losing the snarl as if he'd just realized exactly how his statement had sounded.

"Whatever," I muttered like a petulant teenager before I passed him and slid into the passenger seat of his truck. "Take me home."

He could go fuck himself for all I cared, because I no longer planned to do it.

# Chapter Thirteen

After a tense car ride where I refused to say a single word to Troy, he'd tried to come inside.

I'd let him know I'd had more than enough of his company for one day before promptly kicking him out.

I was sick of men of every sort.

They kept showing up and fucking over my entire life, and so far only one had even been kind enough to give me some orgasms out of it.

The one who never showed up when he was needed, who came and went like a damn ghost. Right, *that* was the good one?

I plopped on the couch after heating up a frozen meal. Just me, a rather large glass of wine and microwavable mac and cheese. Maybe it wasn't glamorous, but it was *mine*. A normal, not weird supernatural life.

I flicked the TV on, wanting to erase the day with some well-deserved vegging out. The world wasn't going to fall apart in the next twelve hours, which meant I'd earned a night of horrible food, alcohol and no thinking.

I switched it to reruns of a show where overzealous moms puts their kids into talent shows.

I loved the show because it was one time when I didn't feel so bad about not having a mom. Sure, I didn't get the whole stable foundation, but at least I hadn't ended up dressed like an aging pop-star lip-syncing a song about strippers when I was six.

Silver linings were important.

Of course, that had me thinking, as it often did, about my past.

I glanced down at the white marks on my arms and remembered how Melinda had been thrown across the room.

What if my parents had given me up to protect me? What if they were running from something and they wanted me safe?

*Yeah, but throwing a kid out on her own without only some tattoos to guide her is a pretty shitty way to go about it.*

Which led me back to where it always did—nowhere.

I had no answers. Whether they were loving people trying their best or junkies who had no business with a kid didn't really matter, did it? How did it change anything about my life *now?*

I took a bite of the mac and cheese, amazed how in a single bite I could have slightly frozen bits and others that burnt my tongue. *Impressive.*

Still, I chewed and swallowed it, pretending it was the best thing I'd ever eaten.

The show flickered, then moved to a breaking news image.

*Why does god hate me? All I want is my trash TV. Haven't I earned this?*

An anchorwoman appeared on the screen, a blonde woman with a respectable white blouse buttoned up, the sort who was conservative enough to not offend Grandma but pretty enough to make Grandpa think of the good old days when he might have scored with such a woman. She had a coffee cup on the desk and a pile of papers, but she stared at the camera instead. "Sorry to interrupt our previously scheduled shows. The following report contains graphic descriptions of violence, so please consider having young viewers leave the room."

The words sent a chill through me. That was *never* the start to good news. It was never 'please have the kids leave the room so we can show off the cutest kitten in the whole world!'

After a moment, the woman nodded, as if sure anyone who wanted to send their kids had. "Police are currently in the Oak Heights area where they have discovered a grisly scene. When walking, a local man found a body. Upon further investigation, six other victims were located in the same area. We now go to Tammy at the scene."

The newsroom disappeared and a new woman came up, a microphone in her hand and her face paler than most TV news reporters were. She spoke with that same nondescript accent, though her words wavered every once in a while. "I'm here with lead detective Harvey Cane. What can you tell us?"

The detective turned his gaze between the camera and the reporter as though he wasn't sure where to look. "We have six victims we know of. We can't release their identities until the next-of-kin are notified."

The reporter broke in. "Can you tell us anything about the cause of death? Or the time?"

"We believe all were killed here, and they were connected. We will need an autopsy before we can give an accurate time or cause of death, but at the moment, it appears to be a matter of severe blunt-force trauma."

My stomach rolled. Blunt-force trauma? So not a werewolf, not a vampire. Could this be a run-of-the-mill human killer?

How lucky would that be? For some crazy serial killer to be at fault. At least that wouldn't be my problem.

Except then the camera panned to the scene. No bodies were left. They wouldn't show those on TV even after warning the kids out. The ground, which should have had pine needles and mess littered on it, seemed raked clear. It was in a circle, one that spread out just past where all the tiny flags stuck in the ground to mark important evidence sat, as if only that one circle had been affected by something.

Like a strong windstorm had sprung up and cleared away the debris.

It could only mean one thing.

Fredrick telling me about similar issues with the vampires and werewolves clearly wasn't the only story.

Only a mage could have done that, which meant this thing was spreading, and the six murdered humans reminded me that others were paying the price.

Suddenly my half-frozen mac and cheese wasn't so great anymore.

\* \* \* \*

The coroner's assistant, Conner, shook my hand. "Not a lot of people get access like this."

"Lucky me. Most people get VIP treatment for concerts, but I get to go see dead bodies."

Conner shrugged and stuck his hands in his pockets as I followed him through the chilly hallways. "Normally we keep bodies, especially if they're connected to an open police case, under tight lock and key. Isn't very often we let anyone in."

Which was exactly the reason I'd reached out to Kase. The coven had to have inroads to law enforcement, and given my star treatment, I'd been right. No doubt keeping their existence quiet was easier with the right people in their pockets.

As we walked through the hallways, I spotted two marks on Conner's throat, the tiny star-shaped scars easy to miss but just as easy to find if I were looking for them. He'd let a vampire feed from him, and judging from the thickness of the scarring, he'd done it many times.

"So, you know Kase?"

He nodded. "Kase likes to keep an eye on anything that might affect the coven. He said to let you see the bodies, so I'm going to let you see the bodies."

My gaze remained on the scars.

He touched the marks, then chuckled. "I'm not used to people seeing these."

"How do they not? You look like a cobra chewed on your neck."

"Part of the magic. Sort of like how humans don't notice the odd things about vampires, like their teeth.

They don't see the bite marks unless they already know about vampires."

I chewed on my bottom lip, thinking about the pressure it would take to break skin. "Does it hurt?"

He opened a door and held it for me. "A little, right at first. Their saliva has something in it that numbs the pain and keeps the blood from clotting. It's why it is so important for them to close a bite afterward, because we can keep bleeding pretty badly without that. After their saliva starts to take effect though…" He didn't need to continue with that line of thought.

It made sense from an evolutionary standpoint. It would be easier to find food if the prey enjoyed the process of being feasted on. Still, it was hard to believe anyone could really like it, even after the glimpse I'd gotten from Rachel's echo.

His gaze went to my neck as I walked through the door. "I'm surprised I don't see any bites on you—unless they're somewhere that doesn't show."

"Excuse me?"

He lifted his hands. "No offense meant. Kase just doesn't deal with humans unless he's feeding off them. Feeding creates a bond, and the vampires don't care for the risk of vampires out and about without that bond. That means if a human is around Kase—or any of them, really—they've got marks."

"Well, I don't. I'm not just a buffet for a set of fangs, thank you very much. He hired me for a job." I paused as something hit me. "Does he feed off you?"

He shook his head. "Kase prefers female donors. Since the process creates specific reactions, vampires like to feed off someone they're attracted to."

The low temperature of the room made the heat in my cheeks all that much more noticeable.

Conner moved on from my question—a good thing because I didn't have to think about Kase feeding off women—before he waved at the metal tables and sheets that covered them. I assumed there were bodies beneath the sheets, but they didn't look right. The normal bumps and valleys I'd expect from a body were absent or twisted.

It reminded me of what the news had said. *Blunt-force trauma.* Apparently, they'd been roughed up enough that they'd lost their natural shape.

The idea made my stomach roll. Again, why was it always dead bodies?

Conner caught the top edge of a sheet, as though to pull it off.

"Wait!"

He froze, eyes wide.

"Sorry," I offered. "I just don't want or need to see all the damage."

"What's the point of seeing the bodies, then? I figured you'd need to, you know, *see* them."

The ground squeaked beneath my shoes, a sign that it had been recently disinfected. "I'm trying to talk to the spirit, so I just have to touch them. A foot is fine."

His expression said he didn't believe me, which was a bit insulting. The man let vampires—who were basically walking dead bodies—bite him and drink his blood for sustenance. Was he really in any position to question the existence of ghosts or if people could speak to them?

Still, him being okay with me doing it even if he thought it was crazy showed his feelings about Kase. Fear opened plenty of doors.

I went to one body and uncovered the foot. It was pale, but thankfully undamaged. I didn't really want to touch anything that felt like a bag of blood and marbles after being pulverized.

Touching it was more difficult than I'd expected. After the last time, after that void, a fear had crept into me that hadn't ever been there before. I'd always understood the afterworld — at least my tiny part of it — and suddenly it felt as though I were on the ocean and had glimpsed my first huge shark. I *knew* there were things below the surface, ones I hadn't been prepared for, ones I wasn't in a position to deal with.

Still, the memory of what Fredrick had said, of Rachel's smiling face, of the reporter as she'd spoken of the dead forced me to move.

I placed my fingers on the foot and closed my eyes, trying to center myself. This time I was slow, careful. I didn't want to fall face-first into that void, and I thought, if I approached it slowly, I could avoid it — maybe glimpse it before it sucked me in.

That electrical sensation over my skin clued me in, let me know it was working. I followed the chain that existed between body and spirit, but at the end of it…nothing.

A frayed edge as though ripped away, but no spirit.

They'd only died less than twelve hours before…

This was impossible.

I pulled my hand free. Connor's eyes were wide, but my throat wasn't sore.

Guess I hadn't screamed.

"Your eyes," he said softly. "They changed."

"They do that," I said as I moved to the next body.

Same thing. Each of the six were exactly the same, as though something had come by and ripped away the soul to leave that tether dangling.

But what could do that? How? Was it the work of that shadow that I'd seen in Rachel's memory? Even if it could, why would it?

How did it all connect?

I pushed my fingers through my hair, realizing only too late I'd gotten dead-germs in it.

The fact I didn't care was a testament to how fucked up the situation was already. Dead people in my hair just didn't register on my list of shit to worry about.

I backed up, trying to think, to recall anything that might link the events together. Something appeared to be controlling supernaturals, forcing them to kill. What did that have to do with the spirits? It was like having all the puzzle pieces but having no idea what they were supposed to make.

I tripped over the leg of a small table, the clattering of tools loud in the room, echoing off the walls. Conner shouted to be careful, but like that helped.

I flung my arm out to catch myself and it landed on something solid and cool to the touch. As I went to stand, that same current went through me, which let me know before even looking what exactly I'd caught myself on.

*Always a body.*

Yet, when I followed that thread—I'd focused so much earlier it seemed autopilot now, I found...*nothing.*

I tore away from the sheet-covered form and stared down. "I thought there were six victims."

"There were. That was a heart attack."

I twisted on my heel to stare at him. "*That* was a heart attack? You're sure?"

Conner came over and picked up the chart that hung from a hook at the end of the table. He flipped through the pages. "Yeah, heart attack."

Everything inside me shivered, an anxiety and fear I couldn't put into words. I grasped the handle of a small door on the wall of freezers and pulled it one open. Inside was another table, but I didn't need to pull it out. Instead, I grasped the foot and followed the trail.

Nothing.

Conner reached for me, but I flung his grasp off. I *had* to know. Again and again I performed the test, careful not to venture too deep, to be trapped by that void again, but it was always the same.

In a room full of dead bodies, all of whom died at different times, different causes, all unrelated, their spirits were missing.

This wasn't a matter of one person or a few supernaturals who seemed to be possessed.

Spirits were being torn away, and that was something that could destroy *everything*.

# Chapter Fourteen

"Gone, like completely missing." I threw my hands up when Grant didn't seem to understand what I was telling him for the third time.

He shook his head. "That doesn't happen, Ava. Spirits are trapped to the body like shackles. When they die, reapers sever that, but there is still a connection between them until they move on."

"Are you really trying to tell *me* how death works? Me? Who's dealt with death all my life? I know exactly how it is supposed to go, but that isn't what's happening, and not just with the people being killed by supernaturals. Every body in the morgue had had their spirit torn away. The edges of the link were frayed. When a spirit moves on naturally, there's no link at all to follow. It dissipates until there's nothing there. There *was* a link on these, but it just led to nothing."

Grant frowned, as though the information was unwelcome.

*No shit.*

I certainly didn't want to think about spirits being snatched away. I *liked* having a basic understanding of my world. I enjoyed knowing how things worked, at least in my little corner of it.

Now it had all changed, and no one seemed to understand why.

I stopped for a moment and stared at Grant. He'd been waiting outside the morgue when I'd left and apparently, I was so used to my new normal that I hadn't thought about how weird that was. "How do you keep finding me anyway?"

He still seemed deep in thought about the current problem, his answer given off-handedly. "I made a tracker for you."

"A what?"

He held up his hand to show a black circle on his wrist with a red dot that pointed at me.

I shifted left, then right, and that mark *moved* over his skin, following me. "How the hell did you do that?"

"Your blood from my knife."

*From the ward spell?* "That's stealing! You can't just take my blood and do whatever you want with it."

"I can, clearly. Besides, you get yourself into too much trouble to actually be able to complain about it. This links me to you, lets me find you and even burns the more you're afraid. It means I can find you and know when you might need me." Grant stopped speaking, as though the conversation didn't interest him. Instead, he'd moved his attention directly on me, and I wasn't sure I liked that any better.

"Why would you do that?"

He shrugged, then peered across the street. "Same reason I do everything. Money. Kase seems to want to keep you alive, and I like the paycheck that comes along with that."

*Ouch.*

I tore my gaze from him. *Fuck him.* If he wanted to have some mark on his arm to warn him about me, well, that was a benefit to me, right?

Also, I planned to watch snake-bite videos at two a.m. every damn day just to make sure his arm burned and woke him up.

Fine, I was petty, but it soothed my pride.

"I know it was a mage that killed those people."

"Of course. Anyone with half a brain could work that out."

"So, aren't you going to do anything about it? Isn't that your job, as a mage?"

He snickered and shook his head. "Not a chance. That's guild work. They police themselves and deal with their own problems. I'd bet they already roasted them."

That made me pause. "Gran said you were kicked out of the guild."

"Kicked out, quit—who can really tell the difference anymore?"

"Why?"

He tucked his hands into the front pocket of his pull-over hoodie. "Let's call it differences of opinion. We disagreed on a few key points and I figured it made more sense to go out on my own. I don't have as many protections, but I don't have the rules, either."

"Yeah, you don't seem like someone who likes rules."

"Rules are for the unimaginative. I got tired of playing by the rules of others."

His words held a story he didn't tell. It was easy to spot it between the syllables, in the way he slowed slightly to speak, a pain there.

What had happened?

Not like he'd answer me. Grant seemed as close-lipped as every other supernatural I knew. They liked their secrets, liked keeping them close to their chest.

Then again, who could blame them? My biggest screw-up could only follow me for eighty years or so. I'd say one hundred, but with all I'd drunk in my twenties, I was sure I'd cut off a decade or two. A supernatural, though, might have to live with those unfortunate things for centuries, even millennia.

Who wanted to be reminded of their fuck-ups for two thousand years?

As soon as everyone forgot, I could totally understand never bringing it up again.

They might not be able to die, but they seemed determined to bury the parts of their past they didn't like.

Grant walked beside me, matching my stride. I could have taken a rideshare back home, but something about walking the streets had always made me feel better. It gave me time to think through the bullshit that rattled in my head, to work it out as I put one foot in front of the other.

Of course, I usually didn't have a mage keeping pace beside me.

Still, no matter how much I tried, how I worked to understand what had happened, I couldn't come to any conclusion. It eluded me.

Where was I even supposed to go from here?

Was there a point in tracking down Olin? In speaking to Paul? If people's souls were disappearing in other ways, then the supernaturals couldn't have been behind it, right?

So *what* the hell was I supposed to do?

I didn't come to an answer — wasn't that the way of things for me? — before a dark growl came from behind me.

I turned to find two black eyes catching the light of a neon sign down the street, making them almost red, and a face I'd never forget.

Olin, and he didn't look all that happy to see me...

I had thought Kase was scary. I had thought Lord Colter was scary.

It turned out I knew shit about scary...

Olin's eyes were entirely black, the white gone. Something dark ran up my spine, similar to the shadow from Rachel's memories but far weaker.

Did that mean whatever that was still controlled him?

It had to, given the eyes, right?

Of course, the snarling vampire a few feet away should probably have had all my attention.

I went for the sharp rod in my purse, because whether or not he was under the influence of someone else, I certainly wasn't going to just roll over and let him kill me.

And his face said he planned to do exactly that.

He rushed forward, his speed astounding, but before he reached me, something flung him back.

Grant muttered softly beside me — spells, I realized — with his hand held out before him. I'd forgotten he was even there, but it seemed Grant was a more useful protector than I'd given him credit for.

He'd trapped Olin against the wall, pinned by the same sort of magic Grant had used on me.

Except, when he'd done it to me, it hadn't hurt. The expression on Olin's face said it wasn't so pleasant for him.

Grant closed in on Olin while I managed to pull the stake from my bag and grasped it in my fist.

Though, the little piece of metal didn't feel quite as formidable when compared to Grant's magic.

Grant leaned down as though trying to stare into Olin's eyes at different angles, as if he could see past the blackness that had consumed them. "You're not there anymore, are you?"

Olin struggled, his wrists moving off the wall before being slammed back against the brick. It was as though a net kept him still, one that was just barely strong enough to hold him.

He bared his fangs, and good lord, if I thought he'd been terrifying in Rachel's memory, it was nothing compared to real life. Then he'd been almost expressionless. He hadn't attacked her as though he'd hated her, but rather with the same fervor of eating a meal—and didn't that thought gross me out?

He stared at *me* like he hated me, though.

Which felt rude. Grant was there, restraining him. Why did I get one hundred percent of his anger? It felt like that should spread out closer to fifty-fifty.

Even still, I walked closer. He had to have answers, right?

"Be careful," Grant said. "He's a lot stronger than he should be."

"Are you telling me you can't hold him?"

Grant didn't turn toward me, but he didn't need to. I could spot his eye roll. "I *can* but the chances of him breaking it, even for a second, are better, and he can do a *lot* of damage to fragile humans in that time."

*Fragile?* It might have been true but seemed rude to point out.

Instead of addressing that, I focused on Olin. "What was that shadow?"

He snapped his teeth together, but no matter how he lunged and squirmed, he couldn't break free from Grant's spell.

"Tell me what that shadow is!" I moved closer, yelling the words into his face.

He broke the hold and flung his hand out. A sharp pain in my side said he'd hit me, but I didn't have time to think about it. I brought my forearms together as I had at my house, when Melinda had attacked me.

Just as it had worked then, he was catapulted backward. Pieces of brick fell down from the impact of him against the wall, and just as quickly, Grant had him pinned again.

"Are you okay?"

I nodded, despite the sharp aching in my side. I patted over me, checking for blood, for worse injuries adrenaline might have hidden.

Olin seemed...calmer, though. His hand gripped something, and I leaned down to look.

*The picture.*

He'd taken the picture of him and Rachel from my pocket.

*That's what he wanted? Just the photo?*

He'd stopped snarling, but that didn't make him look any less dangerous. Not to mention my ribs were the proof enough that he could hurt me.

Still, the action was odd. "He has to still be in there somewhere," I said to Grant. "All he wanted was the picture of him and Rachel."

And that was the exact wrong thing to say because Olin snarled and thrashed again. I wanted to look at him and remind him that he was, in fact, the one who'd killed her, whether he wanted to argue it now or not, but what was the point?

Instead, I pointed at the photo. "Tell me why you did it. You two were happy, so why kill her?"

He didn't move, as if he couldn't recall. Whether it was remembering her, the murder or why he'd done it that confused him, I didn't know.

"It was that shadow I saw, right? The one in the corner of her room. Tell me what it was."

He showed no signs of understanding.

My stomach rolled at the idea, but I didn't have a choice. I didn't really *want* to push him, especially since the more I dealt with him, the surer I was that he hadn't done it but rather whatever was in the room. I could *feel* it, too. The slightest tingle along my spine, like a leftover charge, a shadow of magic. Still, after the bodies, after it all, I needed answers. "You killed Rachel," I said and came closer again. I yanked the photo from him and held it up to his face. "She trusted you, loved you, and you murdered her. I saw you rip out her throat, tear her to pieces."

He went *wild* at the accusation. A sharp curse left Grant before he increased the speed of the words he muttered, but I didn't let up. This was the only reaction I'd pulled from Olin, and as much as tormenting him wasn't my idea of a good time, I needed answers and I wasn't sure where else to get them.

"She's dead and it's all your fault!" Without thinking about how monumentally stupid it was, I reached out and gripped his chin to try to force him to look at me.

The moment we made contact, that electrical charge I'd felt from him sparked. I could *feel* it slithering through him, controlling him.

As soon it happened, the black in his eyes faded a bit, as if the shadowy presence inside him had been forced back.

He blinked slowly, his lip falling to cover his fangs. His gaze remained on the photo I held up, and the longing in his eyes broke my heart.

"Rach," he whispered, the sort of nickname given when people knew each other well. I could almost hear him whispering it in the dim light of the day when he was forced to stay inside and would tug her closer as though to tempt her to stay a little longer.

"I didn't mean to," he continued. "I would never hurt her."

"But you did," Grant said from my side.

It was then I realized he had no idea the difference, that this was Olin now, not whatever was controlling him. I only knew it because of the feel.

Olin nodded, though he refused to pull his gaze from the picture, as though that was all that mattered.

Then again, it was all he had of her, wasn't it? All that remained of whatever they'd had.

"So it seems."

"Tell me what happened," I pressed.

"I don't know."

"*Try.*" I gripped his chin harder, trying to force that shadow back farther, to bring Olin out more. It fought me, struggling blindly as though it wasn't fully aware that I was there but knew *something* was interfering. "Don't make her death mean nothing. *Help* me."

*That* got his attention. He turned his gaze to me finally, a determination there that spoke volumes about how he cared for her. "I don't know. I rested there after…" He swallowed as if he couldn't say it, as though the memory was too painful, a moment he'd never get back, that one fleeting second before a storm. "Then it all went black. No, not black, but rather as though I were in heavy smoke. I saw what happened, the things I did, but it was as though I could only observe, only watch, and only through that smoke."

"Is it an infection? A sickness? Magic?"

Olin shuddered, and that shadow inside him grew. It clawed to regain control, to take over again, and, despite my fighting it, it would win. I had no idea how I was keeping it at bay right then.

"No," he said. "It smells of brimstone and hellfire. It's something…dark."

The shadow, the thing we discussed, gained ground. No matter what I did, I couldn't get ahead of it. The shadow surged forward, throwing me backward with a blast of energy, something stronger than the lingering presence it had been.

He again broke free of Grant's spell, and I had that split-second to get right with god. The way he snarled, the way his eyes lost the sanity he'd found for a moment told me Olin was gone. This was the shadow, the thing that inhabited him, and it had shown it had no mercy.

He lunged, but before he touched me, before he buried his fangs in my throat and tore it free, a fire consumed him, seeming to crack him apart, glowing orange at the seams, and everything turned to dust.

It left me covered in dead vampire and Grant standing there, flames dancing along his hand as though under his control.

*So much for answers.*

# Chapter Fifteen

I leaned forward and hacked. It wasn't ladylike and it wasn't pretty, but damn it, I had Olin ash in my lungs.

*And everywhere else.*

"Can't you just magic this away?" I complained as I handed my keys to Grant to open my front door.

"Sorry, but magic is a limited resource. I can't use it for frivolous things."

"Getting dead vampire out of my cleavage isn't frivolous!"

He chuckled as he opened my door then hung the keys on a hook there. "Think of magic like a bowl. Each time I use it, it takes some out. Do we want to risk an empty bowl if one of the other killer supernaturals shows up?"

I offered him a glare because his perfectly reasonable explanation annoyed me.

I didn't want *perfectly reasonable explanations.* I wanted to get fried Olin out of my bra.

"I'm going to take a shower. I think I deserve that."

"Do you need help reaching anywhere? I hear vampire ash can get into horribly frustrating places." Grant lifted an eyebrow, his green eyes sparkling. If things were different, I might just have taken him up on it.

However, as it turned out, the whole dead person—super dead considering he was a vampire—parts on me killed my libido faster than thinking about Gran in the shower.

"Not a chance," I muttered as I trudged to my master bath.

Grant could stay there. I doubted I could talk him into leaving anyway. No doubt I'd have a better shower not listening for every little sound.

Though, the biggest threat was gone, right?

*Not that shadow.*

The more I learned, the more I had to accept that whatever that was, it was at the root of this all. But what could possibly rip souls away? And for what purpose?

The water washed away the ash, but it wasn't as simple as I'd hoped. Instead, it clumped, and no matter how much vanilla bodywash I used, I could still smell the distasteful scent of burning flesh.

I remained in the shower so long that the water started to go cold. Scrubbing every inch and crevasse of myself took time, and dammit, this wasn't the sort of job one should skimp on. The last thing I wanted was to get into bed later and find a little leftover Olin trapped in the crease where my thigh met my crotch.

I took my sweet time drying my hair and dressing as well. The clock read two in the morning by the time I had finished everything, reminding me that these damn men in my life had not only put me in danger and gotten me wrapped up in things I didn't want to deal with but had also entirely fucked my sleep hygiene.

Still, when I walked out of the bathroom, guess who lounged on my bed, spread out like the best buffet I'd ever salivated over?

"Hey there, shadow-girl." Hunter's gaze moved over my pajamas as if I were dressed head to toe in slutty leather.

"You disappear without a word for days. Do you have any idea how annoying that is?"

"I bet I could make you forgive me." His words dripped lust and promise, and for one long moment...it tempted me. He had delivered the last time, and a few good orgasms always improved my temperament.

However, I knew damn well that Grant hadn't sat on his hands in my living room. No doubt Kase was there, waiting, and somehow, having sex while they were out there was just too far.

"Nice try," I said before walking past the bed — and him — and into the living room.

Sure enough, Grant lounged on the couch and Kase stood by the window.

The moment I walked in, Kase turned, raking his gaze over me as though to check for injuries. I ignored the ache in my ribs. It wasn't that bad, and I wasn't interested in him bleeding on me to fix it. I'd had *enough* vampire parts on me for one night.

"Told you she was fine," Grant said.

"I hired you to keep her safe."

"And I did that brilliantly, if you ask me. She's alive, breathing, glaring. Seems safe enough to me."

Kase stared at Grant with the sort of flat, expressionless look I'd grown used to, which was funny because his sharp words betrayed him. He was not happy, no matter how hard he tried to look as if he didn't care.

So, I decided to try to distract him with what we'd learned, rather than let him stew about *how* we had learned it. "Olin said whatever took him over smelled of brimstone and hellfire."

Kase stilled, tilting his head. "Can you trust what he told you?"

"I think so. I…" I closed my mouth for a moment, trying to figure out what had happened, what I'd done. How was I supposed to explain something I didn't understand? "I *felt* the shadow. It was an echo of what I felt when I relived Rachel's last hours, the thing in the room. When I touched Olin, that shadow retreated at first." I shook my head. "Or maybe I shoved it back, I'm not sure. That's why Olin could talk, just for a minute, before it took over again. It was *him* in that moment, not whatever controlled him. He was telling the truth."

"Brimstone and hellfire mean the underworld," Hunter said from behind me.

Kase and Grant turned their attention to Hunter, but neither reacted. Kase was the one to speak. "I take it you're the hellhound she mentioned?"

"The one and only." Hunter plopped on the couch beside Grant as if the two were old buddies.

"And why exactly are you here? Your sort tends to stick to your own realm."

Hunter nodded toward me. "She caused a bit of a problem when that whole 'reaching for a soul that wasn't there' thing happened. That sort of event gets attention, tells me something is out of balance. So, here I am to figure it out."

Kase huffed softly, as though he didn't care for the idea but could say nothing about it. "Well, as an expert in the underworld, do you have anything useful to add?" Kase's words were strained and annoyed.

Hunter shrugged, as if he didn't notice the animosity. "Clearly whatever it is comes from my realm. *What* it is — fuck if I know. Could be any higher-level demon, but whatever it is isn't anything to take lightly. Playing with the free will of beings from this realm is a serious feat, especially without remaining there. You've got your typical incubi who can create lust. You've got rage demons who can drive people mad, but they have to be in the area to affect anything. Whatever this is seems able to plant some sort of seed of themselves in the victim and control them despite being long gone. That is nothing to fuck with."

Kase shook his head. "Well, that isn't useful at all."

Before Hunter could respond, the front door opened and in walked Troy. I *had* given him permission already, hadn't I?

These wards seemed less and less useful as time went on. I needed to start revoking permission as soon as people left.

*Thank you for coming by, nice to see you, get the fuck out until I decide I want to see you again.*

He took one look at me, then turned his gaze on Kase. "*You* put her in danger!"

"From what I heard, *your* people forced her to do a job that will include getting close to a crazed wolf. Do you have room to talk?"

"She wasn't attacked by a vampire because of me."

"How do you even know about that?" I crossed my arms, a bit annoyed to have *four* men keeping extraordinarily close tabs on me.

Troy looked at me, the same hard edge in his gaze. It seemed he did *not* care for me being in danger. "You stink of burnt vampire and you're favoring your left side. It doesn't take much to put it together." He twisted to fight with Kase, probably because it wasn't like he could throttle me. "You need to leave her alone."

"She isn't yours."

"Yeah, she really is. She doesn't need to wear my bite for it to be true."

Kase's eyes flashed red, a signal that his temper wasn't perfect. "If you even think about putting a claiming bite on her…"

"Then what? Because I don't see one from you on her, either."

The two edged closer, and the guise of being civilized humans fell away.

Kase's movements became slow and smooth, more like a snake than a human. His eyes were rimmed in red and his expression was one that promised pain. Meanwhile, Troy was no better. His eyes brightened, the silver almost glowing. His hands opened and closed, the bones cracking, and he seemed impossibly larger, as though he'd already started to change.

I really didn't care about their dick-measuring competition, especially because, in the end, they were using me like some chew toy and neither had actually tried to impress or romance me at all.

At least Hunter had given me a few orgasms. These lazy freeloaders hadn't even done that!

Troy moved first. Even in the moment before everything went crazy, I knew he'd lunged first, striking Kase with a level of power that made me glad I was not in the middle.

Something wrapped around my wrist and tugged me, landing me on the couch between Hunter and Grant.

"You need to do something," I said as Kase and Troy struck a wall and knocked off a painting. Sure, it was a cheap one I'd picked up at a chain store, some mass-produced image of cherry blossoms I'd always thought would make me a calmer person, but it was *my* stupid painting and they'd ruined it!

"You're right," Grant said and snapped his fingers, whispering a few words.

The two fighting seemed unaffected, however, as Troy flung Kase off him and Kase sailed back, almost faster than my vision could follow.

I was about to tell Grant it hadn't worked when I realized he held a bowl of popcorn now.

Had he really used his magic to summon popcorn? Hunter reached over me to grab a handful.

"You said you couldn't use magic for frivolous things," I stammered.

"I can't."

"You used it to get popcorn!"

Grant lifted the popcorn as though to make a point. "This isn't frivolous, Ava. There is a man-on-man fight here — that requires snacks to properly watch. Get your priorities straight."

My mouth hung open. Every time I thought I had my feet under me with these men, they showed me how wrong I was.

"They could kill each other," I finally said.

"Sure, but they won't." Hunter stole another handful of popcorn and tossed some in his mouth, a few pieces falling to the couch. "Troy hasn't fully shifted and Kase isn't biting. This is just one of those macho alpha dominance shows. Let's all be glad they're doing this instead of actually measuring dicks. Trust me, that just hurts feelings."

I went to get up, but Hunter wrapped an arm around me to keep me there. "Nope. This? This is the sort of thing where an accidental stray punch could end a fragile thing like you. Best to stay out of fights between immortals."

"They're wrecking my place," I complained and winced as they destroyed yet another small table. It splintered into a million pieces, and even though I couldn't for the life of me recall where I'd gotten it from, the loss made me sigh.

"They'll fix it. Hell, they'll probably get you nicer stuff just because they feel bad. Make sure you milk that. I want a large-screen TV here," Grant told me before offering me some popcorn.

And, really, what was a girl to do? I couldn't stop the fight and the two people who could—Hunter and Grant—didn't seem all that driven to do so.

So I took some of the popcorn and joined in on the show.

Apparently saving the world would need to wait for these two to work out their little testosterone-driven fight.

It seemed all men were alike, immortal or not.
*Children.*

# Chapter Sixteen

Once Troy and Kase had tired themselves out — and that had taken long enough for Grant to magic us up a second bucket of popcorn — the sun had started to peek above the mountains.

Blood leaked from Troy's lip, the white of his left eye bathed in red. Not that Kase looked any better.

They'd beaten the shit out of each other and for no good reason.

Which left me at the front door with Troy after Hunter and Grant had left together, like sudden best buds.

"I don't like him here." Troy's voice came out rough and labored.

"It's fine. Believe it or not, I'm not afraid of Kase."

"You should be."

"But I should trust you? Because I saw *two* of you acting like toddlers in there."

Troy shook his head and leaned forward so his forehead touched mine. "No, you shouldn't trust me either. I explained this to you already. Humans don't last long in our world. You need to stop trying to creep deeper into it, because one of these days, it'll grab you and won't let you go."

I sighed, and guilt pulled at me. I had no reason to feel guilty—I hadn't made them act like spoiled brats—but that didn't stop it. "Are you going to be okay? Not going over to your house to die, are you?" Even as I asked, going for funny, the worry bled through.

His chuckle was strained. "No, I'm not going to die. I'll shift into my wolf form once I'm settled in at home, and I'll heal in a few hours."

I went to move backward, but he caught me with a hand around my nape. He brushed his cheek to mine—no doubt it left some blood since there wasn't a spot of him clean of it—and nuzzled my throat. He grazed his teeth over my pulse, and the feeling shot through me like a bolt of pure lust. It wasn't overtly sexual, yet I had a brief moment where I wondered if I couldn't have him then, injuries be damned. I could lie him back, straddle him and do all the heavy lifting myself when it came to sex.

A groan left him, one full of pain, and he pulled away. "In my wolf form I have excellent hearing. If you have any problems, call out. I'll hear you."

I thought he might kiss me—and whether or not Kase was just inside, I'd have let him—but instead he left, a clear limp in his step.

I closed the door and locked it.

Kase wasn't in the living room, and when I followed the hallway toward my bedroom, the splash of water in my master bath let me know where he was.

The shower was probably cold since I'd used the hot water earlier, but given he was as vampire, I doubted he cared.

I went about setting up the room. I ensured the windows were closed entirely, even going so far as to staple an extra blanket across the one window in the bedroom.

The thought of him bursting into flames in the middle of the day sounded horrible. I'd already had one vampire turned to ash around me, and I'd like to leave that number at one.

I did the same to the guest bedroom across the hall, because I did not need him staying in *my* bed.

I also changed into pajamas, more than ready to crawl into my bed and sleep for just as long as the problems in my life would allow. It seemed sleeping at night like a normal person was something I'd have to let go of.

The water shut off, and after another minute, the door creaked open.

I was not at all prepared for the sight.

Kase had a towel wrapped around his hips — which made sense because his suit had been all but trashed — and nothing else.

It showed off his chest, his lean waist, the way his skin had an almost-sheen that came from it hardening with age.

He wasn't as large as Troy or as Hunter, and yet his lithe frame was entirely solid. He held the towel with one hand, and his hair was damp but pushed backward.

Oddly, there was no bruising. A few small cuts, but even they seemed far better than they had been.

"I thought you wouldn't be pleased with the idea of me getting your bedding dirty," he explained.

I went to tell him I agreed until his words hit me.

*My* bedding?

"Do you actually think I'm going to let you sleep in my bed? I have a guest room for a reason, and even though I didn't actually *invite* you to stay over, that's where you'll sleep."

He let out a dark chuckle and walked toward the bed—and me. "I don't think so, Ava. You have proven far too prone to trouble. Even when I hire you a skilled mage to keep an eye on you, you manage to nearly be mauled by a vampire, attacked by a poltergeist and lord only knows what else that you have hidden from me. I believe the only way I will rest enough to truly heal will be by your side, when I am certain you're safe and behaving."

I wanted to argue that none of those cases had been exactly my fault, and that *he'd* been the one to set the entire thing in motion, but what was the point?

Kase was stubborn as the day was long and I could spend time fighting with him—and probably losing—or I could give in and get some sleep.

"Fine," I snapped. "But I'm finding you something to wear."

"I'm not a modest man, Ava. Yet another human thing I don't ascribe to."

*It's to protect my modesty, asshole.*

When I turned to tell Kase there wasn't a chance in hell he'd be getting in that bed naked—and hell seemed a fitting way to put it given our latest discovery—I was greeted with his back.

He'd dropped his towel and all that skin was on display. The sharp cut of his muscles continued on his back, down to his narrow waist and to a perfectly sculpted ass. I wasn't typically an ass woman, but his could make a believer out of even me.

It all shocked me into silence long enough for him to pull the covers back and crawl into my bed.

Now I either had to fight with him some more — and even if he agreed to put something on, he'd have to get out from the covers and flash me again — or I had to accept I had a naked vampire in my bed.

Oh the things I did out of laziness...

Kase looked *far* too comfortable in my bed as I climbed on beside him. He pulled the blanket up to his waist, which still put his entire upper body on display. I tried hard not to stare, to pretend this was some normal, platonic sleepover.

Which hadn't worked out before. Was it even possible to have platonic sleepovers with men this good-looking around?

Kase leaned back, but instead of the smooth motion he usually had, he moved slower, strained.

"Are you hurt?"

Kase shifted. "A bit." Him even admitting it said a lot.

"You don't look hurt."

"My body doesn't bruise the way a human one would because of my blood, and the skin heals fast. I have a few broken bones, though, so even if it doesn't look like it, Troy gave as good as he got."

"Broken bones?"

He huffed as he settled against the headboard. "Don't concern yourself. I'll heal by tomorrow night."

"I thought you all healed instantly?"

"Faster if I feed, but seeing as I doubt you want me calling a donor to come here, I'll simply heal at a slower pace."

Maybe it was selfish, but he was right…

After seeing the lust in Conner's face when he'd discussed being bitten, I sure as hell didn't want some woman to come in and service him. I pictured her with that same smitten look as Conner, then Kase with a smudge of red on his lips, the expression of someone entirely satisfied.

*Fuck that.*

But then I thought about him trying to heal those bones, and how he'd hurt all night, and how he'd healed my hand for me…

*Damn it.*

"What if you fed from me?"

That glow in his eyes came up so fast I pulled back. He tore his gaze away. "You don't mean that, and teasing is cruel. You don't strike me as cruel."

"It's simple, right? Just a basic transaction."

Kase drew a deep breath. "Trust me. It wouldn't be so simple, not with you."

"What does that mean?"

"It means *you* are not just a donor, and there is no way I could stay unaffected."

I stared at him, trying to breathe past the sudden heat in me. Even without him saying outright what he meant, I could read between the lines.

And that he could be so intense even with broken bones spoke volumes about how much stamina he'd have when at his best.

"I don't want you hurting all day when you don't need to." I folded my legs and turned toward him. "We're adults, Kase."

He offered me an indulgent look. "I can tell by your tone you know how you'll react to it. My bite will affect you like an aphrodisiac. Maybe that isn't such a good idea."

"You like to be tight-lipped about everything except this, huh? You won't give me a straight answer anywhere else, but now you want to get into every little detail?" It was easier to attack than admit to the fact that, at that moment, I really *wanted* him to bite me. I wanted to experience that thrill, that desire, and I sure as hell didn't need to discuss it first.

"I'm secretive when I need to be, but not about this. If you offer, I need to make sure you fully understand what it means."

I stared at him, my lips pressed together, as if I could outlast him. Part of me was ready to tell him to shove my offer, that I'd been trying to be nice and if he wanted to be difficult, he could sleep all day with his broken ribs.

Except, I didn't want to do that. I wanted to experience this, and the more I worked on this case, the more I was reminded how short human lives were. "I understand what I'm offering," I told him. "And I'm still offering it."

He nodded then reached out, that same slow motion he did when he didn't want to startle me. His fingers were chilled when he brushed my cheek. His skin was room temperature, but I'd imagine it was my expecting him to be warmer that made me notice he was cold.

He stroked my cheek, then down over my pulse. "You're sure? I don't want you to make a rash choice you might later regret."

"Would you please stop asking? You're ruining the moment."

He leaned in, and I expected a quick bite, that he'd strike immediately. Instead, he brushed his lips over my pulse as he had before. It reminded me of how I smelled my food before trying it, except this time, I had an entirely different reaction.

Lust simmered inside me. Was that similar to what Conner had felt? Did they somehow trick their prey into falling for them before they even used that freaky saliva thing? It probably made getting a meal easier if the meal came so willingly.

And I *really* was ready to come willingly…

I reached for him, but he caught my wrists and held them together. The grip was firm but not tight enough to hurt, a reminder of his strength.

"It's a little early for bondage, isn't it?" My words came out breathy and quiet.

"A bite can hurt at first, and I'd rather you not jostle my injuries by fighting. It's safer if I restrain you."

*Restrain.*

Why was that so damn sexy? Maybe because he was perfectly capable of it. Kase didn't need ropes to keep me still, and for some reason, that worked for me.

"Is that okay?" He rubbed his finger along my wrist, a gentle caress. "Is this okay? You know I won't hurt you, right?" The way he pressed, that he asked to make sure he hadn't bothered me, it warmed me. The grasp of his hands didn't feel confining but strangely safe.

"Yeah, it's okay."

"Good." He moved, and even though it had to hurt his injuries, he shifted me until my back was to him. He tugged my arms so they crossed in front of me, and he could pin them with one arm around me. It didn't let me see him, but that didn't matter because of just how much of him I could feel. He pressed gentle kisses to my throat and over my shoulder. "I've thought about this for so long," he whispered. "Ever since that first I saw you at the shop, when you looked me up and down and turned your back on me."

"So you like people who are mean to you? It surprises me, since you seem to like to be the one in charge. Didn't figure you for someone with a humiliation kink."

"I *saw* you, Ava. After we left, no one else even recalled you but I saw you. The marks on your arms, the ones you don't talk about, that make it so easy to pass you over, but I have *always* seen you."

His words reminded me yet again that for everything I didn't seem to know, others already had the answers. The tattoos, the ones I'd worn yet been ignorant about, even Kase had known what they'd been. I'd never discussed them and yet he'd known the whole time.

"And why did you see me?"

"Because you're *mine*, Ava." He nipped at my pulse, a playful move that left a teasing sting behind. "It was why I suggested we call on you, why I went with you, why I hired Grant. I needed a reason to see more of you, an excuse to reach out."

"I'm not anyone's."

"That isn't true. I wouldn't have seen you, wouldn't be obsessed with you if you weren't meant to be mine, and you wouldn't feel the draw either." He danced the fingers of his free hand over my bare arm, the move a lesson in seduction. I tilted my head, offering myself to him in so many ways.

He could bite me, then we could go just as far as his newly healed body was up for.

As long as I kept it quiet. I didn't need Troy rushing in to try to 'rescue' me.

A long, cool breath escaped his lips and blew over my pulse a second before he bit.

And he was right about it hurting. It was almost shocking how sharp the pain was—though to be fair, he had just buried two fangs into my skin. As quickly as the pain set in, however, it eased.

The lust that had slowed with the pain of the bite simmered to life, and I understood why people allowed this. I knew the moment his saliva came into contact with my blood, though, because a rush of need blew through me. It was powerful, terrifying in its strength and speed. I jerked, as he'd said I would, but it wasn't away.

No, I wanted more. My body burned, my skin painfully sensitive, my cunt drenched instantly. The reaction was like nothing I'd experienced, but it could make addicts out of anyone.

I moaned, arching, offering myself, ready for him to bite down harder, to reach around me and slide his strong fingers into the front of my pajama bottoms and get me ready for what I planned on being a long and satisfying night of sex.

At least, that was what I thought before Kase yanked backward and spat my blood out, leaving a stain of red on the blanket in front of us.

# Chapter Seventeen

I turned, slapping a hand to my bleeding neck while Kase was up and off the bed, moving a lot quicker than he had before. In fact, he used the speed he'd had while fighting Troy.

The water running in the bathroom was accompanied by more spitting and...*gargling?*

I knelt on the bed, too shocked to go anywhere, while Kase acted as though my blood were some shitty liquor he had to grimace to get down.

*How dare he!* My confusion transformed to anger the longer I sat there, as I thought about it.

All the ideas of how this was *supposed* to go swirled in my head. I'd read enough trashy books, had watched the corny movies that all promised Kase would want to bite me and become entirely enthralled by the taste of my blood.

He was supposed to be so turned on that we made passionate, crazy love right after. He was supposed to have to keep himself from taking too much, not spit and rinse like a girl after a blow job!

The water turned off and he walked out, but the full view of his naked body did nothing for me. Not to mention his erection had disappeared like a frightened turtle. A smudge of red he'd missed sat on his lip and reminded me of the topic at hand.

And the worst part? That lust wouldn't go away! It was his stupid saliva that still affected me, that made my body heavy and needy and desperate, even after he'd soundly rejected me. It felt like an insult, mocking me even now.

"Sorry," he said, but he didn't look all that sorry. I suspected it was the way cheating men apologized. He was sorry I saw it, but he would sure as hell spit it out again if he were in the same position.

"I didn't realize you had such fickle taste." I stood, ready to storm out, but he moved quickly to the door to bar my way.

"You don't taste right, Ava."

"It's blood. It doesn't come in too many flavors."

He shook his head. "The blood is to keep us strong, and because of that, we can taste death or illness on a person. *You* taste of death, Ava, as though you've placed one foot in the grave already. Once, when I was still young, I was trapped in a city, pursued by hunters. There was an old man there, dying of god-only-knew what. He had sores all over him, and he coughed as though he could expel his lungs. I fed from him because I had no choice, and you taste like that, like something already half-dead." He shuddered, then took a deep breath as though centering himself. He caught my chin and made me look into his eyes. "Are you sick? Have you been checked recently? Do you feel ill?"

I swatted his hand. "Oh, like you care? You're just mad your meal was screwed up."

"No. I need to ensure you are healthy. Blood doesn't lie, and yours tells me there is a serious issue with your health. You *will* go to the doctor now. The coven has one on staff at the hospital, and I will arrange it."

"I'm not sick!"

He narrowed his eyes. "You will go, or I will call Grant to take you. Should that not work, I will drag you there myself the moment the sun falls." He leaned in until his face was just before mine.

I shoved his chest as hard as I could, because it wasn't as though I could move him. "This was supposed to be different!"

He paused. "How so?"

"You sure made a lot of promises about not being able to control yourself." I waved at his obviously uninterested cock. "But Mr. Flaccid there got scared off by a little blood. And men complain about blue balls."

He pressed his lips together. *Oh, he doesn't like being called out? Too bad.* "We can still have sex, Ava." He came closer, sliding a hand around me, settling on my lower back. "We will just leave feeding off the table."

I pulled away. "Oh, poor Kase will suffer through having sex with me to make up for the fact my blood isn't good enough. I don't think so."

Creases formed between his eyebrows, and I had a feeling no one else in a very long time had managed to make him confused enough for that to happen. "You are honestly upset that I don't wish to drink from you? That I'm worried about your health?"

"Yes. No." I couldn't quite decide. Yes, I was mad about it, even though I had no good reason to be. It felt like a man seeing me naked for the first time and losing his erection. Vampires were *supposed* to want blood above all things, and yet he'd found mine lacking. It felt oddly personal, like a slight I couldn't rebound from.

"Which is it?" His voice had taken on a bored, condescending tone, as if he'd recognized I was being childish, and he no longer wished to humor me.

"How about 'fuck you'. Does that one work?" I turned to leave, and again, he put himself between me and the door. Odd that he didn't grab me, that he was careful to simply create a shield with himself.

"Are you so grossed out by my blood you can't even touch me?"

"Don't be foolish. I'm far stronger than you and don't want to frighten you. You shouldn't leave angry — there's no need for all of this."

"You told me to go to the hospital. I'm just being a good little pet."

"I highly doubt that. You're never good."

I stared at him, not willing to give an inch. I wanted *out* of that house. Away from him, from the stupid moment I'd thought about having sex with him, especially because I knew I was easy enough that he could talk me into forgiving him.

He let out a slow, defeated breath and nodded. "I will call the hospital to tell them of your arrival and message you the address. Go straight there, Ava. I will know if you do not."

"Is that it?"

He narrowed his eyes, and I suddenly missed the times he'd been in the shop when he had hardly seemed to notice me. Maybe because so far, none of times he looked at me had been good. He never looked at my longingly, never smiled. All I ever got were glares.

And disgust. I knew disgust now.

I shoved past him and collected real clothes from the laundry room. Once I was presentable, I walked outside, the warm sun oddly comforting.

My gaze drifted to Troy's house, but fuck that.

I was *not* that girl who needed some man every time things went slightly wrong.

*Nope.*

I was the sort of woman who apparently needed to be poked and prodded to figure out why my blood was so defective even a vampire wouldn't touch it.

*Not much better.*

* * * *

Two hours of that poking and prodding later, and I finally was able to leave the hospital. Of course, I hadn't gone there right away.

It turned out Kase was right. I *wasn't* a good girl. I'd picked up breakfast, walked around a few shops and downed enough caffeine that I could pretend I wasn't exhausted from being up all night.

The hospital had gotten me in quickly—too fast, really. There was an edge of fear to the doctor, and he treated me with *far* more understanding than any doctor had ever. Whatever Kase had told him must have stuck, because he apologized profusely when he had to draw my blood, as though poking me with a needle was the largest insult one could give.

It was times like that I remembered how scary Kase was to other people.

And to me, some of the time, if I had to be honest.

I didn't get the results. Apparently, I was a child, because they forwarded it all to Kase and told me I'd need to discuss it with him. I could have tried quoting HIPPA, but I was pretty sure vampire over-rode HIPPA.

Privacy laws didn't have fangs.

Besides, what I really wanted was some sleep, but since I had a vampire in my bed, that didn't seem likely.

Eventually I gave up pretending to be busy and sat on a bench at a local park. People passed by, kids played on the equipment and over-achievers jogged.

Sleep happened without me even meaning it. I guess when someone stayed awake too long, it stopped being voluntary. I'd only intended to close my eyes for a moment, to ignore the questions and uncertainty and change.

Everyone wanted something from me, and I had no idea if I was capable of any of it. All I'd ever really wanted was a normal life. I'd worked *so* hard for it and yet I seemed dragged farther into somewhere I didn't belong.

Each time I thought I'd found my own normal, it was snatched away, and I was reminded I didn't fit.

Right down to Kase rejecting my blood.

So letting that go, sliding into blissful sleep? That happened without any real thought.

The playground slipped away, the playing children, the faint hum of so many different types of music blending together.

Instead, I found myself in darkness—blissful, quiet, not asking me to do anything darkness. Not the dream I was used to, though. The mist wasn't there, choking me, drawing me into it.

At least, it *was* blissful before an all-too-familiar tingle ran up my spine.

I jerked up, searching that darkness, trying to make out a shadow when I couldn't see anything.

There, in the blackness that sounded me, twin flashes of red. The flames, those same ones I'd witnessed in the corner of Olin and Rachel's room, they were *here*.

Once I saw them, I made out the form...or at least what there was of one. It was the same shadowy figure, without definite boundaries. I couldn't tell size, shape, nothing. It was vaguely humanoid, but that meant nothing.

It neared, and the tingling increased. Whereas what I'd experienced in Rachel's memory was only an echo, *this* was so much different.

Instead of a tingle, electricity ran over my skin, like a million volts of warning surging through me. It told me to run. To fight. To hide.

"What are you?" I screamed into the darkness.

Only a soft whistling, as if wind blew around us, came back. Still, the shadow came closer.

I backed up, wanting to turn and run but unwilling to take my eyes off it. It didn't move with speed, with hurry, as if it had all the time in the world.

I brought my forearms together, just like what had worked with the vampire, with the poltergeist.

*Nothing.*

*Then again, dream tattoos might not have any power.*

I had no idea what the dream rules were. If something attacked me in a dream, could it actually hurt me?

Maybe this was just a meet-and-greet?

It followed me, but as it neared, I realized...those twin flames didn't land on me. It was as if it could sense me but not see me.

*Like that thing in my living room…*

The shadows expanded, swiping out to my left. They missed, further proving my guess.

Whatever this was, it couldn't see me. But the tattoos hadn't worked…

So why couldn't it see me?

I couldn't ponder the question for long before it did it again, and this time, far more direct.

Pain lashed through my arm when it made contact, when the shadow struck me. I screamed and fell to my knees, the sensation like fire burning away at my forearm.

I clutched it to my stomach and tried to scoot backward.

The shadow might not have been able to see me, but it seemed to be able to feel me. It tried again, and as the streaks of black smoke came at me, as I prepared — as well as anyone could — for my short-of-crazy life to end, the shadow struck…something.

Not me, but a barrier, something it clashed against.

A chill ran along my skin before a mist appeared between the shadow and me, and a blink later the shadow was gone, as though driven backward.

The mist remained, and I swore it *turned,* as though looking at me. It neared, lowering as if a crouched figure, then reached.

When it touched me, the chill deepened, a freezing sensation, before it all changed.

The darkness drifted away to a room.

I didn't recognize the room, didn't understand what I was seeing, where I was.

A woman stood there, her hair dark and wavy, her eyes an almost shocking shade of blue, especially against the blackness of her hair. She reached down into a crib she stood next to, humming softly.

I picked myself up off the floor, still cradling my arm to my stomach. She didn't notice me, so I peered into the crib to find a baby, one who could only be a few months old.

It kicked its feet, reaching up as if for a mobile.

Only, there wasn't a mobile there.

The mother hummed a soft song, one that resonated with me, as if I'd heard it before but couldn't place it. It felt so ingrained that I could have hummed along with her, following each note.

The baby's expression twisted, its gaze moving toward the foot of the bed, upset belting from its lungs.

The woman gathered the infant up and held it against her chest. She swayed back and forth, never missing a beat in her song, until the baby settled. She whispered, and I couldn't catch it at first.

It felt wrong to intrude on the moment, on the sweetness between them, something I never had, as if I wasn't meant to even see it. Still, I had to hear her. I *needed* to know what sort of words a loving mother might say to their child.

"Close your eyes, little one," the mother whispered. "They can't hurt you."

*They?*

She clutched the baby closer, a fierceness in her grasp, a reminder that no matter how soft she might speak, how sweetly she might hum, she was also a mother who appeared ready to defend her infant, no matter what. "Just rest, Ava."

*Ava?*

My name.

The scene didn't fade away like some memory, because instead, it shocked me awake. I leapt to my feet, unsteady and nearly taking out a toddler who was wavering by.

A sharp look from that child's mother had me muttering a half-hearted apology — kids fall over all the time, so what was the real risk there? — before I rushed toward my car.

Once inside, I sucked in a deep breath.

Had that been real? Was that some sort of memory? Had the mist shown it to me, and if so, why?

I lifted my hand to start the car, but when I did, I spotted my bare arm.

Where the shadow had struck me, the place that had burned so badly, sat a thin scar. It looked like a third-degree burn that had healed years before, with ridged and twisted skin, going from shoulder to elbow.

Which meant it hadn't been just a dream...

And that *thing* might not have been able to see me, but it sure as hell could hurt me...

# Chapter Eighteen

I sat at the table in the hotel room, more than a little uncomfortable with exactly how nice it was.

This was the sort of room with the layout of a full apartment, complete with a huge balcony, since naturally it was on the top floor.

Not that the top was all that high, but even six stories up offered a nice view.

Hunter crouched beside me, tracing the burn with his finger as he frowned.

Grant sat in the other chair, the room belonging to him. I'd called him once I'd gotten my wits about me. If *anyone* understood what had happened, it would be him or Hunter, but since Hunter didn't seem to have a phone, Grant had been my option.

Of course, as it turned out, Hunter had been there too. While Kase and Troy couldn't get along at all, Hunter and Grant had formed a quick friendship.

"This is hellfire," Hunter said, and for the first time, I heard real worry in his tone.

"What exactly is hellfire?"

Hunter rose to his feet, then started to pace. "Hellfire is, unsurprisingly, fire from hell. But, it isn't fire like you think. It is a basic building block of that realm, which means beings from that realm often are connected to it."

I frowned. I wanted to pretend like I understood what he was talking about—I hated being the clueless one in the room—but given the large, ugly scar on my arm, maybe it was best to actually admit I needed a bit more. "What does that mean?"

"It means what attacked you, whatever you saw in that room, whatever is controlling Olin and the others, it has to be from the afterworld."

"We knew that already."

Hunter shook his head. "We guessed that because of the scent. This is a whole different matter. Look." He rubbed at the corners of his eyes, as though the conversation was taxing. "The number of beings who could do what we're talking about are a handful. We are basically talking about Lucifer and maybe a few of his children. *Maybe.*"

I snorted. "Right. The devil did it."

Hunter turned a serious look on me. "I am not kidding, Ava. Lucifer might not be what you expect from the bible, but don't think he doesn't exist. He is very real, and you really don't want to meet him."

I snapped my mouth shut. *Seriously?* I tried to add that tidbit into what I knew—and again had to admit how little that amounted to. There really was a devil?

Grant spoke up from his seat. "You don't know much about the afterworld, do you? How is that possible when you are connected to it? I know Gran knows all about it."

"I never wanted to learn. I couldn't get out of seeing the spirits, of my crazy dreams. I didn't want to know more, to get dragged any deeper. What did it matter, anyway?" I let out a soft sigh. "It's not like knowing would change anything."

Grant tilted his head, a thoughtful expression across his features as though fitting pieces together. Instead of calling me on whatever he thought he'd figured out, though, he kept on subject. "There are some very scary, very powerful things there. Lucifer is one of them. The afterworld is his domain, and he doesn't venture out of it."

Hunter made a pointed sound. We turned out gazes toward him.

"He doesn't do it much, but he has been known to, at least in part."

I sat back and crossed my arms. "I am so tired of people talking in riddles. Would you just come out and say what you're trying to not-so-subtly say?"

Hunter looked directly at me. "Lucifer is one of the few with the power to influence others, and he's strong enough to do *that* to your arm. What if we're dealing with him?"

Grant pressed his lips together before shaking his head. "What benefit would he have? What would he get out of making a few immortals kill some extra people and terrorizing one human girl? It all seems too low on the priority meter for him to waste his time on."

Hunter did another two lengths of the hotel room before pausing. "I don't know. But I can tell you that marks like *that*" —he pointed at my arm— "aren't the sort of thing that very many could do."

"If it was him, what could we even do? I mean, we're talking about *the devil* here. Is there even recourse, or is this like stopping the apocalypse?"

Hunter snorted. "Lucifer is powerful and old, but he isn't invincible."

I paused, then offered him a questioning look. "Aren't you a hellhound? Doesn't that make him your boss?"

"Not so much. hellhounds are outside of the power structure. Our entire purpose is to keep in what should be in. We're one of the few things in the afterworld that doesn't fall under anyone else's power."

That sounded rather nice. The idea that they had that sort of freedom. Then I thought about the rest of his life. Living in hell, hunting down things that escaped.

*Yeah, no thanks.*

"Does who matter if we still don't even understand the what? Unless you all have figured it out, I still am at a loss to what is actually happening. Where are the souls going?"

Hunter lifted his hand. "I have an idea about that, but no one is going to like it."

Grant offered a sharp look in Hunter's direction. "Please tell me you aren't thinking of the Elder Ones."

"Do you have anything better?"

"Slitting my own throat and seeing what happens to me personally might just be a better idea."

Hunter only chuckled at Grant's statement before turning his gaze to me. "I have a...*friend*." The way he said friend was enough to tell me it was a bad idea. No one needed to pause and use the emphasis he did if it wasn't someone who might just kill them. "Who passes between the living realm and the dead. They'll be able to let us know if the missing souls are there."

"And what is the likelihood that this friend is going to try to kill us?"

"Oh, very high."

* * * *

I jolted awake from a dream, thankful that this time it was only the normal, run-of-the-mill scary dream.

No killer shadows, no memories that I wasn't sure were real, no searing pain or burns. I never thought I'd be so happy to feel as though I were drowning in that mist, but damn, that was like coming home.

The car bumped, and I gazed around the cab to reorient myself. Hunter was behind the wheel, and I'd had my face plastered to the window…

*Along with a nice drool spot.*

"Sleep well?"

I pulled myself from the window, sitting up and shifting the seatbelt away from my throat. "Not really. How far are we?"

He peered out the window, as though the directions were there. Then again, I didn't understand where we were going or how he knew where it was. He hadn't mapped it on a phone—he didn't actually have a phone. After a moment, he sat back. "Another three hours or so. I thought we'd stop at the next place we pass, get a bite to eat? No idea how long the meeting will take, so it'd be better if we ate first."

"Should I update Grant?"

He shook his head. "He knows where we're going. When we get there, he'll show."

The whole idea of Grant being able to arrive places without driving still seemed weird. The rest of us, we had to plan in travel time, but he snapped his fingers and there he was.

Or, at least that's how I assumed it worked. I hadn't actually witnessed it. He'd been adamant he wouldn't spend who knew how many hours in a car when there was no good reason to, and I could hardly blame him. If I could magic myself around, I would never get into a car again.

The next place we ran across happened to be a truck stop diner. There were big rigs to the side and a few smaller vehicles parked out front. The inside was bright white with yellow trim, and a waitress who seated us seemed as though she'd dealt with her limit of shit for one day.

*I feel that.*

The waitress took the menus after we ordered, and I marveled at Hunter's grin. "You are way too happy about diner food."

"You say that because you can eat at places like this all the time. Trust me. There aren't such great options in the afterworld."

"Really?" I frowned as I ran my thumbnail across the edge of the table. "What about the whole idea of heaven? I thought you were supposed to get whatever you want."

He shrugged and leaned back. "Maybe. I've never been to that area of the afterworld."

"There are different areas?"

"Think of it like a playground for big dogs and another for small dogs. You separate them because if you don't, the small dogs get trampled and the big dogs want to play with other big dogs anyway, so you put them in different areas and everyone is happier. Likewise, souls, they're divvied up into a few groupings. They can move around, but if they cause too much trouble — think big dogs knocking around smaller ones — then they get kicked to a rougher group. Hell is the anything-goes area. The ones who can't play nice anywhere else, they get put there. It's located the closest to the living realm, which makes it a border. That's also where Lucifer spends his time, where he has dominion."

I kept my gaze down as I asked the next question. "And that's where you're from?" *Why does that bother me?*

Well, that was obvious, wasn't it? I liked Hunter, and I had trouble imagining him as something from hell. Sure, it was right in the name of what he was, but even still...

"Look at me, shadow-girl."

I lifted my gaze to meet his amber eyes, and that was all it really took to reassure me. I already felt as if I knew those eyes, as though I had some level of trust in them — and him.

He curled his lips into a smile. "Yeah, that's where I'm from, but if I wanted to kill you, I'd have done it already."

"So what do you want? Because you showed up out of nowhere and haven't told me much since then."

He leaned back as the waitress brought our drinks over, not continuing until she was out of earshot. "What do you want to know?"

I thought about all the things I didn't know and started with the easiest to answer. "How old are you?"

He shrugged. "No idea. Time doesn't pass in hell like it does here. There isn't night or day, no years. I wasn't exactly born, so I've been around from the start, but again, time doesn't pass the same way."

"That is an exceedingly unsatisfying answer."

He chuckled before he took a drink of the iced tea he'd ordered. "Count it as the only time I leave you unsatisfied."

His play on words wasn't lost on me, and I moved on quickly before a blush could start. "How did you get *here*, and why did you come?"

"Hellhounds can travel to the living realm all we want. We don't usually—too many rules—but we can. It feels weird, uncomfortable, like wrapping a skin around us, to contain us and make us appear human."

I paused with my cup halfway to my lips. "Wait. What do you really look like, then?"

He didn't show an ounce of shame. That was far different from Troy, the only other person I knew with a different form. Where Troy was uncomfortable with his wolf, Hunter didn't appear to have any such hang-ups about having another form.

"Different," he said, then shrugged. "It's hard to explain. It's a lot of smoke, though."

I froward. "That smoke you used to get rid of Melinda was you?"

He touched his arm where the tattoos sat, tracing over a line there. "These aren't just marks—they're part of me. In my regular form, they're the smoke that surrounds me, that I control. The term hound explains what I do, but there might be a slight resemblance to a dog, I guess. Think wagging tail and long tongue."

I narrowed my eyes at the humor in his voice. "You're just kidding, aren't you?"

His smile cracked wider. "Maybe. Since you probably won't ever end up in hell, I guess you'll just have to wonder."

I blew out a long sigh at his complete non-answer. Funny that for a girl who knew so little about myself, I sure as hell was frustrated by others' lack of forthcoming.

Maybe that was why, though. If I couldn't understand *me* then I wanted to understand them.

"Will you at least tell me why you really came?"

He waited for the waitress to drop off our food before he answered. "I wasn't lying about that. I felt the pull when you tried to summon that spirit, as though it cracked open this space between the realms, and I *saw* you. I'd seen you before, just glimpses, from the spirits you interacted with. I couldn't hear you, didn't know where you were, but I'd see you."

"How can you see through spirits?"

Hunter took a big bite of the omelet he'd ordered, chewing and swallowing before answering. "Hellhounds track not by scent but by spirit trails, sort of like you do. Sometimes that causes us to experience or see things from another's spirit, even if we aren't tracking them. Think of it like a dog catching a whiff of something while walking down a street. They may not be trying to find anything, but they still smell it. Same deal. I saw you through them. It wasn't until that trick you pulled that I could find you."

"So you were just casually stalking me before that?"

He shrugged. "Not my fault so many spirits had memories of you. Besides, even though you fascinated me, I did come because of the danger. I don't think you get just how bad what happened was."

I thought back to that void, to the choking feeling that was worse than any dream I'd ever had. "Oh, I understand."

Hunter reached out and caught my hand on the table, which forced me to look directly into his intense, amber eyes. "You ventured somewhere no one should go, Ava, like diving to the ocean floor without gear or a lifeline. That you came back at all is a miracle, and that you didn't bring anything worse with you, even more amazing. I came because what happened *cannot* happen again. You could have torn a hole between the realms. The things that are in hell are twisted, not just dead people anymore. Trust me when I say *that* isn't what we want getting into the living world."

The seriousness in his expression didn't fit with the jovial man I'd come to know. It was almost fear there, as if he needed me to understand just how close to disaster I had been.

I gulped, especially at the warmth of his hand, the strength there. For *this* man to be afraid terrified me. "Trust me. I have no plans to do *that* again."

He nodded, squeezed once, then sat back. "Good. Because even I can't keep you safe if you do."

# Chapter Nineteen

"You know, a big open spot in the forest with a single tree stump in the center is really a bad sign. This has *human sacrifice* written all over it."

Hunter wrapped an arm around me and pulled me closer to his side. "Well, I mean, what else would you sacrifice?"

His joke didn't help, but I doubted it was meant to.

We had pulled to the side of the road about thirty minutes before and trudged into the densely packed forest. I'd mentioned I wasn't really an outdoorsy girl, but Hunter had sworn we weren't going far. He'd been right, but when I'd spotted our destination, I'd all of frozen because it *screamed* trap.

He walked me through the open space, toward that center stump. It was larger than I'd expected, probably because it was also farther away than I'd thought. I felt nothing, but because I couldn't normally sense magic, it made sense. Still, the outskirts of the area wavered slightly, a signal that it wasn't what it seemed.

"This isn't the magic you're used to," he said softly. "This is old magic, nature magic. You won't be able to sense it. If we had Troy here, he would."

"Why Troy?"

"Werewolves are from the old magic, just like this place. Vampires are connected with the magic of the dead, mages with elemental. They all have their place, and this is a place of nature."

"So why are we here?"

"Nature magic is the opposite of death."

I jumped when Grant's voice came from just behind me, then twisted to glare. He didn't look at all repentant.

"Would you stop sneaking up on me?"

"I like to see that flush on your cheeks." He didn't give me time to snip back before he continued. "Nature magic can give us a glimpse into what's happening, since it seems like something from hell is involved. We can't go ask Lucifer, so we might as well go the opposite way. The person we're meeting can move between the living and dead since she is outside both."

"And you both know this person?"

Grant shrugged. "The supernatural world is smaller than most people realize. There aren't a lot of the Elder Folks around still."

I didn't go back to my spot at Hunter's side. It felt odd with Grant there, so instead I walked between the two men to the center stump.

When I looked closer at it, I realized... "Are those blood stains?"

Grant nodded. "Probably. Okay, sit."

"I am not sitting on blood."

He sighed and dropped his head back as though I were being absurdly difficult. "This is the entry, Ava.

We sit. We make an offering. We go where we're headed." He held his arm out toward the open clearing. "Unless you just came all this way for a pretty view."

I pressed my lips together. I really didn't want to go wherever we were going, and the whole *offering* word didn't sound all that promising.

And yet I didn't have another option.

Really, my lack of knowledge prickled. I was always at the mercy of those around me suddenly, relying on them because I didn't know anything about the world I was in.

I'd been happy to skate by in life, to stay in my lane, but suddenly my lane was so much larger than I'd ever experienced before.

Sitting on the log was the last thing I wanted to do, but when someone was without options, they did things they didn't want to. Because of that, I lowered myself onto the spot and tried to ignore the red stains. "So what now? Do we sacrifice an infant?"

"Do you have one?" Grant asked before chuckling. "No, Ava, this should work." He held his hand out and pointed the finger of his other hand. At the tip, a sharp point appeared, shimmering as if not entirely there. He used it to slice his palm the same way he'd done to me when setting up the ward.

Hunter sat beside me on the log and Grant smeared blood from his wound onto his thumb. He pressed the blood to my forehead, a sticky, warm spot in its place, then did the same to Hunter and himself.

A grimace didn't start to explain my reaction. "Bloodplay is the sort of thing you should warn a girl about."

Grant took a spot to my other side. "The blood shows my offering applies to you both as well. Now, be mindful of what you say. Where we're going, these people have odd customs."

"What does that even mean?"

"It means you should be respectful and think carefully before you speak, only saying exactly what you mean."

Hunter snorted loudly, a derisive sound I didn't really appreciate.

Grant looked past me to Hunter, then sighed. "He's right. You should just be quiet."

I opened my mouth to argue — and sure, I planned to do so in a less than respectful way — when a sudden rush of wind picked up.

I hadn't felt any magic before but I sure as hell did *now*. It was wild, untamed, powerful and chaotic. It swirled around us and blurred out the world.

Grant caught my hand and held it. How had he known just how unsettled I was by it?

Who could blame me, though? Sitting on a log and having it turn into some weird roller coaster wasn't something I had much experience with.

The food from the diner leapt into my throat and I wondered for a moment, if I threw up, where would it go? Back to the clearing? To wherever we were headed? Would it just disappear into the odd space between?

Thankfully I didn't have to test it out, because the log settled and so did my stomach.

The forest was gone — or at least changed. A darker world had replaced the brightly lit clearing, as if a vibrant filter had been added to make the shadows deeper, the greens darker, everything crisper.

Someone approached us, a woman in a flowing dress made of a black fabric with sparks of white that looked like stars in the sky. Silver bracelets adorned her wrists and a multitude of necklaces wound around her throat and hung down her chest.

None of that surprised me, though.

Instead, it was her features I noticed first.

Impossibly cut cheekbones. Dark green eyes. Pointed ears that were sharp and carried back past her head.

She looked similar to what I'd glimpsed of Gran in those moments when her image had shimmered, when I'd glimpsed what was underneath.

"Well fuck me," I whispered.

Grant offered a sharp look, which left little room for doubt about his thoughts. *Right. Be quiet.*

"Welcome," the woman said, her voice with an almost musical quality to it. "I'm Anya."

Grant rose, his hand drawn into a fist as though to stop the blood flow from the cut. "We came to see Serrish."

Anya looked over the three of us, but she stopped her gaze on me. "And why would you bring *that* here?"

*That?* I straightened my back, ready to give her a piece of my mind. Like she had room to talk? With her long ears and weirdly angular face?

Hunter wrapped a hand around my mouth. It seemed he felt even a sharp word wouldn't stop me. *Probably smart.* "She's a medium and connected to the problems Serrish has offered to help us with."

Anya didn't move her gaze from me, and it felt far too invasive, as though she were sliding through my brain and picking it apart. *Wait, can she do that? Can they read minds?* "I was told to expect a human."

*So why exactly is she acting like it's a shock?* She was probably doing that power move where someone pretended to be surprised just so they can show disgust.

*Whatever.* Thankfully she wasn't the one we were meeting.

"Do you know the way to Serrish's tent?" she asked.

Grant nodded.

Anya held her hand out in a flourish so smooth and over the top that I rolled my eyes. "Go then. If you have any other issues, please come see me." She paused, then offered one more dismissive and ugly look my way. "But leave *that* outside my tent."

The words that bubbled up inside me were impressive in the width and depth of their vulgarness. Thankfully, Hunter still hadn't removed his hand.

When we took a few steps away, Hunter finally let me go.

I turned to face him, forcing him to stop. "Did she really call me a *that*?"

"They don't have a great love for humans, Ava. Why do you think they live here?"

"Where is here?"

Grant held his hand out and pointed first to the top, then to the bottom of his hand. "This is the living world, and this is the underworld. He spread his fingers and pointed to the space between. "We're somewhere around here. It's like a tiny universe contained in the folds of the living world. There are a few of them around."

"Like purgatory?"

Hunter shuddered hard. "No. This place follows the basic laws of the living realm. It's like a pocket of space existing there. Purgatory is neither the living world or the dead and it is a place *no one* wants to ever go…and for me to say that?"

He left the rest of it unsaid.

Grant nodded to our left. "Come on, let's go see Serrish. The less time we spend here, the better."

Given their reaction to me, that seemed a fair statement, so I followed when Grant started to move again.

We went down a trail, wide enough for the three of us to walk side by side with rocks lining the way. Tents sat off the main trail, and campfires burned everywhere. People moved, men and women who all looked similar to Anya, with the same features and green eyes. Their hair, their clothes, height and build all changed but those green eyes never did, and they *all* stared at me.

"What are they?" I whispered to Hunter.

He leaned in to answer as we walked. "The Elder Ones. The over-reaching word would be fae, but there are different types — druids, sprits, nymphs. They've mostly kept to themselves, first in out-of-the-way areas and, as humans spread, in pockets like this one."

"Is that why they look so weird?"

Grant snorted. "This is why I said not to talk, Ava. They look different because they didn't start out as human. The ones you're used to, we all started out human and changed. The Elder Ones are born what they are, and while they have exceedingly long lives, most aren't immortal. So this is what they look like."

"So maybe don't insult the beings who can kill us and already don't like you, huh?" Hunter added.

We walked farther, and despite moving through different trails, taking places where it forked left or right, Grant seemed to know exactly where we were headed. At the end sat a white tent, but this one wasn't off the trail as all the others had been. Instead, it was placed at the end, as if the trail always led only there. It was A-framed, with a tall center, sides that sloped down and a center cut in the front flap. On the outside, it didn't appear that it would hold more than a couple people comfortably, and I suspected Hunter would need to bend down to enter it.

Grant held open the flap and Hunter entered first with me behind him.

And the inside was nothing the outside would have prepared me for. Inside the tent was large and spacious, with a ceiling plenty high enough for even Hunter to stand straight and a spread-out, spacious seating area. On a couch that faced us was who I assumed was Serrish. She had the same features as the other fae I'd seen, but somehow, they fit her better. She had long hair so blonde that it looked white and tumbled down in waves to her lower back. Her eyes had the same green color, but she'd used some sort of eyeliner around them to make them pop. She had on a flower dress, much like the others, though hers was tight and low-cut in the front. Instead of bangles up her arms, she had leather cuffs and small pieces of what looked like vine winding up the forearm and to her shoulder.

She beamed as she looked between Hunter and Grant, but that pleasure drifted away the moment she spotted me.

Hunter spoke up to try and head off the complaint. "This is Ava."

Serrish pressed her lips together, but she nodded at the seats across from her.

A hand on the small of my back got me moving, and I ended up seated between Grant and Hunter.

"You didn't tell me what you wanted," she said to Hunter.

"I wanted to ask in person. It isn't something I trusted normal lines of communication with."

Her eyebrow arched up, as if suddenly interested. "Well, you are rarely boring. What brings you here?"

"I believe spirits are disappearing, and I need you to see if they've passed to the other side."

Serrish's long hair tumbled over her shoulder as she titled her head. "Missing? Spirits don't just go missing."

"And yet they have."

"You say that because *she* says so?" She nodded at me as though I were a pet we were all discussing but wouldn't dare talk directly to.

"Yes." Hunter answered it with an absolute certainty that had me turning a side-eye on him. People didn't trust me. They didn't stand up for me. That just hadn't ever been my place in life.

Most people hardly noticed me, and when they did, they thought me odd or dull enough to ignore. Yet Hunter, who hardly knew me, had just made it perfectly clear to a person he and Grant were nervous around that they not only believed me but refused to argue about it.

"Well, I can do as you ask. Is my normal payment acceptable?"

Hunter shook his head. "Not this time."

*Normal payment?*

She looked my way, offering a slow head-to-toe perusal that showed the kind of disappointment people got when meeting the people they matched with online dating. "Because of her?"

Hunter didn't answer.

She huffed, a haughty little sound, like a fancier snort. "I never thought you for that sort, Hunter."

Grant whispered a few words, his other hand out. Serrish didn't appeared worried at all, which said she'd dealt with Grant before as well, and that she trusted he wasn't doing anything against her.

Or perhaps it was one of those times where something was dangerous enough that they didn't *need* to worry. Tigers didn't tend to concern themselves with a kitten snarling at them.

I didn't like being thought of in the kitten group...

A snap happened, then in Grant's hands sat an ugly, pink creature. It shifted as if awakened and startled, and after a moment of him wrangling it, I finally identified the thing.

A hairless cat.

Grant held it out to Serrish, who let out a happy squeal—so much for being ladylike—and took the animal.

"She isn't going to eat it, is she?" The question came out of my mouth so fast I didn't have time to think or recall Hunter and Grant's advice about staying quiet.

She turned a glare my way as she held the cat. "You idiot. We Elder Ones don't *eat* animals. We aren't savages like you."

"Then what's with the cat?"

Hunter elbowed me—*hard*—and spoke through gritted teeth. "Fae don't leave their realms, and they have to repopulate them. A good price is a creature or plant they don't already have here."

"And hairless cats only came about sixty years ago. I figured you wouldn't have one," Grant added, as if to smooth over ruffled feathers.

Serrish held the cat up, gazing up into its eyes as if it were some baby she was already in love with. "We don't, and any sort of feline is always welcome. They strengthen our magic and safeguards. This is more than a fair price for what you've asked." She placed the cat back in her lap and stroked it, while I tried to ignore just how weird the creature looked.

Cats were supposed to have fur, and this abomination made that clear.

"When can we do this?" Grant asked.

"Tomorrow morning. I will set up everything tonight, then rest. The journey there, even in spirit form, isn't easy. I have a place set for the night for you and your...*pet.*"

Hunter grabbed me by the arm, the action quick enough to keep me from responding. "We will see you tomorrow."

We left her with the cat, which was good because she'd started talking to the thing.

The tent she had set up for us was similar to hers on the outside, and inside there were three beds, all singles.

Hunter took one look and chuckled. "She's jealous."

I turned toward him. "What did she mean about *normal* payment?"

I expected Hunter to hem-and-haw about it, to get uncomfortable and tell me it was just one time and I shouldn't worry.

Instead, he cracked a smile that was *far* too proud. "I usually sleep with her as payment."

"Like...once?"

"Oh, no, at least a dozen times."

My mouth hung open for a moment before I snapped it shut. "Doesn't that make you a whore?"

"Sure, but a very well-paid whore. Her services don't run cheap."

"I can only imagine since I know how good *your* services are." The words came out sharp and unhappy. What did I even have to be annoyed over?

It wasn't as though Hunter and I were involved. He'd gone down on me once. That was hardly an important relationship.

He caught the front of my shirt and tugged me toward him, ignoring that I'd crossed my arms and tried *very* hard to ignore him. "I like you jealous."

"You're an idiot."

"No arguments here." He leaned in to kiss me, but the shuffling of Grant behind us in the room made me pull back. Hunter lifted his eyebrow. "Come on. You can't be angry about me shagging people before I ever met you. That seems a bit petty."

"No arguments here." I threw the words back at him, but instead of him getting annoyed, he only smiled wider before he leaned down and nipped my full bottom lip, like a punishment for my difficulty and a reward at the same time.

As soon as he did, when I was ready to forgive him, he pulled away with a grin. "Well, I guess I'll go get us food then. I have a feeling we'll need it."

When he left, I turned to find Grant walking the perimeter of the tent, whispering. It was like at my house—an impressive display. Even without flames or sparks or anything of the sort, the way he moved was captivating. I hadn't realized at my house, but the more I saw of Grant, the more I realized how powerful he was and the more interested I became in what he did.

I wondered if I'd ever have that sort of knowledge or confidence.

Sure, I knew my way around a form eighty-six-B like no one's business, but that was different. Selling life insurance wasn't like this.

Grant, at the door of the tent, sliced his arm with the same sort of sharp point on his finger he had at the stump, and the dripping of blood didn't freak me out as much.

I'd grown used to everyone bleeding all over the place, which didn't feel like much of an improvement.

When Grant finished, he turned as though he hadn't realized I was staring. After a moment, he offered me a cocky grin. "Enjoy the show?"

"How do you do that?"

"Magic?"

I nodded. "It seems like something that would come in handy."

He shrugged, then nodded at the cushions on the floor that looked like a large seating area at the center of the tent. I lowered myself onto one cushion with the grace of a tipsy giraffe, and while he plopped down in a similar fashion, somehow his clumsiness seemed purposeful.

"Magic is something you're born with."

"I thought you said that all immortals are sterile, so new ones have to be turned."

"They are. Mages are sterile, but only certain humans can become mages. Vampires and werewolves, they're made from any human who is infected, but mages are humans with innate magical talent who choose to trade their humanity for power."

"Well, that sounds ominous."

He chuckled before he pulled me around so my back was to him. He set his hands on my shoulders and massaged, digging in so tiny moans left my lips. "It is.

Not all humans who could become mages choose to. It's a trade-off, and even those who choose to try don't always make it. There's a ritual, and it is extremely dangerous. Less than a third of the mages who attempt it make it through."

"What happens to the humans who don't try?"

"They live normal human lives. Some never know anything about our world because they don't have enough power to let the guild know they exist. Others create enough waves in the universe through unintentional magic that the guild locates them and offers them the choice. If they refuse, they have their minds wiped clear of their guild knowledge and they're let go, assuming their power isn't problematic."

"And if it is?"

"Then they're encouraged to join the guild in a way that makes refusing impossible. Most decide to become mages from there, because living in that world but not being a part of it isn't something anyone really wants."

"I understand that." My words came out soft as I thought back to all the times I didn't fit anywhere. I wasn't an immortal, but I was different enough from the humans that I really didn't belong there either.

Living between worlds, never knowing or understanding what I was. It wasn't something I'd wish on anyone.

If someone walked up to me tomorrow and offered me a chance to fully be in either of the worlds, I couldn't imagine passing that up.

He dug his thumbs into the muscles of my shoulders, a delectable loosening of the knots there. "The rest, the words and movements, are just for focus. We don't learn spells—we learn how to harness the power and energies we already have, how to twist the world to our wills."

"Do you miss it?"

"Miss what?"

"The guild. Having a place to belong. If I had that, I don't think I'd ever give it up."

His hands stilled for a heartbeat. "No. That place isn't what people think." When he went back to massaging, his hands tightened. "There's a lot under the surface, a lot no one ever sees."

I yelped when he cranked his hands down, and as soon as it happened, he yanked away. "Fuck. I'm sorry, Ava. I didn't mean to."

I twisted to face him, and the shadows in his eyes made him look far older than he was. He looked like some rebellious barely twenty-year-old kid most of the time, but right then? Yeah, he had a lot more years — and some very bad ones — that had aged him.

He met my gaze, a seriousness that was odd for him there. "I know you want to fit in, Ava, to understand where your place is, but sometimes fitting in isn't worth it. Not all places are worth fitting into."

The earnest way he spoke, that honesty in his eyes, they drew me. Before I could think better of it, I leaned forward and brushed my lips to his.

He tasted of lightening, as if electricity coursed through him, and I felt the full power of it when he kissed me back.

He tugged me into his lap, sliding a hand behind my neck to hold me close.

The roughness of his palm showed scars from how many times he'd had to spill blood, and it only made me want him more.

I parted my lips for him, let him inside me in whatever way he wanted, as I wrapped my arms around his shoulders. His cock pressed against his jeans and I was shameless in how I ground against it.

A throat clearing behind us made me break the kiss, panting and wild and...

*Caught.*

Hunter stood behind us, his eyebrow lifted.

I pulled off Grant's lap, my cheeks heated and my mouth moving in stumbled, halted apologies. "I'm so sorry."

Hunter caught my arm, staring down at me, his lip curled into a half smile. "Slow down. You don't have to start doing the rosary for me."

I frowned. "Was that a Catholic joke?"

"What? Hell-beasts can't make Catholic jokes?"

I blew a strand of hair from my face. "I'm sorry," I repeated. "This has to be sort of awkward."

Hunter gazed between Grant—who still sat on the floor with the widest grin I'd ever seen—and myself. "Sometimes it can be awkward, but I'm sure we can figure out what goes where."

"What?"

"Well, I mean, I'm not great tactician here, but one in front, one behind, you between." Hunter let his half-smile grow into a full one. "Pretty sure we could make it work."

I should have been scandalized by such a suggestion. I was a good—well, mediocre at least—person. I did *not* have threesomes with mages and hellhounds.

I also didn't get involved with four different men at the same time...or at least that was what I would have said a month ago.

But that felt like when I claimed loudly that I was a healthy person while chomping on a bag of chocolate that paired well with my wine—straight from the bottle.

However, I didn't *feel* scandalized by the suggestion. I felt interested.

"You're not jealous?"

Hunter dragged his fingers down my front, over my chest then between my breasts, and even the fabric of the shirt didn't do much to buffer the feeling. "I'm not a jealous man."

"Why not?" I was *not* going to be hurt by that. It wasn't like it was fair to be hurt when my vagina seemed to be fine with this devils-threesome idea. Still, it made me feel...disposable. Like I wasn't worth being jealous over.

He hooked his fingers inside the front of my jeans, just behind the button. "Because I'm a hellhound. I never figured I'd have anything. I'm not a wolf, not a vampire with their whole *mine* shit, who grew up thinking I was going to get some perfect mate. That wasn't my life. So, me finding you at all, someone I can't stop thinking about? Well I don't have a problem sharing."

A delicious tremor ran through me as the declaration, at the promise there.

Grant spoke up, having not moved from his spot. What also hadn't changed was the obvious erection he was sporting. "Life is way too short and fickle to worry about being possessive. As long as I get a taste, I don't care who else is at the trough."

*Well, that is an entirely unappealing phrasing.*

Hunter leaned in and traced the spot he'd bitten with his tongue, as though soothing it. "So, shadow-girl, what do you say? We have this lovely tent and all night. You think you can keep up?"

No, I didn't.

But I damn well wanted to try.

# Chapter Twenty

I hardly had time to reach for Hunter before he was on me. He seemed as desperate as I was, despite his cavalier attitude about it all.

He acted as though it didn't matter, but his kiss said different. He caught me by the nape of my neck and pulled me against him as he walked me backward. A breath later, he had me on my back on the ground, his heavy body above me, his lips against mine.

And I wanted to burn along with him, because he *was* fire. Hellfire and smoke and power, and I wanted it all.

As quickly as it happened, he broke the kiss to nip at the front of my throat, and that was when another hand caught my chin and brought my lips elsewhere.

I let it. Let Grant take the kiss he wanted, let Hunter grasp the front of my tank top and rip it down the center.

What would I wear tomorrow?

*Who the fuck cares?*

Who needed clothing when Hunter pulled down my bra and latched his soft, hot lips around my nipple and sucked?

After a nip, Hunter pulled away and grasped my waist. He twisted me until I was on all fours, then reached beneath me to undo the button of my jeans.

Grant leaned in to kiss me again, his rough hand sliding down over my chest to capture one of my breasts, to tease the damp tip Hunter had had his mouth on.

And why did that turn me on so much more than just the touch? Moments ago, I'd been horrified at being caught kissing one in front of the other, but now it was the hottest thing I'd ever felt?

Maybe it was because that shame couldn't stand against the pleasure, against the promise and the lust that swirled between us.

I didn't want to just take what they wanted to give, though, so I balanced my weight on one hand and reached for Grant's jeans with the other. The button flicked free, but I couldn't pull them, not with my lack of leverage.

Grant chuckled an *eager girl* before he slid off his jeans. A dark thatch of hair started with a trail from his belly button, well-trimmed and looking surprisingly soft. And at the center?

I wrapped my hand around his thick cock, and his deep groan was one hell of a reward. He was solid, his skin hot, the head of his cock slightly thicker than the rest.

He sat back, as though to give me whatever room I needed, and I knew *exactly* what I wanted.

I leaned in and dragged my tongue along the head of his cock, exploring the slit, the edge where it transitioned into his shaft.

Hunter didn't wait around for me to finish, though. He pulled my jeans off, taking the underwear with them. At least he hadn't ripped those, I guess. Once he had me naked, he spread my knees, and I tried to ignore exactly how on display I was for him and just how much he could see — which was *everything*.

I jerked at the first touch of his fingers, which he ran over my cunt to my clit, his other hand grasping my hips to hold me still.

Again, his touch was fire, burning me alive, turning me to ash.

So I focused on Grant, and glided my lips around his shaft, teasing him with my tongue, tasting him and swallowing that down.

He carded his fingers through my hair, cupping the back of my head, urging me forward and backward with smooth, short motions.

"Fuck, your mouth feels good," Grant whispered, his weight back on his other arm.

I glanced up his body to meet his green eyes that seemed to shine, locked on me, pulling me in.

Hunter chose that moment to press two thick fingers into my cunt. Not one, not easing me into it, but making me cry out around Grant's cock by filling me so roughly.

"Damn, that felt nice," Grant said, looking over at Hunter to make it clear he was talking to him and not me.

Hunter's chuckle came from behind me, and even though I couldn't *see* him, I could still picture his smirk.

"She's so tight but slick as hell. What do you think, shadow-girl? You going to let me fuck you?"

Grant pulled me off his cock to let me answer, but when I went to say something, Hunter twisted his wrist and thrust those two damned fingers into me again.

*How does he expect me to say anything when he does that!*

He didn't slow down, fucking me with his fingers hard and fast, as though convincing me, as if making sure I knew exactly how much better his cock would feel.

"Come on, girl. Tell me you want me."

"I want you." My words were absolutely pathetic and yet totally true.

He didn't stop. Instead, he angled his fingers down so they stroked against my G-spot, and I wasn't even close to prepared for the orgasm he pulled from me.

I shuddered, the release powerful but quick. It wasn't the type that happened when a person was edged, when the anticipation lasted so long, when it was drawn out until it was almost torture.

This one hit me fast, rushing through me and leaving me exhausted but wanting more.

"I thought," I mumbled as soon as I could breathe again, "I said I wanted you."

A sting to my hip had me looking behind me to find he'd bitten me. He licked the spot, a fire in his eyes. "Oh, you'll have me, but I want you ready for me."

I snorted. *Typical man, thinking his cock's some sort of gift to women they have to prepare a girl for.* "It's a penis, not the SATs."

Hunter let out a laugh that warmed me, that made this more than just passion, as if we really had some sort of connection beyond the physical.

"You know, I love that mouth of yours," he said as he pressed the thick head of his cock against my cunt.

"Got to say, I agree." Grant used his grip, still in my hair, to pull my lips back around his cock in a quick tug just as Hunter sank into me.

And *fuck* I'd never felt full like that before. My cunt stretched so wonderfully, as if he fit perfectly inside me, while Grant pulled me farther onto his cock then I'd been before.

I moaned, not caring if I sounded like a whore.

Though, really, I *was* taking two men at once, so that term seemed apt right then, and I honestly didn't care.

I was all for team whore right then.

I closed my eyes and let myself fall—into the sensation, into the craziness of it. I wrapped my tongue around Grant's cock, teased what I could, tightened my lips as he controlled the speed and depth. Hunter thrust into me, hard and deep and impossibly perfect.

Even thinking about when the last time I'd had sex seemed like a joke, because it hadn't been anything compared to *this*.

Hunter let out an almost feral sound, something no human could, as he sank deeper into me, forcing me to accept every punishing thrust. Grant pressed farther into my mouth, and I accepted every inch, eager for as much as I could take.

When was the last time I'd felt like this? Free and wild and wanted? I'd spent my life shut out from every single place I'd gone, never fitting in, never accepted into any real group.

It was profound in a way I'd never realized or expected to be *here* with these two, who knew what I was. They'd seen the good, the bad and the really fucking weird over the past weeks and they still wanted me.

Grant groaned low as his cock jerked, as he pulled me back and came. His seed was thick and warm and pooled on my tongue for only a moment before I swallowed him.

He even tasted like electricity, like lightning.

As soon as he pulled free of my lips, Hunter tightened his grasp of my waist and showed he was done playing around. Instead of the measured thrusts he'd done earlier, he fucked me like a man possessed, like the hell-beast he claimed to be. Then again, if he'd tried this earlier, there was no way I wouldn't have choked on Grant's cock.

Which wasn't such a bad way to go…

He stroked his dick against the sensitive walls of my cunt, and I struggled to catch my breath, to gain my footing. He gave me no chance.

He took me with wild abandon, as if he were chasing the only thing that mattered in the entire world, taking me along for the ride.

I gasped, shuddering as another powerful orgasm crashed over me, almost painful in the way it seized my body and made me tense.

Not that Hunter seemed to mind. That otherworldly sound he made, like a feral animal, increased and he fucked me harder, as though he liked the way my body squeezed around him.

When he came, it was with a sound that would have chilled me normally, the sort of one no one with a brain turns their back on, but in that moment, I couldn't find a speck of fear.

I was far too sated and exhausted.

Grant waved his hands and muttered a few tired words before the scrape of wood against the floor filled the tent. The three beds slid until they were pressed side to side to make one large one, and just after Hunter pulled from me, I went to rise.

Moving sounded like the worst idea ever, but hell, I was sure I'd regret sleeping on the floor if I chose not to move instead.

As soon as I went to push myself up, however, strong hands caught my arm and helped. Once I was on my feet, Hunter lifted me against his chest.

Why that felt so nice, I was damn well not going to think about. It would only annoy me and make me feel like some damsel in distress. It was a far better choice to just enjoy it.

We settled into the bed, with Hunter all but tossing me into the center. Warm bodies settled in on each side of me, hard and tempting and already familiar.

I curled toward Grant, sliding my arm around him since he was smaller and thus easier to cuddle against. Not that Hunter seemed to mind. He melded to my back as if any speck of space were personally offensive to him.

"I like this," I said softly, the darkness strangely more intimate than anything we'd just done.

"Good sex is something to like," Grant said with a chuckle.

I shook my head, my forehead brushing his chest. "I've never fit in, never been a part of anything, never been wanted. Hell, I've never been able to just relax and enjoy anything because I always had to work so hard to be whatever I thought I was supposed to be. You — both of you — you know more about me than any other person ever has. It's like…the first honest sex I've ever had."

Grant went still, the sort that happened when a person had one of those 'oh shit' moments.

*Did I say too much?*

I tried to cover the lapse in judgment. "I know it doesn't mean anything, I just…" I sighed. "Forget I said anything."

Lips pressed to the top of my head and Hunter's soft voice followed. "Close your eyes. Tomorrow will come quicker than you did."

The joke helped break the tension, and I smiled, despite myself. To my amazement, I did fall asleep, and fast.

It seemed there were some benefits to going to bed sandwiched between two men, beyond the whole mind-blowing-orgasms thing.

* * * *

I squinted against the light outside the tent, but I couldn't find the sun. A directionless brightness filled the sky, but it lacked a source.

*Best add that to the other million weird things about this place.*

My dress trailed on the ground, just enough to brush the dirt without catching on anything or tripping me. I'd needed something new since Hunter had gone all caveman on my shirt.

It had been sexy as hell the night before, but was a nuisance when I woke with nothing to wear.

Grant had gone out and found me a dress, one that matched what the other fae wore. This one was black with red trim, and swirls of red that came up from the bottom and disappeared near the waist, like flames.

I wasn't a dress-type woman, but it was hard not to like this. I wanted to twirl, to let the billowy skirt flow around as I spun. It made me feel like a little girl again, one who wanted to pretend she was a princess.

Not that I'd had a lot of chances to play that game. It was much harder to pretend that when I was juggled from foster home to foster home as perfect little families who had thought I was an adorable kid realized I was more work than they'd wanted.

A kid who talks to dead people just isn't much of a sell.

Outside the tent, Grant and Hunter waited. They spoke together, voices low, heads nodding. Funny to think the two could become such fast friends.

If only the other two hold-outs could manage it.

I thought about Troy and Kase talking calmly, and even that seemed *far* too unlikely a thing. It would be a miracle for them just not to kill one another.

Grant spotted me first, and his slow perusal of my body lit a fire inside me that had simmered since last night. How was it that one look could make me wonder if we had time to sneak back into the tent and try for a repeat?

We could hike my dress up and...

"No time," Hunter said with a rough, disappointed tone. "Serrish is already waiting, and when I get you naked again, I'm damn well going to take my time."

I blew out a breath and crossed my arms. "Fine."

Hunter dropped his gaze and smirked. "Pout all you want. When you cross your arms like that, it presses your tits together. I rather like it. Gives me a few ideas of what other parts of your body might be fun to put to use."

My cheeks heated, not only at what he said but how he'd said it. Sure, men had dirty talked before, but it was always whispered, as if shameful the dimness of a dark room. Hunter said it without an ounce of shame, as though we were discussing something far less personal and vulgar.

"People could hear you," I said, my voice low.

"They can also see your cleavage, so I'm sure they'd agree with me. Care to ask?"

I narrowed my eyes, since there weren't any words that could adequately explain just how little I wanted him to do that.

He let out a long sigh, as though I were truly frustrating to *him* before nodding toward Serrish's tent. "Come along, then. Let's finish here so we can get back to the normal world where there aren't people who might kill us."

Grant lifted an eyebrow.

"Fine. Where there are other people who want to kill us but at least we have the sun."

"Fair enough." Grant flanked my other side, and we made the short walk to Serrish's place. The same people who had milled around the night before seemed to be out and about again. Many stared at me, and all of them with the same look of disgust.

"Why do they hate me so much?"

"Because you're a human."

"So? I haven't done anything to them."

"Not you, maybe, but your kind. There's a reason they live here, Ava, and it's because humans have been, generally, violent, aggressive and sadistic."

"Well, they need to get over it. I've never done a thing to them. They can't blame me for what others of my kind have done. I'm not them."

"Last I checked, you weren't too trusting of vampires," Grant pointed out.

I went to argue when nothing came out. Damn it, I hated when someone made a good point. "Shut up," I muttered as we entered the tent.

It had changed from the last time. It still seemed to be the same general dimensions, but in the center was a single pillow. Outside of that rested a circle of thick salt. Serrish walked around the outside of the circle, lighting candles and incense that sat on tables near the outside edge of the tent. "You're late," she said.

"Had to find Ava something to wear," Grant said. "She ruined her other clothes."

I shot him a dirty look but kept my mouth shut. After the possessive way Serrish had spoken about Hunter, we probably didn't need to mention that Hunter had actually ripped them.

"Sit." Serrish nodded toward the center of the tent, inside the circle.

I stepped over the salt, like carefully. While I wasn't an expert in magic, I knew damn well not to fuck with a salt line. I lowered myself to the ground, wincing a bit as I did so.

Huh, I hadn't realized just how sore I was.

Hunter offered me a knowing grin, as though that was the sign of a job well done.

Serrish finished lighting candles along the edge before she returned and lowered herself on the single pillow. She was graceful, dropping to a cross-legged position like the best trained yogi around.

She closed her eyes, her back straight and her hands set loosely on her knees. I recognized the stance from every stupid yoga class I'd tried to take, when they opened with people centering themselves.

And suddenly I worried we were wasting our time. Maybe she wasn't useful at all—just some new-age person who was doing exactly what I could do myself.

I opened my mouth to say such a thing, but as though he expected it, Grant elbowed me. At a sharp look from him, I quieted down.

Long minute passed without Serrish doing anything. She breathed slowly, in and out, with an even and unbroken pace. Grant and Hunter didn't appear bothered, but then again it was easier to wait when they knew what to expect.

I had no idea if we were going to do this little sitting-on-the-floor thing for ten minutes or eight hours, and not knowing killed me.

I went to ask—as nicely as I could—how long this would take when her eyes snapped open.

The green was different—clouded, as though something else obscured it.

"What do you see?" Hunter asked.

She didn't answer right away, her pupils locking on nothing, telling me she wasn't seeing anything, at least not through her real eyes.

It reminded me of how Gran said I looked when I allowed spirits to speak through me, which was…unsettling.

"It's empty."

Hunter leaned forward but didn't touch her. "What's empty?"

Her eyebrows inched toward each other, as if she had to concentrate hard. "They aren't here. The spirits, they're not making it through to the afterworld."

She blinked a few times, until the clouds in her eyes disappeared. When she finally seemed back to herself, she looked at Hunter. "You're right. Spirits aren't making it to the afterworld."

"So where are they? Because they're not in the living realm, and they're not in the afterlife."

Serrish looked exhausted as she sat there, as though what had seemed like a quick process had cost her greatly. "You all think yourselves so smart, but you understand so little."

Hunter's voice hardened. "So explain it, Serrish, because we came to you for answers. The spirts aren't in either places, so where are they? And why?"

Serrish let out a long sigh, then held one hand up, her fist closed. A thin trail of fine sand poured from her, despite her not having actually picked up any. I wanted to ask how she'd done it, but no doubt I'd only receive annoyed looks in response to the question, so I stayed quiet.

"This is the normal flow of souls from the living realm to the afterlife. It is slow, steady, controlled. Even in times of crisis, when plagues or war increase that number..." She allowed more sand to pass, creating a larger stream, but still it piled into a neat cone on the ground. "It still remains stable. It has balance between the two amounts. This is how things should work. If something were to disrupt this, though," She paused, and placed her free hand in the stream, catching the specks in her palm. The pile grew, filling her hand, but she didn't stop. "It causes a break in the natural order, and this break isn't always immediately obvious or dangerous. However, it creates an imbalance, and if someone were to use that." She turned her hand over, allowing the large pile of sand that had accumulated in her palm to crash down onto the cone on the floor. Instead of settling in a predictable pattern, it knocked the sand down, flattening it, destroying the calm and steady rhythm.

"So they aren't being stolen?"

"Individual sprits are useless. However, grouped together, they have power. *If* this is what is planned, you don't have much time. The world is a fickle place, and the areas between life and death, where such spirits travel and could be stored, are narrow. It wouldn't take much to carry this out."

"Why, though?" I asked. When she gave me a sharp look, as if I should know better than to speak, I continued. "Everyone lives in either the living world or the afterlife. Why break them?"

Serrish shrugged, the bones of her slim shoulders standing out. "People do terrible things for a few reasons. Some out of spite, some out of fear, some for power and some for pleasure. Without knowing *who* has done this, I can't guess why. There are those, however, who are not so pleased with their place in this system, who feel the balance is anything but balanced, who crave more than they were given. They might be willing to destroy it all if they can't have it."

*Lucifer.*

A familiar tingle ran along my skin. I'd dealt with this damned shadow too many times, judging from how I could feel it before anyone else noticed it.

It stood behind Serrish, outside the circle, large and imposing and dark. Those twin flames flickered, but still it didn't seem to see me.

Whether Serrish noticed it or just noticed me looking over her shoulder, she twisted and jumped to her feet.

At the same time Grant and Hunter saw it—at least it was something for once that others than just me could spot—and they pushed me backward.

"Stay in the circle," Serrish snapped. Despite her small frame, she remained between the shadow and us. "You do not belong here," she said.

The shadow drew back and struck out as it had in my dream, but it only struck the barrier of salt. It couldn't seem to break through.

"This isn't your realm," Serrish said, holding her hands out, palms up. Green sparked from them, the same color as her eyes. "You have no power here, Morningstar."

The name made me press against Hunter's back, a shudder as if it were a name that shouldn't be spoken nor heard.

In fact…the more I thought about it, the surer I was Serrish hadn't exactly said that, as though my brain supplied a name it understood instead of whatever she used.

Even I knew, however, with my lack of formal religion, that Morningstar was another term for Lucifer.

"Go," Serrish said, a glow surrounding her that made me suddenly grateful Hunter and Grant had kept me from opening my mouth around her much. "Go!" She threw her hands out and struck the shadow with the green from her palms. It seemed to vibrate, as if the frequency were wrong, but it didn't disappear.

Serrish left the circle, stepping over the salt and continuing to strike the shadow with more of that green. The shadow lashed out, but she leaned to the side and only took a glancing blow.

The scent of burning flesh told me she wasn't immune.

"This is our realm," Serrish said when she reached the shadow, her body like a beacon of light. "This is the place of magic older than you, Morningstar. I suggest you not venture here again."

The shadow *screamed* as she shoved both her hands forward, into the smoke. Beams of green broke through the darkness, as if they dissolved away the shadowy being.

It was gone moments later, and when she turned, Serrish's eyes were a bright enough green to light the tent. "You brought it here," she said.

"We didn't bring anything," Grant argued. "*That's* what we're trying to stop!"

Serrish pointed at me, and I noticed her nails were longer, sharper than they'd been. Her cheekbones and eyes were more pronounced as well, as though even she'd been hiding how she really looked before. "You brought it here—you let it follow you. You've gotten what you paid for, now take your half-breed and get out!"

*Half-breed?*

Hunter pushed me behind him, just as he'd done with the shadow, as if Serrish might be just as dangerous.

Then again, she *had* sent that thing running without much trouble. I should have been far more believing when they'd warned me of the dangers.

Serrish waved her hand, and I flinched as though what happened to the shadow might happen to me.

Instead of searing pain, however, I turned to find myself back at the stump, with the sun beating down on us.

"She can't do that," I said and plopped myself down on the stump. "We needed more answers."

"The only thing we will get if we go back," Grant said, "is a quick death. She gave us all we were getting. Come on, let's get back to town."

I bit my lip, staring down at the stump, lost. I'd needed more…a direction, an understanding, something.

She'd told me nothing.

All I had learned again was how unprepared for this world—and this fight—I really was. She introduced me to yet again another large portion of it that didn't want me and that I couldn't stand against.

It was a lesson I was really tired of learning.

# Chapter Twenty-One

I sat on a bench across the road from an old brick fire station. Hunter had dropped me back off at home before he'd disappeared.

He did that a lot, was just gone. It wasn't that I needed him around every moment, but the way he went from being such a vital part of my life for a moment to disappearing gave me whiplash.

So I'd brought myself here, to the place I hated to come, because it was the only place I could think of right then.

The bench—old and in need of replacement— groaned when someone sat beside me. The scent of incense told me who it was without me looking.

"What do you want?"

"To see if you survived your little trip," Gran said.

I didn't look at her, choosing to stare at the fire station instead. "You look like the fae."

"Do I? Or do they look like me?"

I blew out a slow breath. "Normally your non-answers are a little charming, but I just don't have the energy today."

She huffed out a small laugh, as though my annoyance were worth it. "I'm older than the fae, Ava. We're connected, but not the same. What I am doesn't matter anymore, since I'm the last. What I am was lost to time long before there were humans or fae or supernatural."

*The last?* The fact that Gran was alone hit me harder than it should have. It made sense, I guess, why she'd taken me in as she had. She understood what it meant to look around and not see anyone like her, to not fit in anywhere.

"I don't know what to do."

"You know more than you think you do."

"You like to say that, but we are beyond the 'believe in yourself' talk, aren't we? This is end-of-the-world shit, and I'm not qualified to deal with it."

She sighed, then leaned back on the bench. "Do you remember the first time you came into my shop?"

I thought back to how young I'd been, how scared. I'd ventured into a few other occult shops, but they'd never felt right. I'd walked in and felt the fraud of the place, that it was just a hipster trend where teenagers went when they wanted to annoy their parents. I had been ten, lost and frightened and so used to keeping things bottled up. No one wanted to adopt or foster a child who saw ghosts, and it had taken a while for me to learn that lesson.

I'd received a flyer for an occult shop, and something had drawn me to it, a need for connection. "You had a cup of tea already set out for me when I walked in."

"And you've always wanted to know if I knew you were coming or if I just happened to have the tea. Why haven't you ever asked?"

"Because I liked the idea that you were waiting for me. I didn't want to know if that wasn't true." I took a deep breath, then asked. "So, were you waiting?"

Gran looked over at me—I could see through my peripheral—and smiled. "Yes, I was waiting for you."

"How'd you know about me?"

"A friend mentioned knowing someone who could use a little guidance."

Another piece of a puzzle about me I knew nothing about. It felt like my life was a game played by others for me. "And this friend?"

"A story for another time, perhaps. The moment you walked in, when I really saw you, I knew they had been right. I haven't always done the best by you, but I've always tried."

I wanted to argue, to tell her she could have given me a home, but what was the point? I'd made it clear from the start I wanted a normal life, and of all the things Gran could give me, normal wouldn't ever be one of them. "You knew about Fredrick. You knew about everything. How does this end?"

She didn't answer, instead choosing to gesture at the fire station. "You come here a lot. Why?"

"It's where my parents left me."

"I know that, but *why* do you come here?"

It didn't shock me she'd know something I had never told her. Of course she knew this was the exact station where my parents had abandoned me, where they'd left me like the worst game of ding-dong-ditch with a really shitty prize.

"I feel like this is the start for me. This is where everything I am, everything I know began. I don't know where I was born, where I spent my first few years, but here is where it changed."

"So why come here now?"

"Because maybe if I stare at it, if I understand something here, I'll figure out what I'm supposed to do, what I'm supposed to be. I feel like I've played a game I don't know the rules to, and coming here is me going back to the start to make sense of it."

Her sigh was unhappy, as if I'd disappointed her, as though I still didn't understand some lesson she'd been teaching me for years. "Starts don't matter, Ava. They never have. They don't change who you are, what you are or what you'll do. You can stare at that station all you want, but it won't ever make sense. Even if you understood your past, you'd still be in the same place."

"Maybe," I admitted. "But I'd have solid footing to stand on."

"Who you were born and who you *are* aren't the same things. You asked me if you'd win, but I can't answer it. Can you win? Yeah. Will you?" She shrugged. "That's up to you."

"No great pieces of wisdom, then? No pep talk that will bring it all together for me?" Even though my words came out like a joke, that was exactly what I wanted. I craved it, for her to tell me something that reignited a belief that I could come out of this ahead, that I could be what everyone needed me to be.

"I watched your mother drop you off here," she said.

An ugly laugh left me as I was so not surprised by that. "So you've known all along who I was? You've known my parents and never told me?"

"I didn't know your mother—I never met her. Still, power like yours is something I can feel, and I watched when she left you here. She closed your orange jacket, pulling it tightly around you, tears on her face. She kissed your head and whispered to you, then said she'd be right back. She watched from a car down the road until the firefighters brought you inside."

"Who is she?"

"What would knowing change? Would you be a different person?"

*No.* I'd be the same disaster who lacked answers as I was right now. Was that her point? That understanding my past didn't change where I was now?

Maybe being angry just gave me an easy out, something to focus on. My shitty life wasn't my fault— it was all because I had shitty parents who had thrown me out.

"When this is all over, will you tell me about her?"

"If we all survive it? Sure."

"If? You are horrible at confidence-building."

She shrugged. "I'm realistic. If you want advice, Ava, I've got only one piece for you. Stop trying to be what you *think* you should be and start being who you are, because fighting this with one hand tied behind your back will kill us all."

I opened my mouth to respond, but my phone vibrated instead. I took it from my pocket to find a text message from Troy.

The werewolf had arrived at the pack house.

It seemed I'd run out of time to find answers.

\* \* \* \*

"The pack owns all this?" We drove on the winding road that was so overgrown, only the twin spots where the wheels touched ground was clear. Short weeds grew up the center on our way to the house where Paul would be brought.

Hunter, Kase and Grant would arrive after the sun set, once Paul was closer, but Troy had wanted to check first.

"They like having space to spread out. Hunting is important for werewolves. It bonds a pack."

"Why don't you consider yourself part of the pack?"

"Because I'm not."

"Why not?"

He huffed, and his knuckles had turned white on the steering wheel. "It's a long story, Ava."

I thought back. "You told Fredrick he remembered what happened to the last person who threatened your mate."

He gave me a harsh look. "You should let it go."

"Why? Everyone wants to dig up my past."

"So tell me about your most painful memory. Let's discuss that, since you're so keen on sharing."

I looked directly at him, giving him no room to wiggle out of the conversation. If he thought he could throw down the gauntlet and get me to back off, he clearly had no idea who I was.

I'd been through *hell* as a kid, and I had no issue spreading that shit out on the table.

"When I was thirteen, I was placed with a couple who seemed nice. Big house, lots of money, that whole 'we really care about you' vibe. My caseworker kept telling me how lucky I was to be placed with them, especially with how *colorful* my past was. That was a word they liked to use a lot, colorful. What they meant was that foster parents would return me all the time because I seemed to talk to people who weren't there, because I knew things I shouldn't and because I just never fit in."

I sighed at how those words had hurt so badly, at how they'd been a deeper tattoo than the ones on my arms, and how I'd worn them all my life.

I kept going, wanting to get the story out, every ugly detail of it. "So the first week went okay. I tried so hard to be normal, to fit in, to be the kid I thought they wanted. However, I started to hear the husband walk down the hall at night. As time went on, day by day, he started stopping and checking on me. I've always been a light sleeper — that happens when you've never had a real safe place to sleep — and he started coming into my room, checking to see if I was awake. I pretended to be asleep, just wanted to act like that house might have been my fresh start. The wife was strict but sweet, they were the picture of what people were supposed to want and I felt like if I just fit in there, everything would change. Then the night came when he sat on the side of the bed, and he ran his fingers across my eyebrow." I shuddered at the memory, at the way it made my stomach roll.

"You don't need to tell me, Ava," Troy said, voice purposely soft.

I let out a soft sigh. "I wanted to fit in so badly that I'd put up with anything if it got me a family, so I didn't say a word. I was on the second floor landing the next day with him and his wife, and we were talking about what to do for the weekend. His eyes went wide, like he'd seen something terrifying. Sometimes I think it was his conscience, but I don't think he had one. He jerked backward and stumbled down the stairs. Maybe it makes me a horrible person, but I had this moment of glee, this thought that with him gone, maybe the wife and I could continue like a family. Not the same family, but I'd still have a place. I wonder sometimes if she knew what her husband was, if I was just a reminder, because she called my caseworker that night to have me picked up." My mouth felt dry, as though I'd swallowed a mouth full of sand through the entire story. "So, yeah, I know what it's like to have parts of my past I'd rather not remember, parts I wish I could bury. The thing is, they don't go away. Even if you move past them, they're like a stain that you can't get out, and pretending they're gone helps nothing."

He reached over and set a hand on my leg—no doubt to be reassuring—but the sensation of being touched after the story made me flinch.

He pulled back, no sign of rejection or anger on his face. "Sorry," he whispered.

His voice was so quiet, like I'd never heard it before, his eyes straight forward, refusing to look at me.

"Are you mad?"

He let out a slow breath, then stopped the car in the middle of the road. It wasn't like other cars would come up on us there, I guess.

When he turned, I pulled back. His eyes were like flashlights—worse than they'd been during the fight with Kase. The lines of his face had sharpened and there was no way his teeth hadn't turned to fangs. He was partway into a transition he was obviously fighting very hard.

He didn't reach for me, didn't get closer, as if he knew better. Whether that was for his control or mine, I didn't know.

"I'm not mad at you," he said, still with that deceptively calm and low voice, though now I got why. I suspected if he spoke the way he wanted, it would be all snarl. "You don't understand what having a mate means, not to a wolf. The thought you were hurt, victimized, that I couldn't and can't do anything about it drives my wolf into a frenzy, makes it bloodthirsty.

I'm not angry with you but *for* you. Don't be afraid of me, Ava."

"I'm not," I said.

He nodded, then drew a slow, deep breath. "I left the pack after my mate was killed. Werewolves, our dominance is controlled by our wolf half. When we're changed, we have to settled into new dynamics. My wolf is extraordinarily dominant, but I've never wanted to lead a pack. The old alpha, he couldn't seem to accept that fact, figured I'd eventually try to take over. I guess he couldn't imagine controlling his wolf that way, so he thought I couldn't."

"And your mate?"

"Sasha. She was human. Sweet, soft, loving, everything I didn't think I could have in my life anymore after I was changed." He spoke with so much longing in his tone, as if he could still see her, as though he wanted nothing more than having her back.

And…I couldn't deny a jealous spark in my chest. It wasn't about Sasha, not exactly, but rather because all the things he said about her weren't me…

It felt like seeing a picture of my man's ex and realizing she was *far* prettier than I was.

I put that aside, though, because it was petty and stupid and Troy's story mattered more. "What happened?"

"Sasha had no idea what I was. I thought I could keep that separate, that I could keep her safe and live a double life. Well, the old alpha decided to strike first. He snuck into our home in the middle of the night."

"He murdered an innocent human over it?"

"I don't think he meant to kill her. I just don't think he cared. I've told you before that humans are fragile, and Sasha was a perfect example. One misplaced strike was enough." He sighed, his shoulders sinking. "I killed the alpha over it, and killed the wolves he brought with him, the ones who had agreed with the action. I think I took out the top eight or nine wolves that night. At the end, I left. When Fredrick took power, he reached out to me, and I made it clear I was done. That was thirty years ago. I knew if I stayed or ever went back, I would never have peace. My wolf would want to lead, and others would sense my dominance and see it as a challenge, and I would forever be fighting both myself and others. So I became a lone wolf."

I wanted to ask more about Sasha, to say something about it, but the way he'd steered the conversation back to leaving the pack told me where he wanted to focus. Showing someone a wound was one thing, and it didn't mean he wanted me picking at the scab.

So I followed his unspoken request and stayed on his topic. "You said hunting was important. Don't you need a pack?"

"I miss it, but after my mate, after everything, I couldn't do it again. It just wasn't for me anymore."

I nodded, understanding. After what had happened at that house, I gave up the desire to find that happy childhood. I'd thought maybe it just wasn't something meant for me, as if I were missing something important for creating it.

I'd still tried to make a life for myself later, as an adult, but I'd given up the picture-perfect childhood.

Troy turned forward again, but he didn't drive right away. He breathed in and out slowly for what had to be five minutes—I suspected he didn't really know how much time had passed. I let him do it, watching, fascinated as his features returned to normal.

Funny that I didn't really *mind* that side of him. It was terrifying — even just a glimpse — but I'd found that monsters often looked entirely human.

"What's it like having a wolf?"

"Tiring," he said. "My wolf is a separate spirit. It has its own wants, needs, drives. It only takes over fully now occasionally, like during full moons or if I lose control, which is rare. But I lose myself at those times. It isn't *me* anymore." He paused, then shook his head. "Don't get me wrong, Ava. *You* would always be safe. My wolf chose you, so you wouldn't need to fear it."

"And if it hadn't been his choice?"

Troy frowned then turned back toward me. His face had regained its previous look, appearing totally normal again. "Is that what's worried you? My wolf might be wild, and I don't trust it in many things, but it was right about my previous mate, and it was right about you, Ava." He still didn't reach for me, as if he wasn't sure I'd want him to. He swallowed loudly, then asked in a hesitant voice, "Maybe we could fit in together. I could be the family you never got, and you could be the pack I can't have. Maybe that could be enough?"

The thought sounded lovely, like offering the one thing I'd wanted more than anything.

I nodded, offering a smile. "Maybe."

No matter how badly I wanted it...I still wasn't sure it was something I could actually have.

# Chapter Twenty-Two

"I have a policy against going into rooms that have drains in the floor." I stood in the doorway of the interrogation room and crossed my arms.

"Try cleaning massive amounts of blood from somewhere without a drain in the floor and you will realize how useful they can be." Kase slid past me and into the room.

"That doesn't make me feel any better. Believe it or not, I've never had to clean up massive amounts of blood."

Hunter passed me as well, taking a moment to slap my ass and draw a yelp from me. Not that he looked repentant, even when Kase and Troy offered him murderous glares over it.

Everyone had found their way to the small house in the center of pack territory, miles from any other building or property line, isolated enough that screams would never carry that far.

The actual room where Paul was to be kept was in the basement, and the room had thin silver chains built into the walls and ceiling to prevent escape. Large hooks were secured to the floor, the sort attached to the ends of cranes, and it again reminded me that I wasn't dealing with humans here.

We were going to have a killer werewolf down here, one I needed to try and have a conversation with without getting myself killed.

"Do you think you can do it?" Kase asked.

I wanted to say yes, that I could force that essence out of the wolf, that I could force it to talk as I had Olin—only better. However, I had no idea how I'd done that in the first place, so what did I know? "Maybe?" The answer wasn't a great one, but it was honest.

"Everything looks good," Troy said after testing each hook, after running his hands over the different areas in the walls and ceiling. His palms were bloodied and burned—a reaction to the silver—but he didn't complain. "I don't think there is any way that wolf could get out of here. We'll have him bound in silver as well, so it should be safe to interrogate him, but, Ava, you will need to keep your distance. One swipe and he could kill you."

"Last time, with Olin, I had to touch him."

Troy shook his head. "Not a chance."

"We'll work it out," Grant offered instead. "Between the four of us, you don't think we could restrain one silvered werewolf?"

Troy narrowed his eyes but didn't respond.

Understanding him better, I knew exactly where his mind had gone. It wasn't the place to reassure him, though, not in front of the others, so I let the subject drop. "When will he be here?"

"An hour or so. They've reached the back gate." Troy stretched his hands as if they still ached, but the skin had already started to knit back together.

On the main level, the house was nice but not overly large. They probably kept only security teams up top. The benefit was that they did have a few rooms with two beds per a room — so plenty for us if we had to stay a few days.

The pack hadn't been happy about having all of us there, but Troy had explained it was a non-negotiable part of the deal.

I suspect he only did so because he knew more people meant less danger, and his fear of anything happening to me was bigger than his jealousy or suspicion.

"This is going to be a long few days," Troy said. "Wolves don't break easily, so we should all take a break before he gets here."

Muttered agreements sounded, and we all exited the small, dark basement. The boys went to pick out rooms, and perhaps because they knew how difficult the situation was and how not-useful a fight would be, none of them tried to make a claim on me.

Instead, I ended up in my own room, flanked by them. Kase and Troy each took their own rooms while Grant and Hunter chose to bunk together.

They went about securing the windows to keep the sun out while Grant set up wards. In thirty minutes, the entire place was ready for however long we needed to stay, and I went outside for a much-needed breath of fresh air.

I loved the desert, but in town there was still enough light pollution to hide the stars. Out here, the sky stretched forever in each direction, a huge black ocean with sparking light.

I sat on a large boulder not too far from the house and marveled at how insignificant it made my problems seem.

Which was silly, since if Serrish were right, if we didn't fix this problem, even those stars would blink out of existence.

"Do you know why I choose to live here?" Kase asked when he walked up beside me.

His voice made me tense, especially after our last interaction. My neck still itched from where he'd bitten me—then soundly rejected me. Being unwanted sucked, but having his saliva turn me into some desperate horny mess while he remained uninterested made it all the worst.

"I always thought it was weird you would pick to live somewhere with so much sun."

He leaned against the boulder to my left. "The night sky. Other places don't have this view. Since I can't ever see the day sky, since sprawling cities bathed in light isn't something I can have, I chose the best night sky there was."

I pressed my lips together as his thoughts mirrored mine. Still, I moved onto the thing I knew we had to discuss.

"So, am I dying?"

He shook his head. "No. You appear to be in perfect health."

"Maybe you just have bad taste."

He let out a tired sigh. "I am sorry for hurting your pride, Ava. It surprised me and..." He paused for a long moment before continuing in a soft voice, "frightened me. I had a moment of terror that I finally had you and you were sick, that I would lose you so quickly."

"Not sick, just defective." I shook my head and spoke again before he had a chance to try and make me feel better — or try, because I doubted he could. "That fae woman called me a half-breed. Hunter and Grant wouldn't tell me what she meant."

"They probably don't know."

"That's evasive."

He leaned a hand on the boulder so he could look up at the sky with me, because he was *not* the type to stretch out on a boulder. "Half-breed means a lot of things to the fae. It simply means, at its core, not pure. They often use the term for humans with any sort of other blood in them."

"But I thought immortals couldn't have children. So how could I have blood from something else in me?"

"There have been cases, rare though they are. Mages using unsanctioned magic, werewolves or vampires who are pregnant when changed, some of the fae who can reproduce with humans. Sometimes the fae simply use it when they mean a human with talents that imply somewhere in their lineage, they had something else, because they enjoy any insult they can use against humans."

That was a wholly unhelpful answer. It didn't tell me anything new about myself, didn't give me answers.

"I wish I could explain what you were, Ava. I believe all our lives would be easier if we knew, but I'm not sure we ever will. There are times when things simply happen, when there is no explanation."

I thought back to when Melinda had sat on my bed, and it seemed like a lifetime ago. "You know, just before this all started, a spirit came to me, and I told her the same thing. She wanted me to reassure her, to tell her there was some great purpose or plan to make her death mean something, but I couldn't say that. I told her things happen and you have to make peace with it."

"There's truth to that. I've seen many new vampires try to make sense of the world, of why they became what they were, of why they would watch their old lives drift away, their loves ones die, and if they couldn't accept that, if they couldn't make peace with the change, they never lasted long. Eternity is daunting if you need it to make sense."

But...I still wanted it to make sense. I wanted to close my eyes and know my suffering had been for a reason.

I kept the thought to myself. Knowing something and accepting it were two different things and they happened on their own schedules.

"So what now? I can't imagine you signed up for wanting anything with a human you couldn't even feed from."

He twisted so he could look down at me, though the darkness hid his features. That didn't stop me from feeling his glare. "You believe all I wanted from you was blood?"

"Seems like a driving factor, yes."

"I have donors, Ava, and other avenues for feeding. You are more to me than a meal." The way he spoke made me shiver. It was honest—and hungry—and since he couldn't stand my blood, it was a hunger for something very different...

"So what am I? Because so far, I've brought you trouble, you can't feed from me, I don't listen to you—" *And I'm currently sleeping with other men.*

The thought happened so fast that I couldn't stop it, but at least I'd kept it from pouring out of my mouth.

"And you're sleeping with other men."

"How the hell did you know I was thinking that?"

"It wasn't hard to guess, Ava. I'm not blind."

"Well, so what's the answer? With all of that, I just can't really see the benefits from your point of view."

"I can't say the situation is...*ideal*. However, with you being human, I also doubt you would willingly stay locked safely inside during all daylight hours, when I couldn't be there to protect you."

"You've got that right."

He didn't acknowledge my snarky response. "The reality of my situation has required me to make adjustments. I am only capable of being in half of your life, at best. Should you lose a loved one, the service would likely be during the daylight hours when I could not attend. When I worried you were ill, I had to send you for tests alone as I couldn't accompany you. That is the reality of what I can and cannot offer, and it means I have been forced to recognize some benefits to such an..." He paused as if looking for the right word. "Arrangement. It isn't what I expected, but perhaps it is what would work."

"So you're saying you're fine with it?"

"I am saying that if the choice is between sharing you and losing you, I am willing to try whatever lets me have you."

It wasn't his words that got me, it was how he said them. Kase was a hard man to read, and a harder one to trust, however in that moment, I believed every word.

I leaned up, slipping my hand behind his neck, and offered him a slow, sweet kiss.

He flinched, then caught my hands and pulled them away. Before the rejection could set in — and boy it was about to — he pressed me back on the rock and trapped my hands above my head. "Can I kiss you?"

"Yes, you stupid—"

He silenced the rest of my tirade with a kiss that made my heart speed and my back arch. The man was *sinful* with those fangs, with the way he moved his lips against mine, how he took me over so wonderfully until I was mindless.

But as fast as it happened, he stopped.

I wanted to complain, to tempt him back, but the glow of headlights in the distance clued me in.

The werewolf was here, which meant we had a job to do.

So even though I'd rather stay there and never stopping kissing Kase, it seemed we needed to be responsible.

Besides, if we didn't fix this, if we couldn't save the world, well that would put a damper on how much more of Kase's skills I could test out.

And that was something worth saving the world for.

# Chapter Twenty-Three

Troy helped with the transfer, and I only caught a glimpse of a struggling body as they'd worked him downstairs since they kept me far away. He stayed in the basement for a long time, since there wasn't any chance that he'd let me enter that room without being absolutely sure Paul had no way of moving. Even after the other wolves who had come to help left, Troy remained out of sight.

The sun had started to peek above the mountain ranges, which meant for the remainder of the day, Kase was stuck inside. I'd sat outside and watched it after Kase had retreated, like some last hurrah.

Maybe it was the stress of the upcoming interrogation, how I still had so few answers about anything, trying to judge so many different personalities, that everyone looked as me as if I was supposed to understand or know anything and I just didn't. Whatever it was, I felt overwhelmed and stretched too thin.

Once I couldn't sit still anymore, when I couldn't ignore the reality of the day any longer, I headed for my room. I needed a few minutes of silence to recenter, to close the door and pretend for just a moment that I had no one relying on me but myself.

I'd let myself down enough times that I was a pro at that.

How I'd gone from having no one care where I was or what I was doing to having people needing me, to having people depending on me for things that felt far too important.

The door to Kase's room sat cracked open. I knew he'd planned to attend the interrogation, but perhaps he'd wanted a little rest as well before that.

Voices floated out of the room, and I paused. *Grant.*

I'd recognize his voice anywhere. Then again, Grant was in charge of dealing with the wards and much of the magical protection, and Kase had hired him, so they had to be friends, right?

Still, the lowness of their voices set off alarms in my head, something that said this wasn't right. No one spoke like that when everything was on the level. I stopped at the door, closing my eyes to drown out all the other senses and focus on their words.

"How safe are we here?" Kase asked.

"Safe enough. But if we really are dealing with Lucifer, no wards I have are going to make a difference."

"He won't come himself. It's not his way. He doesn't like to get his hands dirty. Do you think Ava can actually drive back his influence?"

"She's done it before. I don't think she knows how she did it—it seemed like instinct. Still, Olin went from mindless to speaking."

"What does that mean? What is she?"

There was a slight pause, then Grant's voice seemed to come from a different place in the room, as if he were pacing. "I don't know. I did every test on the blood I got from her and everything I find reads human or inconclusive."

*My blood?*

"I didn't hire you for you to not give me answers. You told me from day one you could figure it out. That was why I hired you and not a guild mage, because you swore you could determine what she is."

"Of course I said that. I've never had a person defy every test I know before. It's like me asking for you to put a vampire into the sun so they'll burn, but you do it, and they don't burn. We're dealing with someone unprecedented here."

Kase made a soft sound, one that came out like a growl. "I swore to Colter that I would figure out exactly what she was. I can't go back empty-handed, and you don't want to anger the coven elders, either."

My stomach rolled with each word they exchanged.

Grant had been working for Kase the entire time. Not just to help, as I'd been led to believe, but because they wanted to know what I was. It had been a ploy from the start, and I'd been the idiot who had fallen for it.

I looked down at my hand, at the scar there from where he'd sliced me. He'd needed blood for the wards, but I remembered the careful way he'd sheathed the blade—covered in my blood—and had put it in his satchel. I remembered the way he'd winced after I'd told him that I finally fit in when we'd been tangled up in bed with Hunter. I was nothing but an easy target and a job.

He'd known all along he was betraying me, that he was working for Kase to uncover my secrets for a price.

And Kase?

He'd acted like I mattered when I'd been nothing but a job for him, an errand from his precious coven leader. All the times I'd thought he wasn't led around by Colter were my own stupidity.

His words came back to me, the ones he'd told me that first night after I'd woken up. '*Keep asking questions and you'll end up dead.*'

He'd told me I'd never dealt with him before, and it seemed I'd underestimated how right he was.

I pushed open the door, and the creak of the hinges caused both men to swing their gazes my way.

Guilt rushed across their features.

I didn't need to yell, to say I'd caught them — it was written all over their faces I'd heard them exactly right. There was no misunderstanding, nothing for them to explain away.

I shook my head and wrapped my arms around myself. I'd been so *stupid* to actually trust any of them.

Four men had fallen into my life out of the blue at the exact moments I needed them, and I didn't realize how insanely suspicious that was? I forgot for a moment that I didn't *get* things like this?

"Wait," Kase said when I stepped backward.

I held my hand up to stop him. "Do you really think there is *anything* for you to say right now?"

He stilled, then pressed his lips together as if he had to keep himself silent.

Troy's heavy footsteps made me turn, and the tense expression on his face reminded me we had bigger problems…

Like a killer werewolf in the basement.

"He's ready," Troy said.

I nodded and turned my back on Grant and Kase, not needing them to see exactly how wounded I was.

* * * *

The man downstairs wasn't really a man anymore. I tried to look calm when I saw him for the first time, as though it didn't entirely freak me out, but he made Troy look normal those times when he'd started to shift.

I recalled Gran once telling me that werewolves didn't look like men or wolves when they turned, and she'd said it with a rare hesitation in her tone that said she wasn't a fan of the sight.

I finally understood.

Paul's face was hardly recognizable, with sharp, high cheekbones and lips pulled up to reveal a mouth full of sharp teeth. His eyes were bright and amber, and his face angled as though a snout had started to form.

He was huge, larger than any man, and with thick black fur covering him. His arms were longer than they should have been and his large hands were tipped with vicious looking claws.

He was every inch the monster people pictured werewolves being.

Heavy chains of silver wrapped around him, and manacles kept his hands behind his back. He was on his knees on the ground, a muzzle over his face made of leather and steel, fastened behind his head.

The chains hooked to two anchors drilled into the cement, and despite the way he twisted, he couldn't move.

I tried not to think about Troy like that. Would he look the same if I ever saw him fully shifted? Would he have that same anger in his eyes, that violence?

A hand touched my arm and I jumped, so focused on Paul that I'd failed to realize Hunter had walked up to my left. He didn't pull away, instead giving me a moment to recognize him and relax.

"He shouldn't have much range," Troy explained as he walked past me. His words were sharp and careful. Maybe he was thinking the same thing, comparing himself to the beast bound there. "I had him muzzled, and his hands are bound in the thickest silver we could find. That should keep him from being able to do too much damage."

"Has he said anything?"

Troy shook his head, standing beside Paul, a glow in his eyes that said he didn't care for this. "According to the wolves who transported him, he hasn't said anything. He just snarls and lunges, mostly. He hasn't seemed to sleep, hasn't shifted back to human, doesn't respond to even pack dynamics." At my confusion, he continued, "Dominant wolves and alphas can usually force some amount of submission. No one can reach him."

I let my hands fall to my sides and shook them out, like trying to release the tension. It felt like the first time I'd tried to follow a spirit trail, when Gran had explained how to do it, had told me to slow my breathing and focus.

I suddenly wished Gran were there. She always managed to make me feel not quite so strange, not so out of my element.

Instead, I was all on my own.

Paul struggled as I approached, and Troy put a gloved hand on the chains that wrapped up and around his shoulders to hold him still.

I shook my hand once more, hard, then held it out. Paul's skin was burning hot when I touched it, as though he had a raging fever.

My eyes closed as I concentrated and tried to ignore that a werewolf as tall as I was when he was kneeling wanted to tear my throat out.

*Focus on the positive.*

Like the fact that I had backup.

*Backup who betrayed you.*

I shoved that all away, the questions, the worries, the things that wouldn't stop circling in my brain as I tried to sort it out and make sense of it all.

That shadow was there, inside Paul, swirling around. It retreated from me as it had that last time, as if it didn't know what or who I was.

That made me frown. Shouldn't it? We'd done this before, with Olin.

*Maybe the shadow isn't connected to the person anymore. Maybe this is a piece it breaks off and leaves in the person.* Like the stinger of a bee.

I tried to push forward, to force the presence backward.

"Where am I?" A rough voice asked the question, and as much as I wanted to answer, I could only focus on one thing—keeping that shadow back.

Thankfully Kase stepped up. "What is the last thing you remember?"

Paul's eyebrows moved, but the expression seemed all wrong on his monstrous face. "I was sleeping, under the moon, out in the desert."

"And?" Kase pressed.

"Something was there, a being. It walked toward me."

"What was it?"

The shadow surged forward, but I pushed it backward.

Paul cried out, as if the battle pained him as well. "I don't know. It reached out and burned me, from the inside. It woke my wolf, removed any control I had of it." Paul arched forward as if something inside him were chewing to get out.

No matter what I did, the shadow gained ground. I tried to push out of the room, the thoughts of what Paul said, what it meant, and focus only on doing *whatever* I had done before, on trying to force back that shadow.

It kept winning, though.

"What does the shadow want? What does it have to do with the missing spirits?"

Paul howled, a terrifying sound of pain that no human could manage. "I don't know. What it did to me, it wasn't controlling me. It just took away all my control, that of my wolf, so that everything I saw I wanted to kill and eat and bathe in its blood."

The shadow surged forward so powerfully that it knocked me backward, throwing my hand off Paul as surely as if it had been there. I fell to the ground, the air knocked from my lungs, and Paul had reverted to before, back to snarling and twisted and rage.

I stared at him, at the flames I saw in his eyes, the ones that matched those in the shadow, in the thing that was too powerful.

"Try again," Kase said.

I stood and reached out, but this time the moment I set my hand against his chest, as soon as contact was made, that shadow lashed out and knocked me backward. This time my head struck the ground, disorienting me for a moment.

Fear crept in, doubt. *What am I thinking? I've been the one to turn my back on this all my life. This isn't my place.*

Hunter was there to help me up—Troy stared at me with the sort of intensity that said he was fighting with himself to stay where he was. Then again, a tiny bump was a lot less dangerous than a raging werewolf.

"Again," Kase said. "Concentrate this time."

"That's enough," Hunter snapped, facing Kase. "She's had enough."

"We need answers, and this is our only method to get them. This is bigger than all of us."

"I can do it," I said, rubbing my hand over the back of my head where it ached.

I wanted to prove I could handle this, that I could do what they needed, that I wasn't useless.

"You don't need to," Grant chimed in, despite Kase's sharp look in his direction. "We can figure out something else."

"Like what? Does anyone have any better ideas?"

"I could try using my wolf," Troy said. "Paul didn't react to more dominant wolves, but those were casual tries. I could try to force it."

Hunter shook his head. "Bad idea. If you try to do that, you could just as easily end up in the same condition he's in. We don't know if this can pass from one person to another, but I don't think we should go screwing with the chance by having you create that sort of link."

Troy opened his mouth to argue, but I spoke up between them. "I want to try again."

Troy's lips pressed together, a clear sign he wasn't happy about the choice, but he nodded.

I tried to breathe in, to ignore the pain in my head to ignore the rapidly spreading sense of failure as though I'd tried and screwed it up already.

I used my other hand—the one I'd been using felt as though it had been burned. I took one big breath before placing my palm on his cheek, beside the muzzle, and I focused everything I had into driving back that shadow.

And for a moment it worked. For one second the shadow retreated, but like a wave it crashed back into me with even more force.

This time Hunter caught me, which was good because I would have hit the ground and skidded.

"Enough," Troy growled out, and one look at him made it clear. We were done.

He had his territorial, 'don't fuck with me' face on that said he'd had enough of seeing me tossed around. No one argued with him—what was the point?

I rubbed my eyes and pulled away from Hunter. I didn't bother to look at Kase or Grant—I really was in enough pain—as I walked up the stairs.

"Ava?" Troy said, a question in his voice.

"I'm just going to lie down for a little bit," I said. "That wore me out."

No one spoke again, and I was glad.

I really didn't need to think about my failure anymore.

The mist came when I fell asleep. It always came, so why it surprised me each time, I wasn't sure.

I choked, gagged, tried to cough it out of me. Sometimes the drowning was worse and sometimes it was better, but it was always there. When it was good, if was like walking through a room with smokers in it, and when it was bad, it was being pulled under the water.

This time it was in the water.

Across the way, some of the mist moved, coming closer, the gray of it almost shaped as a person but not quite.

It reminded me of what I'd seen that had driven back the shadow. I'd spotted them before, in this place, but they had never noticed me, to care about me.

This one reached out, and the mist retreated. I could breathe.

"What are you?" I gasped out the words, grateful to be able to speak, to draw air in.

It didn't answer, only stood there as though it expected something from me.

"Was what you showed me real? Was that my mother and me?"

I got the sense it nodded, but it was impossible to be sure.

"Why did you show me that? How would you even know?"

Nothing. It felt as useful as any other interrogation I'd done recently.

Hell, I was asking something in a dream. It was probably nothing more than my own manifestation of fear. It was telling me what I wanted to hear, not what was real.

It showed me a woman and a baby because I craved being wanted so badly that it concocted that.

"You're just a big grouping of trauma and neurosis, aren't you?" I sat, the hard ground beneath me. It felt like packed sand with tiny rocks, but I didn't bother to look. Who really cared what the ground of a dream was made of?

I was just exhausted, even mid-dream, and standing felt like too much work.

"I'm so tired of not being enough," I admitted. Why not use the thing as my own personal sounding board? It wasn't like it could go tell anyone else. "I can't do what I need to do. I'm letting everyone down, and I'm just…" I sighed and leaned forward. "I'm not enough."

The mist creature settled before me, as if mimicking my stance. It moved its hand, and the mist changed between us.

It solidified to create a scene and showed a bird in water. It flapped its wings, struggling against the current of a stream, but before long it disappeared beneath the current. After that, it showed the same bird hopping on the ground after a snake. The snake twisted, rearing back and striking. It wound around the bird, and eventually the bird went still.

*Quite the pep talk, subconscious.*

The last scene had the bird in the air, its wings out. It dove, angling the wings back, its feet forward, and it caught a squirrel on the ground.

After that happened, the mist faded back into the normal swirling nothingness.

I frowned, trying to make sense of what I was trying to tell myself. "You know, it would be more useful if you—well, I—could just tell me what I need to know, instead of this nonsense."

The figure didn't respond, as if it had given me all I needed in that pseudo-metaphysical lesson.

I sighed and shook my head. I was the cause of all this so why did I think I'd have the answers? Hadn't I proven I wasn't trustworthy when it came to good choices?

Something echoed through the mist. A roar?

The figure rose, a slow movement that didn't signal concern.

I'd never heard anything in the mist of my dreams before, which made me frown.

It happened again, and that was when it hit me. It wasn't in my dream. It was something from the real world, something that made me jerk awake.

Whatever was making that noise was in a killing mood, and I doubted it was going to be friendly with me.

# Chapter Twenty-Four

The third time the sound happened, I stumbled from the bed, still groggy, my head still aching, my ears ringing. It went beyond fear, down to something primal inside me where my ancestors knew to flee from whatever made that roar.

Hunter busted into the room, a crash downstairs. "Time to go."

"What happened?"

"Nothing." He grabbed my arm and pulled me from the room. "We need to get."

"What do you mean? What is that?"

Another loud bang, then a howl. It came from the basement. "Did Paul get out?"

"Not exactly."

Sun streamed in the window and I pulled against his grasp. "What about Kase? He can't go out in the sunlight."

"Fuck Kase. Fuck Grant. I am getting you as far away from here as possible." He grabbed me around the waist and hoisted me over his shoulder, which dug painfully into my stomach.

That was when it hit me. He hadn't mentioned Troy. *That sound is Troy.*

I knew it, like a sinking realization, as though there were something in the inhuman roar that I recognized of the man I knew.

"He tried to control Paul's wolf," I whispered.

"Yeah, despite me telling him it was fucking stupid. We thought a crazed Paul was bad? Troy makes him seem like an unhappy puppy."

I shoved at Hunter's back. "I can't just leave him."

"Yeah, you really can. I'm not about to let you die here."

I kicked once more, then did the only thing I could think of. I brought my forearms together.

Everything spun, and Hunter let out a string of curses that were so creative as to impress me.

Not that I waited to hear it all. Even after I struck the ground, I grasped the nearest thing I could—the couch—to drag myself to my feet and take off toward the door.

I didn't have to make it that far, however, before the door shattered into a million pieces. A bleeding, snarling monster emerged, covered in blood—far too much to be its own.

I recognized him. Even beneath the fur and the behind the blood-lust eyes, I saw *Troy*.

Not that he saw me.

He let out another roar, the daggers that tipped his fingers held out as if in warning.

He charged forward, but before he could reach me, something slammed into his side. Troy and whatever had hit him skidded into one of the bedrooms, and the curtain was torn off the window in the struggle.

They moved fast, but the sickly scent of burning flesh told me what my eyes couldn't follow.

It was Kase who had stepped in, who fought Troy despite the sun.

"Go," he shouted at me just as Troy took him to the ground. This wasn't like the time they'd fought before, when they'd traded blows like some show of dominance.

This was real. They were going to kill each other if someone didn't do something...

Troy tossed Kase to the side, and Kase hit the wall so hard that the window broke.

He didn't move.

Hunter approached from behind — I had no idea where Grant was — and Troy locked eyes on me.

The flames danced there, the ones that I'd seen, that had mocked me.

*It can't have him.*

Troy was mine. The shadow could go back to hell as far as I was concerned.

I brought my forearms together, just as I had with Hunter, and thankfully it worked against Troy. His massive frame was thrown backward, but I didn't give him time to settle. I rushed forward — hoping I'd stunned him long enough to reach him before he could swipe those claws at me.

I hit him at full speed and set my hands on his cheeks.

The mist came back to me, that memory, the bird.

The lesson...

I stopped fighting it all. I stopped trying to win by being something, by proving anything. Instead, I accepted it. Accepting what I was, even if I didn't have a name, even if I didn't understand it, I embraced it. The mist I'd run from, the fears of being different, I released them all.

The shadow that snaked through him tried to surge forward, to knock me free, but I wouldn't let it. I reached into him, used whatever power I had to grasp that shadow, the wrapped my fingers around it and yank it free.

It scratched at me, clawing, leaving burning pain, but I didn't relent.

It couldn't have him.

Finally, I fell backward, not thrown like before but this time from pulling that shadow from him.

The shadow moved in the room, as though a fish thrown from its bowl, before it dissipated.

And I collapsed, my knees striking the floor and everything going black.

* * * *

Fingers stroked through my hair, gentle and sweet. They drew me awake, despite the throbbing in my head, the aches in my body.

I opened my eyes to find familiar amber eyes staring down at me. "You worried me." Hunter's long hair hung down, wild and so much like him.

A soft groan from the side made me frown, and when I twisted to find Kase seated, his back to the wall and his eyes closed, it all came back to me.

*Troy. The fight. The shadow.*

I scrambled up, despite the way it made me light-headed.

A quick count told me everyone was there, but it took a slower second pass to check on them all.

Someone had hung a heavy blanket up over the window, to keep the sunlight out, but the burns on Kase were still obvious. He opened his eyes, which had dimmed, then gave me a half smile that didn't reach his eyes.

Grant stretched out on the floor, a cut on his lip and another on his forehead. Hunter reached out and kicked him, and despite looking all but dead, Grant lifted his hand and offered a thumbs-up.

Lastly, Troy sat in the corner, his legs crossed, his body hunched forward. He stared down at his hands — which had returned to normal, as had the rest of him.

I took a step toward him, wanting to reassure myself that it had worked, that he was okay, but as soon as I did, he nailed me with a hard look that froze me in place.

"Are you back?"

He huffed and looked down. "You should have run, Ava. That was a stupid risk you took."

Him lecturing me was the best thing I'd ever heard. It meant he was really okay.

I dropped to my knees beside him, wanting to breathe him in, to touch him until I was sure I'd saved him.

Except, when I touched his arm, he flinched as though I'd burned him.

I yanked backward, looking at my hand. Nothing.

*Maybe he just needs a minute. Are werewolves sensitive after shifting?* A more sinister thought emerged on the tail of it. *Maybe he saw what you could do and decided he doesn't want you anymore.*

I pulled away from him, moving back to the center of the room so I could see them all.

"Paul?" I asked.

"Dead," Hunter told me, the least injured of any of them. "Partially digested as well."

Troy snarled but said nothing.

"It worked, though. I *can* fix this. I can drive the shadow out."

Hunter nodded. "So it seems."

"So why aren't you more excited? This is the first win we've had…" I quieted down as none of them would look at me. "What aren't you telling me?"

Hunter reached into his pocket and drew out a small box. "This appeared just after you passed out. I thought about getting rid of it before you woke up."

"What is it?"

He sighed softly, then held it out. "It is from Lucifer. A message, one that can find its target anywhere, in any realm."

I took the small box, lifting it so I could study it. What I'd thought were detailed carvings from farther away I realized were actually bones, set in the aged metal like jewels. A clasp at the front held it closed, a ruby on the latch.

"If you wanted to get rid of it, why didn't you?"

"Because when Lucifer finds the urge to go through this much trouble to send a message, you don't want to see what happens if he has to send it twice. There is no time when *that* is a good thing."

"What does it say?"

He shook his head. "I can't open it. Only you can."

I took a deep breath and pressed open the latch. The top flung wide, and blackness poured from the box.

I jerked away, but the box floated in the air instead of dropping, and a dark figure stood in the room.

At least…it seemed like it did. As it cleared up, going from shadow to man, I realized I could still see through him, and his eyes didn't quite meet mine.

It was almost like a recorded message?

When the man solidified, he looked nothing like I'd expected. He looked to be in his thirties, with jet black hair brushed back and bright red eyes. His lips were black and twin horns ran from his temples and curled over his ears. "Ava Harlin." His voice was crisp, elegant, and it sent a shiver up my spine. "You have been summoned to my court to answer for your actions."

He disappeared, dissolving along with the blackness until the box fell to the ground.

"Answer for *my* actions?" I repeated, as if I could argue directly back to him. "What actions do I need to answer for?"

Hunter set his arm on top of his knee as he sat on the ground. "Well, if he's behind this, you screwed up his plans. That would piss him off, I'd imagine."

"Can I ignore this?"

"Not really. Lucifer isn't known for patience. If you don't respond, if you don't do what he's commanded, he will send things after you, things I can't protect you from."

I nodded, trying not to freak out. I'd just saved Troy. I'd outdone that damn shadow.

*I can handle this, right?*

The box shifted on the ground, a hissing coming from it.

Everyone froze, and even those who had their eyes closed opened them. Flames poured from the box, but the flames weren't red. They were black.

Hunter cursed and grabbed me, wrapping his body around mine as though he could shield me from whatever was happening.

It seemed pretty rude for Lucifer to summon me and immediately kill me, but that was a complaint I could formally lodge later.

*Especially because I'll be dead…*

The flames spread through the room, but they didn't seem to catch anything on fire. Troy, Grant and Kase cried out, pained sounds that I was sure would keep me up at night.

Some licked across my leg, my arm, the few places where Hunter didn't fully surround me.

As quick as it happened, though, it stopped. *Silence.*

I shoved at Hunter, who uncurled from me. Grant, Troy and Kase all appeared unharmed, all on their feet as if they hadn't been lounging about moments earlier. I guess that sprang them all into action.

We weren't in the room anymore. In fact, we weren't inside at all. Trees surrounded us, everything dim as if lit by a moon that wasn't in the sky. A breeze carried the scent of brimstone on it, and something hungry and angry and *large* howled in the distance.

Smoke thick enough it could be caught in a person's hands cover the ground.

"Where are we?" I asked even though I had a sinking feeling I already knew.

Hunter crossed his arms, staring out toward where the sound had come from. "It looks like Lucifer wasn't willing to wait around and see if you'd show up. Welcome to hell, shadow-girl."

# Want to see more from this author? Here's a taster for you to enjoy!

## Grave Concerns:
## Hell Raising and Other Pastimes
### Jayce Carter

### *Excerpt*

So, hell was pretty much what I'd expected.

Troy sat across from me in a small cave we'd taken shelter in, still avoiding looking at me, turning the spit with something cooking on it over the fire.

I had decided against asking what it was they were roasting, because I doubted any answer to that would make me happy.

If it were some strange hellbeast, I'd be grossed out, and if it were a cute, fluffy critter, I'd be sad.

Some questions were better left unasked, such as "Do I look fat in these?" or "Do you think my sister is hot?" and "What animal did this come from?"

Hunter came into the cave looking far too happy, as though he'd been waiting anxiously for just this moment. Hell, he was almost *skipping*.

Kase, on his heels, appeared significantly less pleased with the turn of events.

"I love the smell of brimstone in the morning." Hunter set down an oddly shaped cup in front of me.

I took a closer look at the dish, the white of it standing out against the dimness of the everything else. "Where'd you get this?"

"Don't worry about it. Drink. You mortals get parched fast out here."

His answer didn't ease me at all, so I lifted the cup closer to the fire. The white took a moment to place, and once I did, I couldn't unsee it. "Is this bone?"

Hunter groaned and sat cross-legged on the other side of the fire. "I *told* you not to worry about it."

"You can't seriously expect me to drink out of a bone cup."

"I have skulls, if they're more your style."

I was ready to yell at him for the stupid joke until I realized he probably wasn't kidding. Somehow, the idea that Hunter had a collection of fine china made from bones in hell seemed right on par for him.

Especially the way he had no shame over it.

"Drink," Kase said, nodding toward it. "I doubt you want to die of dehydration while in hell."

"At least it'd be a short trip if I did," I muttered before closing my eyes — it'd be easier if I didn't have to actually see the cup — and drank the water in big gulps. I figured if I finished it off quickly, I'd have to touch the thing for less time overall.

Which was a stupid reaction since I'd touched dead bodies plenty of times.

But I'd never use them as flatware. There were some lines a person didn't cross.

The water was warm, stale and tinged with an odd taste that made me want to gag a bit as I downed it.

Still, once I finished it, I handed back the empty cup. "Why would Lucifer drop us *here*? I thought he wanted to see me?"

Hunter shrugged. "He might figure a good test would be worth it. Anyone who can't survive a few days journey in hell isn't someone important enough for him to meet in person. Or maybe he intended for us to get dropped in his Court, but something went wrong. Magic doesn't work quite right on you."

"Things aren't supposed to just go wrong for Lucifer."

"Then you don't know Lucifer. Remember the whole fall from heaven thing? He's had things going wrong right from the start."

And, again, that made me feel no better. I liked the idea that at least Lucifer had his business figured out. The thought that he was as powerless and fumbling as the rest of us gave me a moment of thinking, *If* he *can't get shit right, what chance do I have?*

I sighed and crossed my legs, leaning forward. *Great.* We were stuck in hell, had no idea why I was where I there and now even the guy who ran it all didn't seem to have a good grip on specifics.

The only person happy about our circumstances was Hunter, who grinned as though he couldn't have planned things any better.

Then again, it was his home.

Grant was still outside, setting wards so we could get a good night's sleep, or at least the best one could expect in a cave in hell.

Not that there seemed to be any *night.* It reminded me of the pocket realm I'd met the fae in, except it didn't get lighter or darker. It remained a constant depressing level of dim, which ranked around the super overcast and rainy level.

When Troy finished cooking the food, he tore free a piece and held it out for me. Instead of thinking too much about it—I was really hungry—I popped it into my mouth, surprised to find it rather good.

*As long as I don't consider what it might have been before being spit roasted or how many legs it might have had.*

"Do you think he'll try to kill me?" I asked.

"I doubt it," Hunter said. "If he wanted to kill you, he could have done it without this much work. Lucifer doesn't do anything without a reason. He calls it efficient—I call it lazy."

"Maybe he just wants to be able to watch me die in person," I muttered around another bite of food.

"We won't let him hurt you," Kase said.

I gave him a withering glare in return. I didn't get over betrayal so easily. We might have been in an entirely different realm, but I wasn't ready to forgive him for lying to me, for hiring Grant to figure out what I was, for manipulating me. Maybe his words would have reassured me if I didn't already doubt his loyalty so much.

He looked as though he wanted to discuss the matter, but a glance around the cave reminded him we had an audience. Kase's ego would never want to air dirty laundry with others in earshot.

The perfect Kase didn't want to not look so perfect.

"You know, you all don't have to be here." I forced the words out even though I really didn't want to say them. Still, it was only fair to give them an out.

"What?" Grant asked as he came into the cave.

"Well, you can make portals to and from hell, right? You might have gotten sucked in here on accident, but you don't *have* to stay."

"Actually, we do," he said.

"Don't give me that. There's no reason for you all to risk your lives just because I evidently have an appointment with the devil."

Hunter shook his head, a smirk across his lips. "No, shadow-girl, what he means is that when Lucifer yanked us here, it placed a tracer on us. *All* of us. None of us can portal back until Lucifer removes it. The magic just won't work for a portal. I could cross the boundary, but I couldn't take anyone with me."

I blew out a breath, ashamed to admit just how relieved I was by that. Sure, I had to give them an out, but the thought of them leaving, of trying to make my way across hell by myself hadn't been one I relished. They were stuck with me for now, and it was far more reassuring than I wanted to admit.

"How long until we reach Lucifer's Court?" I asked, trying to change topics.

Hunter plucked a piece of meat from the creature and ate it with noisy bites. "Three days? Maybe five if we need a lot of stops. We ended up right at the boundary line, so it's a long walk. If it were just me, I'd make it in a day, but you all couldn't keep up."

Troy snorted. "Maybe not them, but I'm quicker than you think."

Hunter offered Troy a wide grin. "Yeah, but you'd keep up — *maybe* — if you were in your wolf form. Sadly, you've got some performance issues about that one, and on two legs you're as slow as the mortal."

Troy narrowed his eyes but didn't respond.

*Fine by me.* Honestly, I'd love for them all to shut up.

It was bad enough they bothered me at my house, when they stopped by constantly and threw my life into chaos, but out here, I didn't even have the privacy of a bathroom or the occasional moments of peace.

It was twenty-four-seven testosterone zone.

So I ate another piece of food before a yawn told me I needed rest.

The cave floor was hard and there wasn't anything to use as a pillow around. I groaned and twisted, my shoulder sore from where it dug into the ground.

Troy had taken a spot far away, as though he wanted to avoid me as best he could—just like he'd done since I'd saved him.

The ungrateful bastard. Next time maybe I'd let that freaky shadow take him over.

After checking the wards, Grant had leaned himself against the doorway of the cave, his legs stretched out and his eyes closed. He'd picked there, at the threshold, like a guardian.

Funny, since Grant, with his twenty-year-old appearance, massive number of tattoos and rebel hair style, appeared the least dangerous.

Hunter had chosen to rest outside, like some dog in the yard. He'd taken a large hunk of the meat and claimed to like sleeping under the stars.

Not that there were any stars…

"Come here." Kase's voice was soft in the darkness, and close enough I jumped.

How he could move so quickly, I didn't understand. He'd managed to shift around so he crouched just above where I lay.

I pressed my palm against the cave floor and pushed myself up. With the fire gone, I struggled to see Kase, so I glared in his direction best I could. "Sorry, but that doesn't work."

"What doesn't work? You need sleep, and you won't get any tossing and turning like that."

"You think this is my first time dealing with men? Let me guess, I'll sleep *so* much better all curled up beside you. And I'll sleep better without any pants. In fact, a few orgasms will put me right out." I made sure my voice sounded as insulting as I meant it to be.

Which was stupid, because no matter how much I disliked him at the moment, a few orgasms *would* help me sleep.

Just not from him. Not that he'd proven himself capable of delivering them anyway. His only attempt had been pathetic.

He sighed before sitting on the ground, his back to the wall. He removed his jacket and balled it up in his lap. "I'm not offering orgasms, Ava, and since my body doesn't run warm, there isn't a reason to curl up beside me, naked or not. However, I am, at the very least, useful as furniture."

I wanted to argue that I was sleeping just fine, but the ache in my shoulder called me a liar. Still, the thought of touching him made me wonder how stupid one person could be.

His entire reaction to me was bad enough — I wasn't sure I'd ever live down him spitting out my blood as if it were tainted — but the idea that he'd been lying to me was what really stuck.

He'd hired Grant to spy on me, to go behind my back and figure out what I was. He'd even said the entire thing had been for the coven, not him. How on earth could I just forget that?

Still, his lap was as good as anyone else's, and I *was* tired. I slid up, wincing when it aggravated my shoulder.

He set a strong hand on my back, helping me to adjust, until I was on my side, my head pillowed on his lap, his jacket creating more cushion and a useful barrier between me and any erecting that might happen.

Not that that seemed a problem with him.

When he ran his fingers through my hair, I swatted him away. "Knock that off."

He let out a soft sound, all annoyance. "I'm trying to help."

"I didn't *ask* for help, did I?"

"You haven't ever asked, and yet here I've been, doing it anyway. I am in hell, literally, for you."

I sighed, having nothing to say back to that. When I closed my eyes, he dragged his fingers through my hair again, and this time I let him. Just because I was mad at him didn't mean I had to forgo the nice sensation, did it?

It wasn't like he was getting anything out of it. Might as well enjoy it while it lasted. I doubted many nice things happened in hell.

"I didn't mean to hurt you," he said, voice low as if we could have a private conversation in such a small space, surrounded by others. "I hired Grant before I knew much about you."

"But even after you got to know me, you didn't feel the need to mention it? To call him off?"

"I knew you wouldn't be happy about me invading your privacy like that, and as I spent more time with you, I found out you hold grudges. It seemed a pointless argument to risk, since if you never found out, you would have never been angry."

I shifted and *accidently* elbowed him in the crotch.

He let out a rush of air—it seemed not everywhere on a vampire was impervious to harm—before groaning. "I have learned my lesson, Ava. I do not intend to lie to you again."

"And so I'm supposed to be okay with it? What was this all? What was it when you tried to feed from me? Just more research for the coven? At least that explains why you couldn't keep it up."

"No. It wasn't ever for the coven."

"That was what you told Grant."

"Because I prefer not to expose potential weaknesses."

"So I'm a weakness now?" I went to rise, because his lap was *not* worth me getting any more hurt than I already was.

He set a hand on my shoulder and pressed me back down, reminding me just how strong he was. "Stop it, Ava. Stop fighting with me long enough to listen. I have thought about you since I first saw you in that shop, and that obsession hasn't ended. When I asked around and found out what little I could, it still wasn't enough. So, yes, when given the chance, I hired Grant to discover more about you — not for the coven and not for Colter, but for myself. You can be angry with me for as long as you'd like for that invasion of privacy, for the lies, but do not mistake it for something it wasn't. I hired you for the job with Olin because you could do it, I wanted to feed from you because I couldn't stop thinking about it. I *want* you because I have since I first saw you. Besides, you shouldn't be so angry with me when Grant found nothing useful out."

"Maybe that's why he got kicked out of the guild, because he's a terrible mage."

A snort from the doorway said Grant was listening, but I pretended it was a random sound so I didn't have to think about our audience.

Kase went back to the gentle stroking of his fingers through my hair, and, despite my better judgment, it relaxed me. His voice, smooth and unfailingly calm, was even worse. "He ran every test he could, did everything he knew and he could not identify what you were. No matter how much I researched, who I threatened, I discovered nothing. You are an enigma, Ava."

"And that's why you're still around? Because I'm a very interesting puzzle, and you're old and bored? Or because I could be potentially useful to you?"

"No. I don't think I care what you are anymore. Originally, it was a mystery, but I've discovered you are trouble no matter what you might be."

"That doesn't explain why you're here *now*."

"You're smart enough to figure that one out. I'm not sure there are many reasons a man goes to hell for a woman."

I opened my mouth, but nothing came out. Kase and I, we never talked. We didn't admit anything. Where Troy liked to come out and say what he felt, and Hunter didn't feel deeply enough for the need to have a conversation, Kase and I liked to exchange things in non-speak.

He didn't say he cared, and I didn't say I liked that he was there.

Even still…I couldn't quite accept his words. I recalled Colter, remembered the coven house, and knew I had no idea where his loyalties really lay.

He might be a great piece of furniture, but that didn't mean he wouldn't kill me if he needed to…

\* \* \* \*

I wiped my mouth after coughing and gagging some more.

As it turned out, werewolf and vampire physiology weren't as affected by the smoke and ash as mine. Kase and Troy had no problem trekking along, mile after mile, while breathing in that junk.

Hunter lived here, so it didn't bother him.

Grant coughed on occasion, but his immortality made him sturdier, which left me as the one who kept throwing up because the ash coated my esophagus and made me gag.

I wiped sweat from my forehead, already sick of hell.

Hunter passed a waterskin to me, the outside made of a leathery material that looked suspiciously like scales. I'd opened my mouth to ask Hunter what it was made of the first time he'd had it, but he'd told me it was better I didn't know.

That seemed the general theme of hell. What was moving in the distance? What were those things flying above us? What was the shrieking?

*Better not to know.*

I took the water from Hunter and drank in large gulps, ignoring how warm it was.

*Everything* was warm. The breeze, the water, even in the shade, the rocks were hot to the touch.

Still, it was better than nothing, and the constant ash meant even warm water was helpful in clearing it away. Plus, he hadn't tried to give me anything made of bone to drink from again, so I'd take the weird scale bag as a win.

"How can you figure out where you're going here?" I handed back the waterskin.

Troy was far to the front, and Grant and Kase had taken up the rear. Hunter moved between the group, as if herding us all in the direction he wanted us to go.

"I feel it." He pointed behind us. "That's the way to the barrier, to the points between this world and the living world, and in the other direction, at the center, is Lucifer's Court."

"I thought you weren't controlled by him."

"I'm not. It isn't his power that draws me, but the fact that it's the center of hell, the draw point of the power in this place. It's where hell connects to the other realms of the afterworld. Lucifer built his palace there *because* it was the center. It isn't the center because he's there, no matter what he'd like to think."

A screaming echoed in the distance, died off to a whimper, then to nothing. I twisted to peer in that direction, even though I knew I wouldn't be able to see it, and I probably didn't want to.

Spindly trees rose around us in each direction, looking like dead things in the middle of winter, but they grew so densely they still obstructed the view.

"Relax," Hunter said.

"How am I supposed to relax when things sound like they're being eaten?"

"Well, they probably are being eaten." He grinned when I offered him a shocked look. "However, the point is that they're getting eaten because I'm not there to protect them. This is my *home*, Ava, and believe it or not, there isn't much here I'm worried about. At least, not anything outside of the Court."

"Forgive me, but you don't look nearly as imposing as those things I've seen before, as whatever is *eating* that poor creature. You're just a man and some smoke. I mean, a good-looking one, but I don't think monsters are going to be like 'he is sure handsome. Guess we won't kill them.'"

"I still look like this because you won't like me as much in my other form. Plus, no usable penis like that, and I'd really love to use mine on you, so I choose to keep looking like this."

The casual way he said such things silenced me and made me think about how much I agreed.

Not about not liking him in another form, but about how I wouldn't mind a repeat of our time together in the tent.

Or in my bed.

Really, so long as we were both naked, I wasn't picky about the locale.

Another howl came through and woke me up.

We were in hell. That was *not* the best time for quickies.

He lifted his head and inhaled, slowly, tension filling him.

When Hunter looked nervous was about the time to panic...

I inched closer to him, unable to help it. I would much prefer to be nearer to him for reasons that had nothing to do with orgasms right then.

Well, other than I'd like to live long enough to have more of them.

"Fuck," he muttered softly.

"What?"

Something in the distance came into view, but just barely. It wasn't a shadow, not like the thing that plagued me, that we chased, but more like mist. It reminded me of my dreams, of the things I saw in them.

It sped over the landscape as if it weren't fully there, the hazy appearance of a spirit.

Hunter pressed closer to me, though he didn't wrap an arm around me, as though he wanted both hands free to face whatever approached us.

The thing slowed when it neared us, and this time I could make out a shape. It was a dark figure, though not wholly corporeal or solid, covered in dark, floating cloth, including a hood that obscured its face. It had sleeves so long, hands couldn't be seen. Nothing but the mist-like robes were visible, floating despite there being no breeze.

It paused before us, and I could *feel* it looking at me. The sensation crawled over me like ice, something frozen and sinister.

A growl left Hunter, but the thing took no notice of him. It came closer, shifted as if to see me better. After another moment, it rushed away with the same speed it had arrived with, and Hunter let out a heavy breath.

Kase came over, Grant behind him. "Please tell me that wasn't what I think it was."

"Wish I could."

"They never show up," Grant said. "What the hell is going on?"

I elbowed between them men. "For those of us who don't have a field guide to hell on hand, what was that?"

Hunter pushed his hair from his face. "A reaper."

"The thing that severs the connection between body and soul?"

Hunter nodded. "Yep. Reapers are one of the few things that *nobody* fucks with. Even Lucifer leaves them alone. Because they aren't alive or dead, they don't belong to the living or the dead realm. They don't *belong* to anyone."

"They're from purgatory." I might not have seen one before, but I did understand what they were. They were, in a way, cousins of mine, something connected to the thing that seemed to make me different.

Kase was the one to answer, nodding. "Reapers don't take notice of the living or the dead. They're more like scavengers than anything else, beings that do their job and ignore everything else."

"It was looking at me."

"I mean, it stopped, but—" Hunter started to say.

"No. I felt it staring at me."

Grant cursed under his breath. "You do not want a reaper taking an interest in you. They're essentially invincible because they aren't alive—never were—and they don't have actual bodies to harm. If they want to snatch a soul from a body, they can do so with a touch and no one can do a thing about it."

I thought about the way it had seemed to look past my skin, into my spirit, into the part of my that wasn't corporeal, and I shuddered. Just when I thought there wasn't anything worse, that we had reached the end of bad shit that could ruin my day, it seemed like the universe wanted to throw another one into the mix.

Sure, soul-snatching mist creatures from purgatory.

What the hell was next?

Home of Erotic Romance

Sign up for our newsletter and find out about all our romance book releases, eBook sales and promotions, sneak peeks and FREE romance books!

# About the Author

Jayce Carter lives in Southern California with her husband and two spawns. She originally wanted to take over the world but realized that would require wearing pants. This led her to choosing writing, a completely pants-free occupation. She has a fear of heights yet rock climbs for fun and enjoys making up excuses for not going out and socializing.

Jayce loves to hear from readers. You can find her contact information, website details and author profile page at https://www.totallybound.com

**The Omega's Alphas**
Owned by the Alphas
Shared by the Alphas
Saved by the Alphas
Protected by Her Alphas
Caught by Her Alphas
Tamed by the Alphas
Claimed by the Alphas
Exposed by Her Alphas
Trained by the Alphas

**Ready or Not**
Fake It 'til You Make It
Opposites Attract
Third Time Lucky

**Grave Concerns**
Grave Robbing and Other Hobbies